A
BALM
IN
GILEAD

A Novel

MARIE GREEN MCKEON

A BALM IN GILEAD
Copyright © 2014 by Marie Green McKeon.

White Bird Publishing
E-mail: whitebirdpub@gmail.com

PUBLISHER'S NOTE: This is a work of fiction. Names, characters, places, and incidents are either the product of the author's imagination or used fictitiously. Any resemblance to actual persons, living or dead, businesses, companies, institutions, events, or locales is entirely coincidental.

Cover design: Rachel Caldwell
Interior design: Karen Giangreco
Editing: NY Book Editors

ISBN 978-0-9904338-2-8
First Edition

To Jack, with love and gratitude,
and in memory of my mother

CONTENTS

There is a balm in Gilead
to make the wounded whole.
There is a balm in Gilead
to heal the sin-sick soul.

—from an African-American spiritual,
based on Jeremiah 8:22

PROLOGUE

It must have been about seven years later that I came upon her: an anonymous co-victim, a secret companion who, like me, bore the brunt of a terrible crime.

It was a chance encounter a good number of years after what my friends, family, and law enforcement gingerly and euphemistically referred to as the "attack." We would speak of it in a near whisper, as if speaking louder might resurrect all sorts of horrors. Certainly by the time I saw this young woman, a long enough period had passed so that few people would even broach the topic of the crime, or the series of events that followed. It wasn't necessary to dredge up the past, really. Everyone—including me—believed that this brief but ghastly chapter in my life was over.

I was waiting my turn in the doctor's office, my head aching and feeling as pumped up as a balloon. I suspected a sinus infection and I had been waiting for about forty-five minutes for a doctor to confirm it. At first I resisted touching anything in the waiting room for fear of smearing my germs about. I became so bored that I convinced myself that it was probably a non-contagious infection and began flipping through the old magazines that were scattered on the wide table separating the banks of occupied chairs. Soon I was bored with this activity, too. Still, there seemed nothing better to do than to reach over and sift through dated issues of *Good Housekeeping*, *Time*, and, curiously, *Bon Appétit*. I was thinking that someone in this practice must be into cooking, when I happened to glance up at the newly arrived patient who was picking her way through the crowded waiting room.

She was young, attractive but pale, with a look that could only be characterized as stricken. Sinking into the vacant seat opposite me, she pulled a book from her bag and buried her face in it, leaning over so that her long, silky hair became a screen that hid the book jacket.

I couldn't help staring. Something about her was recognizable, I thought. It could have been something in her expression that looked familiar. After less than a minute of reading, the young woman picked her head up and sat back, as if reading was too much for her. Holding a finger in her book to keep her place, she leaned her head back against the wall and closed her eyes. She seemed exhausted and sad.

I glanced at her book, which was held at an angle that let me read part of the title. I could make out the words *rape victims*.

She's just like me, I realized. Immediately I felt the old, weird rippling sensation in my face: the skin flattening against my cheekbones like I was on an amusement park ride, the cartilage in my nose vibrating like a tuning fork. You couldn't exactly say it was like someone striking your face. It was more of a phantom pummeling, like a ghost was punching me.

My face carried the memory of my attack. The rest of me could manage to forget, but my face had total recall. In the immediate aftermath, I experienced this sensation all the time, sometimes from the most innocuous occurrences. It rarely happened anymore. Except that here in the waiting room, without warning, the muscles and bones were bringing back everything I wanted to forget, from the first powerful, surprising blows to my terrifying escape. Once again, my face betrayed me.

I looked again at the young woman. From the raw, bruised look of her, I could tell this girl had recently gone through her own experience. I'm not sure how I didn't recognize the symptoms immediately—the impression of a piece of butchered meat that had been thrown unceremoniously from a cold storage locker, and then kicked into the street to be run over by traffic. I didn't need a doctor to diagnose her as a member of the same secret club that I belonged to.

I thought about talking to her. I really did. I pictured myself getting up, moving around the big coffee table, dropping to my knees at her feet. I would let her know that I understood perfectly because I had been through a similar experience. I would tell her . . . tell her what? Keep your chin up? That everything would be okay?

I was a coward for not saying anything, for letting her suffer alone. But I couldn't. I couldn't risk waking the sleeping monster inside me, not after all my hard work to normalize my life. And it was normal. I was very proud of that fact.

So I sat there watching the inner turmoil playing out on the girl's waxy face before I had the sudden thought that I could be wrong. She's just here to see the doctor about a physical ailment, she's not feeling well, and she's reading this book for a college sociology course. It's a coincidence. She's not my secret companion after all.

No, I thought. No, my first reaction was right. Even so, it was better not to take the chance. I had a history of projecting my problems on others. I recalled, with embarrassment, that brief period early in my recovery. It was long after the physical injuries had healed, after the trial. I was seeing one of the psychologists my parents were always sending me to. This doctor suggested that talk might be the best therapy. I think she meant within the context of some sort of support group, but for several months I had the bright idea to tell my story, to expel it, to rid myself of it for good.

The first time I ventured a complete narrative of my attack and the subsequent trial was an exceptionally poor choice. It was during an evening out at a local club with a group of friends. I didn't want to go; they insisted it would help. A boy, with whom I was only slightly acquainted, sat next to me at the large round table and offered to buy me a drink. I'm sure he was expecting bantering or flirting, not a confession.

I don't know how I got started or what brought it on. All I knew is that, while halting at first, the story eventually poured from me like a rush of water down an unclogged drain. I talked faster than I thought possible, my words tumbling over each other. I began experiencing that facial distortion. At times I had to cup my hand around my nose to stem the tuning fork vibration. Midway through, I had a more violent physical reaction, and my whole body began to shake uncontrollably. I wrapped my arms around my torso to try to control the tremors. I went on like that, talking and talking and barely stopping for breath, all while clutching myself and occasionally, spastically, grabbing at my face.

I stopped only because I had run out of words. When I looked up, the face of my listener registered with me for the first time. He had the look of a traveler stuck on a bus or plane next to a nutty passenger. I had to give the guy credit for not bolting from the bar halfway through my story. But then again, I was blocking his exit.

Over a period of several months, I couldn't stop the strange compulsion to buttonhole strangers, the merest of acquaintances, anyone, really. I would tell my story to anyone who would sit still long enough to listen. It didn't matter how it affected the listener. The point was to cleanse my soul. It was verbal bulimia and, once finished, I was spent but relieved, momentarily free.

In the end, only one person listened to the story with true interest. It turned out to be the last time I felt the need to relate it for a long time.

She was an older woman, a captive audience on public transportation, so it could easily have gone bad, the way it did with my first listener in the bar. It was during a long New Jersey Transit ride into Manhattan, when I was once again with a larger group. There were few open seats in the car, and I slid into one next to an elegant woman who reminded me of a small bird. She had bright brown eyes and a bird-like way of cocking her perfectly coiffed head. It didn't take long for me to find an opening to launch into my tale, and she appeared somehow calm rather than fidgety as she trained her bright eyes on me. She asked a few questions. It was clear she was neither put off nor unsettled.

This person had had a similar experience. I was quite certain in this realization as we solemnly shook hands good-bye at Penn Station. I watched the woman walk away on her bird-like legs and thought, *What, did you think you were the only victim in the world?* The woman might have said that herself. Instead, kindly, she had only listened.

My friends that I had traveled with were urging me to join them, but I lingered a moment to watch the woman make her way across the crowded floor. Perhaps the woman felt my gaze because I saw her stop and search around. She spotted me, sent a brief smile, and disappeared into the sea of commuters.

It was after this telling that I gave up the practice altogether. After that, I rarely mentioned the attack to family or friends, to those who were with me throughout the ordeal. Most of the people I met afterward—especially those I met after my talking cure, as I came to think of it—knew nothing about the experience. I liked it that way. It helped me to see it all as a mere aberration, however unfortunate, from the ordinary progression of my life.

I remembered all this as I watched the woman across from me at the doctor's office. Maybe I owed this person the same kind of assistance that the bird-like woman on New Jersey Transit had given me. It was probably an unspoken rule of our secret society. You help the next victim, pay it forward.

I shifted in my seat and started to sweat. Despite the fact that this person was clearly drowning in her own despair, I couldn't make myself get up to help her. I couldn't even reach out a hand. Something held me back. A voice inside said, *You've done more than your share already.*

I became angry, suddenly and unreasonably angry. I was even angry with the girl across from me. It should have been enough that I had suffered and—thank God—survived a brutal attack, but the fact remained that I had done more. I had done everything I could, everything I was asked to do, to try to stop the creep who had done this to me, so that others wouldn't have to suffer the same fate. I listened to all of them—the police, the lawyers, the health professionals—when they went on and on about how it may be a bit of rough going through the legal system, it's no day at the beach, but you've got to do it. You've been given a big gift, you know. You have the power to stop this guy from hurting other girls. All you need to do is to go into court and tell the truth and everything will be fine.

Except everything didn't turn out fine.

No, I've managed to successfully shove those old demons into some secret closet where no one—most of all me—had any business entering. I had tried valiantly to do the right thing and let justice take its course, and it all went wrong. What could I, one little victim, do? I was damn lucky to survive the attack, even if it meant I had to endure the subsequent humiliation of the courtroom. I certainly couldn't have stopped the chain of events from unraveling the way it did.

I felt tears welling, and angrily brushed them away. But the anger was no longer directed at the victim across from me, or the well-meaning people in my past, or even the horrid judge who presided over my case. I was angry because now I realized it wasn't good enough that I had survived. A certain truth also survived. Little pieces of this truth had been buried all this time in that dark closet. It was the truth was that it wasn't really *over*. I may have accomplished a semblance of a recovery, but it wasn't going to be over until there was more than recovery. Someday there would have to be a reckoning.

The door opened and the nurse appeared. She glanced down to check the file in her hand. "Quinn? Quinn Carlisle? We're ready for you now."

I rose and walked toward the nurse with my head high, and not even a glance at the waxy-faced girl across the room. It was time for me to move on.

CHAPTER ONE

Early April 1987: a university campus, Pennsylvania

I should have known when I woke without the alarm.

My eyes fluttered open of their own accord. I assumed that my inner clock had roused me ahead of the buzzing of the clock radio, which I kept in a far corner of the bedroom. The strategy behind this positioning was a simple one: it forced me to get out of bed in order to shut off the alarm.

Even though I was like any other college student who keeps late hours and has trouble waking early—I had fallen into bed the previous night after one o'clock, exhausted both from working late and then trying to squeeze in some reading for a literature class—in my fuzzy haze, I thought waking on my own made sense. Of course today I would wake naturally, because today I needed to get to the bus stop on the other side of the campus. My body knew I needed to get up in time to catch the morning bus home.

I was stretching my limbs to full length to try to push the fuzziness away and to gain full consciousness when I froze. Something was wrong with the light.

My bedroom in the semi-basement apartment has one small casement window. But even from my severe angle of view from the bed, the sun seemed too high in the sky for it to be near dawn.

I bolted from the bed and lunged at the clock radio. Its rectangular silent face stared back at me. As I held it, the large numbers clicked from zero-nine-five-nine to ten o'clock. I had overslept by two and a half hours.

I checked the top of the clock radio and groaned. I had forgotten to switch on the alarm. This morning, of all mornings, when I had to get home for the funeral.

I stood there a minute, swaying, still clutching the radio, and considering my options.

The obvious choice would be to call my parents for a ride. But I didn't have the heart. My mother was distraught over the loss of her mother, whose funeral I was supposed to attend. My father would be busy supporting my mother and helping with the funeral arrangements. He would not be able to miss the wake this evening. My brother, Frank, could drive, but was without a vehicle, having recently totaled his in an accident. Our parents had been holding fast, refusing to lend him the family car on principle. They certainly wouldn't trust him to drive the six-hour round-trip to retrieve me from the university.

I compiled a mental list of friends and acquaintances (lengthy), who owned cars (much smaller), and whose homes were relatively close to mine (nearly nonexistent).

There was one other option. I could ask my roommate to drive me home.

Judith was from Ohio, so she didn't live anywhere near my family. But she did own a car. Maybe she would like to explore my part of Pennsylvania. We could invite Judith to stay at our house. Come for the funeral, but stay for the after-party! It was an insane idea, but I had to try.

As usual, I struggled to yank open the cheap bedroom door. The wood tended to warp in the damp apartment. In fact, most things felt slightly wet, which was not exactly comfortable, especially during the harsh winter we had only recently emerged from. But the place was more spacious than typical student digs, and we had yet to see any vermin, which gave me some comfort. I was a little wary of my living quarters, since the guy from the third floor said both ends of his apartment floor were listing toward the center. Since then, I've been worried that his bathtub might come crashing into our apartment. Even with the safety hazards, living arrangements like this, on the fringes of the university, were more desirable than the cramped and noisy dormitories. I should have been satisfied with this place, but what really made me feel trapped was my roommate, Judith.

I tugged hard on the door and burst into what served as our living room. The heavy shrubbery that covered the single small glass block window allowed little light to filter into the room.

"Judith?" It came out in a whisper. I could see the door to her bedroom was ajar. I peeked in cautiously because you never knew if her boyfriend was over. But the room was empty.

Great. Normally Judith spent Wednesday mornings the same way she spent every waking moment that she wasn't in class or with her boyfriend: studying like mad. She was always hunched over the small metal kitchen table, and would growl if I had the audacity to pour corn flakes into a bowl or—heaven forbid—if I stirred soup in a pot and scraped the spoon along the bottom.

"Must you make that racket?" Judith hissed once, keeping her eyes glued to a textbook page almost entirely covered in hot pink highlighter. "Some people are trying to study."

"Yeah? Well, some other people like to eat once in a while." To prove I was only joking, I tossed the spoon up to the ceiling with the intention of catching it. I missed. Actually, I ducked when I saw the spoon heading directly at my face and was forced to chase after it as it clattered to the floor near Judith's feet. "You skipped highlighting a word there," I told her on my way under the table.

Judith's absence today could signify that most rare of occasions: when Little Miss Stiff-Necked took her nose out of her books and let herself have some fun. I felt a little guilty at my uncharitable characterization. But it was difficult to like Judith, mostly because Judith detested me.

I wasn't quite sure where this hatred, with its great depths, came from. Among my friends, the general consensus was that Judith was jealous. It infuriates Judith that you're popular, my friends told me. She wishes that she were like you.

There could be some truth in that. Most of the time Judith had only her boyfriend, Sal, for companionship. Sal idolized her, but he could be whiny and annoying. He got on my nerves during his lengthy stays in our apartment.

Judith and I weren't acquainted when we agreed to take the apartment. In my first two years of college, I had several roommates I hadn't known prior to sharing a dorm room or an apartment, and those situations had turned into fast friendships. I guess I had expected this arrangement to follow the same pattern. But this roommate deal wasn't working out at all, contrary to what Eloise, the mutual acquaintance who had brokered the arrangement, had predicted. "Judith has this place. She needs a roommate. You need a place and would be a great roommate."

I headed to my room to pack. There was nothing left to do but see if I could catch the next bus. Hopefully there would be a next bus. They ran irregularly despite all the college students in the area.

I was shimmying under the bed to retrieve my good black shoes, when the door rattled open. As soon as I heard Judith drop her keys on the kitchen table, I pulled myself with difficulty from under the bed and leaped out of the bedroom, blurting out my request. "Thank God you're back. I have a huge favor to ask and I promise I'll never ask anything again."

Judith looked annoyed. "What is it?"

"I know it will really be an imposition—"

"Quinn, just tell me." Judith was unpacking her book bag in her usual intense, deliberate manner. She began to rifle through one of her many notebooks, glaring at the pages. That's when I remembered that Judith had recently mentioned something about cramming for an important test.

I stumbled over myself. "You know my grandmother's viewing is tonight . . . you do know my grandmother died? Anyway, I missed the bus and I was hoping you could . . . that you might drive me home . . ." My voice trailed off. It sounded pathetic, even to me.

Judith's withering look didn't help. "You've got to be kidding. I have classes the rest of the week."

Judith plopped herself on the kitchen chair and began arranging her study materials with precision. "As a matter of fact, I have plans and a phenomenal amount of studying to do. If you're too lazy to get up in time for the bus, that's not my problem."

What a bitch. I stifled the impulse to say it aloud. My mother's voice echoed in my head: *No matter how rude someone is, never sink to their level.*

I headed back to my bedroom to finish packing. Glancing back, I saw that Judith was already hunched over her textbooks.

Well, she had taught me a lesson. It was, after all, a lot to ask someone to drive two hundred miles out of her way. But let's face it. Judith was too mean-spirited to drive two hundred feet.

It was later than I had anticipated and already well past dusk on Saturday evening when I finally arrived back on campus. The Greyhound bus had dumped me in the unpaved lot that served as the bus depot. I had been forced to scamper down the steps of the bus, my bag providing so much momentum that I nearly fell out. The ill-tempered bus driver had made it clear that he wasn't planning to linger in this godforsaken university town in the middle of nowhere.

"You best get off quickly if you don't want to end up in Pittsburgh," the driver announced as he slammed on the brakes. One second I was perched at the top step, hanging on to a metal pole, and the next moment I was on the ground, barely landing on my feet as the bus pulled away.

Coughing out the last of the diesel fuel exhaust from my lungs, I looked around the depot. Rather, I tried to. It had been cloudy and damp all day, and now a thick, black night had overtaken the campus.

Sighing, I hoisted the long strap of my purse over my shoulder and picked up the boxy, fabric-covered suitcase. It was light but awkward to carry, as I had discovered the other day after Judith gave me the brush-off. On the return trip, the mile or so to my apartment seemed an impossibly long distance.

I was exhausted, and not just from the stress of getting home or the uncomfortable bus rides. It was the emotion of the last few days. Not that I wished death on anyone, but if it had to be someone old and also a relative, why didn't God see fit to take, say, a very old, never-seen great-aunt? I hadn't been prepared to lose Nana, who had moved in with us after my grandfather died twelve years ago. She had been in failing health for the last two, but I had refused to acknowledge it.

At the funeral, I nudged my brother and whispered, "Remember when we talked Nana into buying all those lottery tickets? You had her convinced that your mathematical mind could figure out the winning numbers if only you had enough to work with." We chuckled, but I had to look away when I saw Frank's eyes starting to water.

As children, Frank and I had basked in the pure pleasure Nana took in us for our smallest accomplishments at school or in sports, or in her fretting over our slightest illness. I don't think either of us felt that one was favored over the other. But I secretly felt a special bond with my grandmother that was mine alone. My unusual first name, Quinn, was my grandparents' surname, my mother's maiden name. "Don't you pay any mind to what they say about your name," Nana would tell me, smoothing my hair when I ran into the house sobbing after another merciless teasing on the school bus. "Did you know that I'm the one who suggested your name to your mother and father? I'm proud that you're carrying on the Quinn family name, and you should be, too. I'll tell you, nothing made your grandfather happier."

I walked through campus, switching the suitcase from one hand to the other, and thought of my mother, considering the effect the past few days must have had on her. They had to have been intensely difficult. Yet she had endured the funeral and its trappings with the stoicism she was famous for. She reminded me more than once to "put on a polite face." One was required to chat calmly with extended family members and friends of my grandmother, most of them strangers, along with cousins, neighbors, and other mourners. It was all very taxing, and I apparently hadn't inherited my mother's ability to dip into a bottomless reservoir of strength. When it was time for my father to drive me to the bus station to return to school, I was relieved.

On the drive to the station, my father was uncharacteristically sensitive to how I was feeling. Under normal circumstances, my dad would be unaware of a hurricane swirling about him.

"Are you all right?" He kept glancing sideways at me in the passenger seat. "You can always go back tomorrow or next week, you know. So you miss a little bit of time. Not a big deal, right?"

I pointed to the windshield to get him to watch the road. "You always get upset at the idea of me cutting class. Let me repeat, 'I'm not paying an arm and a leg to send you off to college only to have you cut class.'"

"Well . . ." My father looked sheepish.

I bit my lip. I should have known better, especially because it was only recently that I had come to the conclusion that everyone reaches sooner or later: my parents were not perfect.

I made a weak attempt to recover. "I do need to do some studying before classes on Monday. So I really should get back." My father reached over and patted my arm. Maybe I should stay, I thought. But it seemed too late to change my mind.

At the station we embraced awkwardly, and from the bus window I twisted around to wave good-bye. My father, looking suddenly—frighteningly—frail, tried to smile as he waved back. I thought, *He looks as sad as I feel*. It was a mildly shocking revelation that my father felt the loss of his mother-in-law as deeply as the rest of us. Something else I hadn't given him credit for.

It was warm for April. Because the university was nestled in a valley amid the Appalachians, which tended to be cool in the spring and summer anyway, the unseasonable temperatures were especially unusual. Even now as evening was falling, it was still humid.

I continued to trudge along. My arm, the one carrying the suitcase, felt like it might come out of its socket. Perspiration began to trickle down my back. I thought about stripping off the linen jacket I wore, but that would require stopping and rearranging my luggage.

Plodding on, feeling damp and uncomfortable, I peered up at the tall trees. In daylight they were a majestic backdrop to the campus. Now they threatened to swallow me. The university's labyrinth of paved walkways had some streetlights, but the light couldn't seem to penetrate the shadows. Every few feet as I stepped out of the light, I had to slowly and carefully put one foot blindly in front of the other.

Entering one of those pools of light, I suddenly had the odd feeling that the campus had completely emptied. I stopped, disoriented. I wasn't quite sure if I was heading in the right direction or even if school was in session. Nothing felt right.

I shivered despite the humidity.

I set down the suitcase so I could push up the sleeve of my jacket and check my wristwatch. I don't know why I thought that checking the time would help me get my bearings. Surprisingly, it did. I took a deep breath, got a firm grip on my bag, and set off as briskly as I could, the clunky suitcase battering my leg with every stride. I needed to hurry. I told myself it was because I had promised to phone my mother as soon as I got home. I didn't want her to worry.

"Hey. Do you have the time?"

It was startling. A moment before it had felt like I was alone in a postapocalyptic world. Then out of nowhere, there was this clean-cut boy smiling at me in the artificial light of the street lamp.

I assumed that he was a student because he looked like everyone else on campus. He wore jeans and had on a dark windbreaker despite the heat. He looked friendly enough. Fluttering around the edge of my mind, however, was the unnerving thought that there had been absolutely no sound or movement before he had emerged from the shadows.

His smile was wry and engaging. He tapped his wrist. "Time?"

"It's almost eight."

I turned to resume walking but his voice stopped me. "Are you sure?"

My reaction was natural, but for years after I would curse my stupidity. I had looked at my watch not a minute before, but his question made me second-guess myself. In one reflexive motion, I adjusted the suitcase without setting it down, and bent awkwardly to push back my sleeve for another look at my watch. In the same instant, in a move that might have been choreographed, he had me in a locked embrace.

"Don't scream. Don't say anything. I have a gun and I will kill you."

It was odd. I had the luxury of long moments. Time expanded, stretching into minutes or even hours. I had time to think, to plan my next step, to remember, to rage. I was only nineteen and I was going to die. I was shocked that this was it, this was how my life was to end, over barely past childhood. I considered simply closing my eyes and acquiescing. I could just let it happen.

But as soon as the thought came, I rejected it. I had to fight. The question was how, with my arms pinned to my sides and my face smashed against his jacket. In a strange way, I was calm. Maybe I could get out of this. I became aware of him cursing and calling me foul names. I could smell something sweet and sickening on his breath, some kind of alcohol. Maybe he was drunk. Maybe I could take advantage of that. He wouldn't be in control of his reflexes.

Still pinned, I was trying to come up with a strategy when I heard the rumble of a vehicle. A bus. And it wasn't far away.

Air brakes sounded a telltale screech. I managed to twist my head from his chest. I could see it. It wasn't the long-distance Greyhound bus that had dropped me at the depot thirty minutes ago. It was the shuttle bus. I hadn't realized I was that close to one of the service roads that crisscrossed the campus. The bus seemed so close in the frightening darkness, but at the same time too far away. Certainly it was too far away for the driver or any of the passengers to notice a pair of students locked in a struggle.

I heard the bus gather steam and resume its rumbling. And with that sound, something snapped in me. The bus represented my last, desperate hope, and now it was leaving.

The cry came unbidden, from deep inside. It was more a wail, a long, agonized keening of someone who knew she was about to die.

"Shut up!" My howl made my attacker both nervous and angry. Already I had managed to violate the rules he had set. I caught a glimpse of his features twisted in fury just before the blows landed.

His closed fist smashed my left eye, my nose, the side of my head. He continued to scream at me to shut my mouth, even though at that point he was the only one making noise.

You really do see stars, I thought. Tiny pinpoints of light were spreading out in the sky. His fist caught me on the cheekbone. I was reeling. I would have fallen if the attacker had not been holding me upright with one hand while he hit me with the other.

I have to do something. I have to figure out something. As I struggled to think rationally, I was on the verge of passing out. I struggled to remain conscious.

The attacker had switched tactics. Now he no longer struck me and his voice was comforting. "It's okay, Linda. Don't worry, Linda. I'll take care of you." The hand that had been punching me was now smoothing my hair.

I was woozy but seized the opportunity.

"Come on. Let's go find Linda." I tried to sound excited at the prospect. Linda was a long-lost friend. I would help him find her and make everything okay.

I had spoken the same way an adult would to a child. Astonishingly, he reacted just like a child.

"Okay," he said. He didn't release his grip, but he allowed me to lead him in the direction of the road where the bus had been. We shuffled along in this stranglehold dance. I strained to pull him toward the main thoroughfare that I realized, now that I had my bearings a little, must be close by. There, we were more likely to encounter other people and cars. That was where I had a shot at finding help.

At first it seemed that my attacker was cooperating, walking with me in drunken, dizzying loops. With our arms in a tangled embrace, we circled together in a dozen crazy steps for every foot we advanced. I tried to control my breathing, which became more labored the more I struggled to move his weight in the right direction.

Just when I thought we were getting somewhere, my attacker shifted gears. It was as if he woke up and realized where we were headed. In an abrupt shift in momentum, he pushed me the opposite way. I knew this direction was not good. I could sense a perilous darkness lay ahead. We moved into a lighted area again, and I saw we were heading directly into some overgrown brush and trees. The thought playing over and over in my mind was *Don't go there, don't go there.* I dragged my heels on the ground to try to slow him.

I was so intent on resisting that his next punch was unexpected. He let me go at the same time his fist crashed toward my face; I could not hold my balance. The back of my head bounced off a patch of grass. My lower back and legs slammed against the concrete pavement.

The impact stunned me. The next thing I knew he was climbing on top, straddling me. *This is it,* I thought.

But my body wasn't ready to give up. I fought back. Grunting, I made a massive effort to heave him off me; and when he didn't budge, another. I stopped for a moment, panting. He was motionless and seemed in some kind of stupor. He was tremendously heavy. It was getting hard to breathe. I began to worry he would crush me to death.

Panic was starting to rise. I could sense the opportunity to escape slipping away. Using all my strength, I managed to lift one hip a few inches until I felt him tilt to one side.

Something clattered on the pavement. I managed to twist around to look and saw his head pop up. He was awake or out of his stupor or something. We both stared at what had fallen from my jacket pocket. The object was clearly visible in the light from the street lamp. It was a knife. Actually it was my knife, a little novelty switchblade that I had chosen as a souvenir when I went with my parents to New York City two years ago. I had selected the knife to shock my mother, who had ignored my protests that I was too old for family outings. My mother had been less than impressed with my choice of souvenirs, but failed to be shocked. She merely grimaced at me when I smiled and slipped the knife in the deep pocket of my jacket, the one I now wore.

Now, as we eyed the weapon for what must have barely been a second, I knew what I had to do. So did he, but I had a head start. Also, my hand was miraculously free. I grabbed the knife and hit the button that popped open the blade.

There was the edge, glittery and sharp in the yellowish light. I held it against my attacker's neck in the most threatening manner I could, considering my position: flat on the ground, with a thick wet sticky substance—blood, I realized—running down the side of my head and pooling in my ear.

We looked at each other, the knife between us. I could see his eyes turn to slits. What I didn't see in them was any fear.

Do it, I commanded myself.

I tried to will my hand to thrust the knife toward his carotid artery. It should be easy, like slicing butter. But it was proving impossible, as impossible as turning the knife around and using it on my own neck.

"Go ahead and try. You can't." He was goading me.

Suddenly the tables were turned. My hand no longer held the knife, and he was pressing the blade against my neck.

His laugh was a short ironic bark. "I knew you couldn't do it." He pressed the knife point harder. I wondered if the skin was starting to split. "Maybe I should just slice your head off."

If this whole event, this attack, would change my life forever—and it would—then the moment with the knife changed the entire event. It was the fulcrum. I was desperately trying to halt a brightly spinning top, trying to slow it with my fingertips, and in that one instant I had an opportunity to stop it, to take control and save myself. But I had let the moment slip by.

There was nothing else to do. I closed my eyes and allowed it all to happen.

CHAPTER TWO

A decade later, moving on

After nearly ten years, I had it down to a science. Each year I would hold a little solitary vigil on the anniversary of the evening I stepped off the bus and had the bad luck to encounter Dennis Price. Usually my remembrance was nothing more than a brief walk or a quiet moment. Once or twice I made a visit to a chapel. It was always a private, silent affair. I didn't waste time reliving the horror. But I did indulge myself on that one day to mourn. Mourning was important because something had been killed in my attack after all. I had survived, but my innocence had not.

You can't remain a child forever. That's how I would usually end up rationalizing it. *Innocence has got to go sometime*, I would say. But I couldn't help thinking on each anniversary that it all had seemed a particularly harsh introduction to a brutal world where people tried to kill you and the justice system was anything but just.

Technically, it was during the second year after the attack that I began relegating the ordeal to a solitary day of remembrance. The first anniversary was too soon to put any real distance between myself and the trauma, and between me and Dennis Price. I was still struggling with the nightmarish aftermath, especially Price's trial, which took place not long after the one-year mark.

It wasn't long after the trial ended in chaos that I came to an important realization. Charlotte, a friend from high school who was attending a different college when I was attacked, became the unlikely source who stuck with me during the worst of this period. Why Charlotte tried to help, and especially why she persisted at it, was beyond me. My bitterness didn't make me a pleasant companion.

"In movies, the bad guys always go to jail. Yes, sir. Justice prevails in Hollywood no matter what," I complained to Charlotte on one occasion. We were waiting in the dim theater for the film to start. I was still on summer break, just a few weeks after the trial. Charlotte still seemed a little stunned by the whole story. All summer she had been visiting me almost daily, insisting that we needed to get out of the house and "do something." Usually when she came over, I was sitting lethargically on my parents' living room sofa, wrapped in an afghan despite the late summer heat, half-watching daytime television.

"You can't just sit inside all day," Charlotte had said for about the fiftieth time when she arrived on this particular day.

"Why not?" I yawned. I was overcome with exhaustion even though I had slept until noon.

"It's not healthy." Obstinate, Charlotte insisted that I choose among a list of activities she had compiled, which included walking in the park, bicycle riding, shopping at the mall, and going to a movie. I reluctantly agreed to the movies. That seemed the least obtrusive. I figured I could just sit there.

"In movies the bad guys end up dead more often than they go to jail, don't they?" I could tell Charlotte was trying hard to keep her response mild. I grunted and stared at the blank screen. I was still cross.

Charlotte sighed. "Quinn, I know it was a horrible experience," she began.

"No. You don't know. You can't know."

"Okay. Have it your way. I don't know. But humor me and just try to look at it from a different perspective. You got through it. It's over. I know you can't snap your fingers and forget it, but hanging on to your pain isn't going to let you heal."

Finished with what she had to say—probably something she had wanted to say for a while—Charlotte turned to face front just as the lights dimmed and the movie screen came to life. She wasn't the least interested in my comeback. I watched her profile in the flickering light, more than a little shocked. This was a different, more mature Charlotte than the teenager I had spent so much time with.

Right there in the dark movie theater, her statement was like a powerful light breaking through the haze I had been stumbling through. I made a decision. It was time, I told myself, for me to give up dwelling on it, harping about it, and repeating the story to anyone who would listen. My self-prescribed talk therapy wasn't helping; it was only letting the chain of events define me. I had to move it all to where it belonged, the realm of the unspeakable.

I settled back in my seat and, under the booming sound of the movie, I whispered a little vow to myself. I would return to the land of the living.

It wasn't long, maybe another year, before I was avoiding thoughts of the attack with little effort. I went from being trapped by an invisible monster whose claws dug at me, stopping any kind of functioning considered close to normal, to feeling that the whole experience had diminished to a bad nightmare dissolving at dawn. Other than the anniversary, I didn't allow myself to give it any serious thought.

I decided to rid myself, as much as possible, of anything left from the attack. At first I dutifully attended the therapy sessions that my mother insisted on, but after several months I canceled an appointment, then another one. Then I just didn't go. I phoned my father to ask him to stop paying for the sessions and extracted a promise that he would not tell my mother. My mother grilled me anyway, either guessing or wrenching the truth from my father. I came clean but assured her, yes, they had helped. I just didn't need them anymore.

"I'm fine. Really," I told her. Surprisingly, I *was* fine. At least, I considered myself to be so. I was reasonably happy. At times I was very happy. Other days, not. Just like a normal person, I thought with secret pride.

Granted, there was the pre-attack Quinn and the new Quinn. But then, an event like that changes a person. Maybe in some ways it wasn't so bad. For example, I was now much less naïve about the world. And I was very security conscious. Now when I walked alone—and I congratulated myself for being able to walk alone, just like everyone else—I was no longer oblivious of potential dangers lurking around every corner. Granted, I was a little obsessive, locking and double-checking the locks on my windows and doors. I never entered a car without scanning the backseat for intruders. Sometimes, I was embarrassed to admit, I even looked in the trunk.

That was just using good judgment and sensible precautions, I told myself. The world wasn't the pleasant, safe place I imagined it was as a child, where people who wanted to hurt you lived in a far distant corner, if they existed at all.

Once the trial was over, I didn't waste time dwelling on the fate of my attacker. What became of Dennis Price—whether he continued on his merry way to perdition, or whether he was so relieved that he dodged a prosecutorial bullet that he repented and straightened his life—I didn't know. Or care.

I never could decide whether mentally compartmentalizing the attack was a healthy thing to do, or if I was simply in denial. *Well, whatever works,* I would tell myself. The important thing was that I seemed to have recovered, at least enough to carry on with life. Still, I frequently had the sensation that I had stepped out of a building engulfed in flames, only to find to my utter amazement that I was not just alive, but barely singed. I discovered that I was okay.

I was convinced that Charlotte had set me on a path to healing. Eventually I reached the conclusion that I had made a miraculous recovery. Years went by. Life became relatively uneventful, even a bit boring, which was fine with me. That's why I couldn't understand why, without warning, the approach of the tenth anniversary of the attack jolted me like electricity. I didn't even wait for the decade milestone: by the ninth year, I was completely rattled. I began to suspect that I wasn't as emotionally healthy and whole as I claimed. Maybe I never would be.

The ninth anniversary was different in other ways. I wasn't my mournful self, purposely reopening an old wound. Instead I was filled with a cold dread. My stomach twisted tighter as the day wore on. By evening, I felt physically ill. I sat cross-legged on the living room floor and lit a stout sandalwood candle. I breathed in the scent, trying to calm my nerves and settle my stomach. This was worrisome. It didn't seem related to my annual wallowing in self-pity, or concern that I was closing in on my thirtieth birthday. I didn't care much about age, since I had long ago left my youth behind. What worried me was that this reaction might signal the return of all the old anxiety.

"Shit." I said it with such force that the word extinguished the candle. I had my head propped on my hands and was watching the smoke spiral from the candle when Alex walked into the room. He stopped and looked at me oddly. Still distracted, I wondered why until I realized that I was staring at him like he was a complete stranger, instead of the person with whom I had been living for the past year.

Alex and I were, I suppose, a couple. It had started as friendship, then a matter of convenience, and none of that had changed much for me. Mostly I liked Alex because I felt more secure when he was around. Recently I noticed, with some discomfort and even more guilt, that Alex frequently talked about us in the first person plural. As in "we'll do this together" or "we should talk about our plans."

"I would think you'd like having a relationship with no strings attached," I would say lightly. But he didn't take the hint.

When this topic came up with more and more frequency, I would look at Alex curiously. Most of my attempts at relationships did not last very long because I suspected that most guys instinctively knew something was off-kilter. They guessed that there was some huge baggage, even if I thought I was hiding it well. Maybe Alex was a little less sensitive. Even after a year of our being together, he still didn't know about my past. Neither did he appear to even guess that I was damaged goods.

His expression as he looked at me over the candle was half-quizzical, half-doubtful. Dear Alex. I was so fond of him. Even if he couldn't see the truth about me—even if I went on pretending that we had a future together—this wasn't fair.

I sat up straight and looked directly into his eyes. "I want out," I said.

The morning after the ninth anniversary, the day after I upended my life by breaking it off with Alex, I expected to feel some kind of remorse for my impulsive decision. Instead, I felt good. Well, at least relieved. And that was better than I had felt in a long time.

I woke before the alarm and raised my head to look at Alex, who slept quietly, his back to me. I still felt no regret. That was promising.

I lay back and tried to assess exactly how I did feel. I was calmer and less anxious. That was also hopeful. Maybe it was proof that I had, for once, made the right move. I had to find a place to live and start over, but so what? I began to make mental lists of what I needed to do when I realized, startled, that I would be on my own for the first time. I had never lived by myself. It was always my parents' home, or with roommates, or something. The prospect of setting off alone struck me as exciting, and that in itself was unusual. In the past—even as recently as the previous day—the idea would have scared me to death.

I tucked my arms under my head and stared at the ceiling. Maybe taking stock was good for me after all.

When the day came that I was to move into my very own apartment and strike out on a brave new life, I had lost not only the sense of excitement, but my courage as well.

"I don't know if I can do this," I confessed to Suzy. I was hunched over the steering wheel of the mid-sized U-Haul truck, driving hesitantly.

"Of course, you can. It's not like it's a stick shift. Give it some gas." Suzy was a fellow graphic designer at the ad agency where I worked, and the closest I had to a best friend in

Maryland. She shot an annoyed look from the passenger side of the truck's cab. Suzy might have had a soft heart, but she was famously impatient; she didn't brook nonsense even on a good day. She had been gracious in arranging for her husband to care for their two small children so that she could take me to the truck rental center and help with the move. But she hadn't counted on the whole process taking so long.

"Hey, I'm going the speed limit. But what I meant by not being able to do this was, maybe this move isn't such a hot idea."

"It's a little late now, isn't it?"

I nodded. But I miserably considered that I just wasn't cut out to be someone who could live on their own. It was possible that I was always going to need the protection of sharing my living space. I had a sudden dark vision of myself as old, alone, and terrified. I shuddered, but it was hardly likely that Suzy would have noticed with the violent way the truck was vibrating. It didn't matter though. Suzy was the only person in Maryland I had told the story of the attack to. She knew why I had cold feet.

"At my age I should be able to be self-sufficient." This was more or less mumbled into the steering wheel. I was surprised Suzy had heard me.

"If you're afraid of being on your own, maybe you should get a dog."

I rolled my eyes.

"You'll be fine," she added gruffly.

I'll be fine, I said to myself as we bumped along, repeating it until I believed it.

It wasn't that I didn't enjoy living in Chestertown. I had fallen in love with this little Maryland town, instantly charmed by the houses with their white pillars and large porches, and gardens hemmed in by picket fences. I hadn't for a moment regretted moving here from Pennsylvania a few years ago. That move had really been picking up stakes and starting over, I reminded myself, even if I had felt continually protected, first by sharing a large house with a group of young women and then moving in with Alex.

I first discovered this area on the Eastern Shore of the Chesapeake while driving through a rural area of southeastern Pennsylvania and accidentally wandering into Maryland. Even though I had grown up in Pennsylvania, I had always considered the state, with its thick woods and scenic roads, beautiful but somewhat forbidding. Just crossing the border into Maryland gave me a feeling that was very different. The bright fields and gently rolling hills were welcoming in a soothing way.

When I left college with a degree in fine arts and graphic design, my first jobs as a designer were close to home in the Philadelphia suburbs. I always assumed I would stay in the area—my extended family traditionally stuck close to home—until that Sunday drive took me into Maryland. A few weeks later, I made another trip deeper down the Eastern Shore and happened upon Chestertown on the day the town was celebrating the reenactment of its Revolutionary War tea party in which, according to local legend, colonial patriots protesting excessive taxes had thrown crates of tea into Chestertown's small harbor. I bought an ice cream cone and wandered, enchanted, among the tourists and families and teen actors in colonial garb. Everyone seemed *happy*. It was like a throwback to a more innocent time. By the end of the day, I had decided to live there. Within the space of a few months, my job, living arrangements, and moving all fell into place and I was a full-fledged resident.

The process of finding my own apartment, post-Alex, turned out to be just as smooth. After only a few excursions, I took a place on the third and top floor of a renovated elementary school that dated back to the 1920s. From the outside it still looked like an old-fashioned square school, but the inside was transformed. As soon as I saw it, I knew this was my new home.

The best part was the large skylight in one room. That room was intended as a bedroom, but I saw its potential as an art studio. This, I was sure, would inspire me to pick up painting again. I had let that slip for a long time with the excuse that my day job as a graphic artist kept me active in art. But I knew that work wasn't the same as painting, which was once such a compulsion for me. I looked at the natural light flooding the room from the skylight, and felt again the creative tug.

I interrupted the rental agent in the midst of her spiel about the building's amenities. "I'll take it," I said.

By seven thirty in the evening on moving day, everyone had long since gone home. I was bone weary. But I willed my body to carry one more box from my car.

I was trying to balance the box and pull open the heavy glass door in the building's main entrance, when I stopped and turned to the sky that was fading into night. The air wrapped around me in a perfect warm-bath temperature. I had to savor it, if only for a moment. It was springtime. You could practically smell the rebirth.

Perfect timing, I thought. *I'm starting anew.* This was a good sign.

But still I had to shake off the familiar nagging feeling, that tiny animal clawing at my insides and making me question whether I would ever be normal. I couldn't go down that road right now. At least the unreasonable fear that threatened to paralyze me during the drive with Suzy this morning seemed to be gone.

I stood another moment, trying to recapture the sensation that had made me stop in the first place. But it was like trying to hold on to the edges of a dream.

I turned and let the door slam shut. Slowly, because my leg muscles were aching, I again climbed the stairs to my apartment. Before I inserted the shiny, fresh-cut key into the lock, I glanced up and down the hallway, an old habit. *Better safe than sorry*, I said for God knew how many times in the last decade, and pushed open my new front door. I half-tumbled into the vestibule, which was crowded with more cardboard boxes than I remembered packing.

I reached over and flipped an overhead light switch. "Let there be light," I said to the empty apartment.

My voice echoed. *Of course it would*, I told myself. *No carpets or curtains to absorb sound*. Still, the excitement and that satisfying sense of independence seemed to be slipping away under the harsh dome light in the cluttered hallway.

I looked at the uninterrupted chaos of boxes and bags, the furniture left cockeyed wherever it was pushed or dropped. Despite the mess, the place seemed sterile. The windows, devoid of window treatments, were black squares reflecting the night. I was tempted to switch off the light again.

I took a deep breath. This could all be tackled tomorrow. All that was needed at the moment was a toothbrush and a pillow. In fact, I could make do—

Wait. Did I lock the car?

I looked around desperately as if the clutter held the answer. I was always so security conscious. I not only locked everything in sight, even if I was leaving only for a few moments, but I double-checked and triple-checked that I locked up. But now, after the endless trips to the parking lot and back, I couldn't be sure. I had the awful mental picture of leaving the car doors wide open and the key in the ignition.

I gnawed a broken fingernail. I really didn't want to venture out again. I was exhausted, my friends had gone home, and night had fallen. But I couldn't risk leaving my vehicle unlocked all night. For all I knew, the neighborhood might have been experiencing a rash of car thefts.

Obvious choice, Quinn. Get going. And please leave the fingernails alone. I might finally be on my own, but I could still hear my mother in my head.

I went back to my front door, opened it just wide enough to poke my head out, and peered up and down the hallway. Empty. It was probably my imagination, but now that daylight was gone, the place had an entirely different feel. A little eerie.

With another deep breath, I stepped out, pulled the door shut, and locked it in one seamless movement. I marched toward the stairwell, at first at a sedate pace. But not even a few steps from the sanctuary of the apartment, anxiety was climbing up my throat, threatening to choke me. When I reached the steps I ran down them as I gripped the pepper spray canister attached to my key chain.

I reached the foot of the stairs. *Thank God*, I thought as I lunged for the crash bar. The door fell open on its own. I nearly tumbled out from my momentum.

A tall, powerful-looking man looked down at me, as startled to see me as I was to see him. He had a goatee and a shaved head that should have given him an air of intimidation but for the eyeglasses that made him appear friendly. Still, I automatically tensed the hand holding the pepper spray. Without even realizing it, I raised my arm to point the spray at him. His reaction, unexpectedly, was a grin.

"Don't shoot."

I flashed a smile of my own. The man could have been a mass murderer, but his demeanor was disarming.

"Sorry," I mumbled, sticking the pepper spray halfway in my pocket, my finger still on the trigger. "Better safe than sorry." I thought about it a moment. "I guess that saying kind of contradicts my apology."

The man laughed. "No, I know exactly what you mean," he said. I shot him a look. He knew what I meant? He sounded so sincere that it occurred to me that maybe he did understand.

"You're a new resident, I guess? There aren't a lot of units in this building, so after a while the new people sort of stand out. So, let me stop being rude and introduce myself. I'm Joe Armstrong and I live"—he reached around and patted the apartment door behind me—"right here."

His sudden movement made me flinch. To Joe's credit, he didn't react.

"Conveniently located near the front doors, so I suppose I'm the default sentry. If you need anything, just holler."

I nodded, still nervous. He had taken a step back after reaching for the door, but he still seemed a little too close. "I'm Quinn," I said as an afterthought. I avoided glancing down to see if he was extending his hand. He might take that as invitation to shake, and I was busy visualizing him grabbing me in mid-handshake and yanking me into the apartment. I still had my hand in my pocket, firmly on the pepper spray. This person may have appeared innocuous enough, but so had my attacker.

"Uh, I'd better be going. Forgot something in the car . . ." *Damn. Why did I say that?* I edged closer to the crash bar.

"Hey, if you want, I can watch from the entrance here. You know, make sure you get to your car and back okay. Or I could walk you to your car. Whatever you're more comfortable with."

I stopped and looked at him. He seemed earnest despite the macho look. For instance, he wore an expensive-looking leather jacket over sharply pressed dress slacks. It was like he was trying to come across as tough but another persona kept oozing out. I couldn't help but find this endearing.

"Really? You would do that?"

"I can understand that you don't want a perfect stranger following you to your car. But I do have a good view from here. On the off chance something should happen, you know?" He looked embarrassed. "I mean, I could be there in a flash."

I suddenly seemed to be doing all sorts of things out of character for me, but I decided to take a chance. Something told me that it was okay, that this person was trustworthy.

"I would appreciate it. I just want to run to my car. It's the one parked right over there."

Joe nodded and pushed open the door. On cue, I dashed to my Toyota. As soon as I reached it, I looked back and saw him at the top of the steps leading up to the front doors. He was a comforting, solid figure, silhouetted in the floodlights that bathed the building's facade in a white glow. He did look like a sentry.

I don't know what possessed me, but I waved to him. He held up a hand in response.

The car doors were locked. But the rear window was partially open. Cursing myself, I methodically checked the seats and floors for cartons or stray items. I had just taken a half a step to return to the building when I thought to look in the trunk. Inside was a large grocery bag full of kitchen paraphernalia, including perishable food.

"Look at this," I muttered, hefting the bag. I shut the trunk lid with a satisfying click, and doubled-checked the locks on the car doors. It was only then, standing there for a moment in the still parking lot, that I realized I had none of the usual panic I ordinarily would have experienced. I was methodically moving about, feeling calm and *normal.* There was hope for me yet. I felt a sudden urge to whistle, sing, or something.

Instead, I took a last careful look around and returned to the building, my pace intentionally measured. I thanked Joe and politely refused his offer to walk me up to my apartment. He could very well be the nicest guy in the world and trustworthy enough for a parking lot run, but I wasn't willing to throw caution to the wind. *Not on a hunch and a briefly held sense of serenity*, I thought as I climbed the steps to my apartment one last time. I resisted the temptation to look back and check, but I was pretty sure he still stood there at the bottom of the steps, watching me.

CHAPTER THREE

Early April 1987: a university campus, Pennsylvania

Among my family members, I was not generally perceived as someone who handled the unexpected. Any time I came close to an emergency, I had one of two reactions: either I froze, or I fell apart.

"For God's sake, Quinn," my mother would say when I couldn't catch a glass falling from the table. I would also fail to jump out of the way of the crashing shards as the glass hit the floor. I just didn't seem to have the same instincts other people had.

"I certainly hope you aren't planning a future career as a first responder," my mother would say, pushing her hair from her face as she always did when exasperated.

I could clearly remember one summer afternoon as a seven-year-old, when the two sisters who lived across the street, Peggy and Cynthia, and I ventured to the creek that ran through the neighborhood. Visiting the creek was expressly forbidden by our parents; I'm pretty sure that's the only reason we wanted to go there. After we climbed a fence of thick wire rope cable and teetered at the top of the steep embankment, I could see why we weren't allowed there: the creek was an ancient and frightening thing. There was hardly any water; mostly it was a deep fissure in the earth. We were looking at this slash of a creek from the top of the embankment, when Peggy inexplicably panicked. She took off like a rabbit. Cynthia lunged after her, tried to jump the cable fencing, and cut a deep gash in her thigh.

Peggy ran to her house and began beating on the front door, followed by a bloodied, screaming Cynthia. I only heard about it later. As usual, I had remained rooted to my little patch of earth, frozen, unable to move.

I was being attacked, I thought, as I bumped along. But it was incomprehensible. The stranger had stopped me as I walked across campus, asked me the time, and grabbed me when I looked down at my watch. That could not have taken place very long ago. A few minutes maybe, but it was difficult to tell. Time continued to expand.

It was clear, though, that the experience had begun to take on different dimensions. The attacker had control of both the knife and me, and so the world had changed. In fact the world had changed quite literally.

I became aware that the ground was racing beneath me. There seemed to be an endless crashing with branches. Sticks were whipping about my head, pebbles and rocks scraping my back and legs. I was being dragged through the foliage and underbrush by my hair. I worried he would pull it all out.

If only I could get my wits about me. I wanted to beg him to stop, even if just for a minute. I thought I heard screams in the distance, and that seemed very odd—*was another girl being attacked on this same campus at the same time?*—until I realized I was the one who was screaming.

"Shut up," he grunted. He was breathing heavily from the effort of dragging me. A piece of my jeans must have ripped near the hip, causing the brush and rocks and what felt like a million sharp objects to tear into my flesh. My body was bumping, ripping, hurting. He let go of my hair and pulled me by the wrists, but this was worse. My arms felt like they would come out of their sockets.

At last he stopped. I could hear him panting. I squinted to try to see where I was. It appeared to be a wooded area, but I could see an expanse of lawn up ahead and the fluorescent lights of a building through the darkness.

"Get up." He yanked on my arms again, pulling me to a standing position. I yelped.

He grabbed my face with one hand and pulled it close to his. He spoke through gritted teeth. His breath stank. "We're going in there and I don't want you to make a peep. Or you're dead. Understand? Dead."

I managed the slightest of nods. My heart was thumping so hard, it threatened to bang its way out of my rib cage. The only clear thought I had was that if I could just stay outside, I might have a shot at being rescued. The feeling in my gut told me that if he got me inside, it would be all over. The problem was that I had no idea how to stop him or how to get away.

He pushed me in the direction of the building, holding my arms twisted behind my back.

The building began to take shape as we neared it. I recognized it. We were at a group of dormitories on the east end of campus. These were very familiar to me because I had lived in another building in the same group during my first year at school.

At the rear of the building, we came upon a fire door. These emergency exits were usually locked and inaccessible from the exterior. But this one was open.

Maybe I could delay the inevitable. I could hope for a break, for someone to come by, anything. I tried to make myself as much of a dead weight as possible. He wasn't the least bit fooled, and hissed a stream of rebukes and threats into my ear. Still, he was forced to half-drag me up a full flight of stairs and down a long corridor. I took the tiniest shred of pride in that, even as I realized that it was to no avail. We didn't encounter a single person. The building might as well as have been vacant.

Of course it is, I thought bitterly. Students would be away for the weekend or out at parties. They wouldn't be wandering the halls of a dormitory on a Saturday night looking to help a girl who was about to be raped.

We stopped in front of a door that looked exactly like every other one. Still firmly clutching me, he cocked his head and listened. I could only guess that he was making sure no one was inside. Abruptly, he pushed open the door and pulled me in the room in a single motion.

Once inside, I couldn't see how he would have suspected anyone to have been there. The room was stripped bare except for the obligatory dual beds, and the beds consisted only of mattresses. There were no linens or blankets. No books, personal items, or clothes were in sight. None of the wall posters that decorated every dormitory room. It didn't appear anyone lived here.

Without warning, my attacker half-twisted like a discus thrower and shoved me toward one of the beds. I missed the bed and landed hard on the bare linoleum floor. He looked down at me with disgust.

"Get undressed. Now."

Once again, I thought, *This is it. I'm not going to survive this.* I procrastinated, waiting as long as I dared. I rose slowly only when he began making impatient gestures with the knife.

"Okay," I mumbled. Without taking off my jacket, I began to slowly unbutton my shirt. I gave a short desperate look around and noticed the window. It was covered with the same ugly plaid drapes found in every dorm room on campus. Although the curtains had been pulled across the glass, a sliver showed where the edges failed to meet. I could make out another dormitory building and a few squares of lit windows. Lights that were cold and distant, offering no help.

I can't do this. My legs were shaking.

I was shocked by the hard slap to my face. I found myself looking at him, staring stupidly, barely registering the stream of threats pouring from his mouth. I struggled to gather myself, struggled not to cry. My muscles were starting to spasm. I was trying to undress faster, but it was difficult to move. My attacker had lost patience. With one swipe of the knife, he sliced through the fabric of my blouse. The blade hit skin.

The knife hadn't cut me deeply—in truth it had barely scratched me—but it was too much. I lost control. I wailed and wept and flailed my arms in the air, not caring if he used the knife again. It was a tantrum of utter futility, no better than shaking a fist at the heavens during a thunderstorm. I felt myself sinking beneath some invisible roiling torrent.

Before I knew it, I was immobilized, wrists tied, and a cloth stuffed in my mouth.

It was in this state, ironically, that the reality of the situation struck me. To get through this, I would have to compartmentalize, and maybe just remove myself mentally. I forced my body to go limp and prayed that I would die.

The remainder of the night was far from a blur. I was acutely aware of everything. I was stubbornly holding on to the idea that if I could mentally catalog every detail, it would somehow help later, when he was captured. That is, if he was captured. And if I lived. Part of me wanted it over with—just kill me and be done with it, I would think several times during the night. But another, deeper part of me believed that not only would I survive, but that there would eventually be justice.

In the meantime I had to get through it.

Years later, my friend Penny would tell me about giving birth using natural childbirth breathing techniques. "Before I had the baby, I really didn't believe any of that breathing stuff would work," she told me. "You don't think you can possibly get on top of the pain. But you can. The contractions come in waves. I would breathe and focus and somehow it was all manageable. Just like swimming."

I don't have children, and as a result of the attack, I will never be able to, but I knew exactly what Penny was talking about. During my ordeal, I must have instinctively resorted to breathing my way through it. I managed to climb on top of each wave of terror and ready myself for the next one.

There were a few points though when the fear was overwhelming, such as when he inexplicably doused me with ammonia. The fumes burned my eyes and lungs. My immediate thought was that it was flammable and that he was going to set me on fire.

He didn't set me alight, but he did use the knife. I tensed every time, expecting a deep plunge, but most of the cuts were quick slashes across my torso and arms. Most were superficial, although they stung from the ammonia. The one exception was when he used the knife to make deep and deliberate cuts into my forearm, concentrating there for what seemed like a long time. It wasn't until later that I discovered that he had carved a word into my flesh.

"You know what, Linda?" he said as he cut me. He might as well have been a tattoo artist, chatting with a client.

My name's not Linda. For an instant I was afraid I had given voice to the thought, even though I was still gagged.

"I could cut your eyes out. That's an option. Then you couldn't go around identifying people. People like me. What do you think of that, Linda?" Suddenly he had hold of my head and was pushing the tip of the knife against the soft tissue around my swollen left eye. I tried to squeeze my eyes shut tighter. My throat was raw from trying to scream through the gag.

Then suddenly, he released me, leaping back and laughing crazily as I wept. *This isn't fair,* I thought. *I'm not Linda. I'm not Linda.*

It occurred to me, as I lay on the rough, scratchy mattress, that it was becoming increasingly hard to gauge the time. A few minutes could have passed, or maybe a million years. I didn't know why it bothered me, other than that perhaps I was cling-ing to the idea that if I was aware of time passing, I was still in command of something. My senses, I suppose.

I must have fallen asleep briefly or passed out. That would explain why I lost track of things. But there was none of the confusion of awakening, or any hope that I had just been dreaming. I knew exactly where I was. I had awoken into the middle of a nightmare.

Dawn was creeping across the rectangle of the plaid drapes. At some point the harsh fluorescent ceiling light had been switched off. The grayness of morning was beginning to lighten the room's shadows.

I was cold. I was also uncomfortable. My arms were tied to something above my head. I tried shifting, but that felt worse.

Part of the problem was that beneath me was some sort of sticky substance. I managed with some effort to twist my head and peer through my swollen eyes. I saw that the substance was blood. Other than that, it was hard to figure out how injured I was. At least he had taken out the gag so I was able to breathe.

I was still alive. But nothing else seemed to have changed. I was still in the same dorm room, still in the same situation. I couldn't see my attacker, but I doubted I was lucky enough that he had disappeared.

Painfully, I twisted around to check. He was on the floor, asleep.

Just then, his eyelids fluttered and opened. By reflex, I immediately shut my eyes. It was silly, like a child closing his eyes and pretending he is invisible. And it was a completely ineffective defense.

Quickly he was on his feet and shoving me. I felt nausea rising into my throat, and for a moment I wasn't sure if I could keep it from exploding from my mouth. I gagged. God knew what he would do if I vomited on him.

I struggled to speak but my lip hurt. *It must be cut*, I thought calmly. I tried to moisten my lips and made one final effort to stage my own rescue.

"If you . . . if you'll just untie my wrists, maybe I can . . ."

I looked away and waited, unable to breathe. It was a very long moment. I felt him looking at me.

Without a word, he began to undo the knots around my wrists. My arms were finally free. I lowered them and began to rub my stiff bicep muscles.

"Okay," I murmured, mostly to expel my breath. I could sense his impatience growing again. Slowly I pulled my legs toward my torso to get into a semi-sitting position, pretending to be cooperative. I allowed my hands to inch toward him.

I reached and reached. Then, abruptly I leaned back and reared my legs. Adrenaline flowing, and with strength I didn't know I possessed, I kicked with all my might.

In my mind, I was kicking with the force of a Thai boxer. But the result was a disappointingly weak effort. I had wanted to inflict maximum damage, but the most I could manage was a dull impact from the flat of my bare feet. But luckily I had caught him off balance. That, more than the force of my kick, sent him skidding onto the linoleum.

I didn't wait to see what he did. In a single movement I was up, wrenching open the door, which, miraculously, was unlocked.

The next instant I was in the hallway, bruised, blood-encrusted, and, as my grandmother used to say, screaming bloody murder.

CHAPTER FOUR

1997: Maryland

Some time went by before I saw Joe Armstrong again. I saw other residents frequently and we would exchange brief pleasantries. No in-depth conversations yet, which was fine with me. I was busy, both at work and getting settled in my new place. I also was spending most of my free time in my extra bedroom–turned–art studio happily resuming my sketching and painting. With all I had going on, there was little time to get cozy with the neighbors.

After that first night, I hadn't even given much thought to Joe. So, when we nearly collided one morning several months later near the building's front entrance, I thought he looked familiar but it took me a moment to register who he was.

"Oh. Hello." I had pulled up just short of crashing into him as he turned away from his apartment door.

"Whoa. Guess we're both running late for work, aren't we?" He was downright cheery. *Probably a morning person*, I thought.

"Sorry about that," I murmured.

I would have guessed that Joe might appear differently in daylight. But he conveyed the same solid appearance, the kind that would have been imposing but for his pleasant demeanor. Friendly in an arm's length sort of way.

I felt a sudden sharp embarrassment about my actions that night. I could now see that I must have come across as clingy and fearful. I dropped my eyes and examined the tops of his shoes. They were black dress shoes, very shiny.

"Were you in the Army or something?"

"As a matter of fact, yes. How did you know?" He seemed amused.

I pointed at his shoes. *God, this is getting awkward.* I managed to mutter, "Good morning," and pushed open the door.

Joe might have called after me; I wasn't sure. My face burning, I marched double time toward my car, keeping my gaze directly on my Toyota. I didn't want to catch sight of him as he made his way to his car and be forced into more stilted conversation. I didn't know what was worse—rudely pushing past him to get out the door like I was at some kind of Macy's sale, or running away. At this point he was probably thinking I was out of my mind.

I concentrated on getting myself into the Toyota, locking the doors, buckling up, and adjusting my sunglasses. I was determined not to look around until it was necessary. I put the car in reverse and, when I finally turned to look before backing out of my parking spot, I stomped on the brakes harder than was necessary. There he was, sitting in his car, patiently waiting for me to proceed.

He gave a big smile and waved me on. Sighing, I inched out, and lifted my fingers in a tentative wave as I drove off.

I related the whole experience to Suzy when I got to work.

"He's probably a totally normal person. A nice person, even. Then I go and act like he's Attila the Hun." I propped my elbows on my desk and looked at her. It was fascinating, in a way, to watch Suzy, a bundle of nervous energy who constantly moved at top speed.

"Give yourself a break." Suzy managed to sound interested in the conversation as her eyes darted around the computer screen, her hand manipulating the mouse. She had an astounding ability to juggle all aspects of her life, including her various roles as graphic artist, friend, mother, and wife. She claimed her multitasking skills at work came from being extremely efficient with her time. She had to leave precisely at four thirty each afternoon to pick up her two little boys from day care.

"I just don't have time to waste," Suzy explained to me shortly after I started at the agency. "My family commitments don't give me the freedom to stay late to finish a project, like you might. When we're busy, I've got to use every moment of the day. It's all very necessary, once you know how Helga is."

I did come to know how Helga, our boss, was. Our mutually held fear of Helga had become the foundation of my friendship with Suzy.

"Let me get this straight." As she spoke, Suzy continued moving and clicking the mouse. "You run into him the night you moved in, and he protects you from unseen forces in the parking lot. You two have a brief moment when everything seemed all cozy and warm. Then today you see him and treat him like a pariah."

"Pretty much."

"Most likely, he's wondering where he went wrong." Suzy glanced over for a second, not breaking from her work. "He could be looking for an opportunity to ask you on a date. That's what it sounds like to me anyway." She refocused on her computer screen.

"I don't think I'm ready for that. Maybe I'll never be ready."

This statement seemed to startle Suzy to the point that she actually stopped what she was doing. She turned to me. "Oh my God. Was it that horrible with Alex?"

I shifted, sorry that I had opened this line of conversation. "Not at all. In fact, Alex was too much of a safety net. That was one reason I wanted to end it. I was hiding behind him."

Suzy resumed her work without comment.

"It's just," I added belatedly, "that I'm trying to be on my own. So far, I like it. I'm not as afraid as I thought I would be. And I'm not sure I'm cut out to be the other half of a couple."

"Then why care about why kind of impression you're leaving with this guy? What's his name again? Joe?"

She had a point, but I shrugged it off. "I don't want to look bad while becoming a spinster."

Suzy laughed. I tried to change the topic by launching into the story of an old widow in my neighborhood when I was growing up. The woman was a recluse in an ivy-covered Tudor house that was very mysterious. The local kids would whisper that she was a witch.

"Benny Smithson in particular never shut up about her," I told Suzy. "He said she could cast a spell if you got within shouting distance of her house. He claimed to have it on good authority from his parents."

"Sounds like a story his parents told him to keep Benny in line. And she probably wasn't a witch at all. Just old and alone, the poor thing," Suzy said.

I was becoming convinced that it would be the same for me someday. Old and alone. But why, I wondered irritably, did old and alone sound unbearable, while young and solitary seemed so independent and free? At least it did to me.

On a lovely Friday evening in June, I was driving home from work, exhausted.

It had been a long week. Helga, reveling in her role as creative director of the agency, spent the majority of the time a nervous wreck and admonishing us while we worked feverishly to prepare campaign ideas for one of our most difficult clients. Helga, always insecure about her own artistic abilities—in Suzy's and my opinions, she possessed none—was particularly vicious during these types of preparations, and we struggled to come up with creative approaches that met her approval. In this latest project, I had the role of lead designer, but Helga cast aside every one of my designs. I was forced to start anew so many times that I just wanted it over with.

Now at last, it was. We had not only survived, but won the contract. I was grateful that the reaction to the design concepts was positive. At least it was a bit more than a luke-warm response, anyway. Helga took full credit for everything, of course. At one point during the meeting, as we all sat stiffly around the conference table, Suzy caught my eye and gave a slight grimace and the tiniest of nods in Helga's direction. Helga was Helga.

A luxurious weekend stretched before me. I was looking forward to nothing more strenuous than flopping onto the sofa and reading and watching movies. I drove slowly, visual-izing a glass of iced tea in my hand with a fan blowing cool air over me.

It was nearly seven thirty when I pulled into the parking lot. The sun, sinking lower, washed the front of the apartment building in golden light. I nosed the car into what had become my usual parking spot and smiled. It felt good to have my own place with my very own parking space. I'd finally found my real home.

I leaned over to gather my purse and work bag from the passenger seat and automatically reached for the door handle without looking. My hand hit air. Startled, I looked up and saw Joe Armstrong holding my door open. I gaped at him.

"Guess I startled you." He seemed jubilant at having accomplished this. "So," he added perfunctorily, as if we saw each other daily, "how was your day?"

I got out of the car slowly. "Okay, I guess."

"A beautiful evening, isn't it?" Joe was nodding and smiling. He seemed much more vivacious than before. In fact, he was borderline bubbly. I began to wonder if he had been drinking.

"I know it's pretty forward of me, and I'm not usually like this." My confusion was probably evident. "The thing is, I just received a big promotion at work. That means it was a great day for me and I really would love to share it with someone. I was wondering if you would do me the honor of helping me celebrate. I'm thinking beer and pizza at La Taverna. Not quite champagne and fireworks but it's short notice, you know?" It came out in a rush.

Say something, I told myself.

I wanted to respond. A big part of me wanted to throw caution to the wind and say yes, I'll go have pizza with you because you seem to be a perfectly nice person. But as usual, I started overthinking it. My mind raced with thoughts that wouldn't have been polite to say aloud, such as it's not a good idea to start anything, or I really need to continue my solitary life. Yet here was this man I barely knew who looked for an instant like his face might start to crumble if I said no. If that happened, I didn't think I would be able to stand it. Conflicted,

I remained mute. Awkward seconds passed until it became almost unbearable.

"Well," Joe said slowly. "Like I said, it's short notice. That's okay."

I watched helplessly as he crossed the wide parking lot to his own car. Even from a distance, I could see his shoulders slump. For some reason, that slight movement spurred me into action.

"Wait!" I called. Hurriedly, I grabbed my bags, locked the car, and trotted after him.

"Wait a minute," I called again, breathless. He didn't seem to hear me. He was already on the far side of the lot. "I'm going to get shin splits by the time I get there," I grumbled to myself. Because of the client meeting, I was wearing a pencil-slim skirt and high heels, an outfit that made jogging difficult. My handbag slapped me with every stride. I could feel my hair, which had been pinned back, coming loose.

"Joe!" I yelled. It was unnecessarily loud, because by this time I was only a few feet from him as he was starting to open his car door. He turned to me just as the toe of my pump caught a large crack in the blacktop. My purse went flying in one direction, and my shoe in another. I would have landed on my face but for Joe catching me.

He gently set me upright. "Are you okay?"

"I always seem to be crashing into you." Embarrassed, I rearranged my skirt, then bent to search for my shoe. "Trust me, it's not on purpose."

Joe retrieved my shoe and purse, and handed them to me. "I'm beginning to think you must have played football. What with the tackles, and all." He held out his arm so I could lean on it to fit my shoe back on. "What would you say if I asked you again about dinner?"

Other than my decision to leave Alex and strike out on my own, this was probably the second most impetuous move I would ever make. At the moment, it felt remarkably right.

I smiled. "I would say that you talked me into it."

At the start I had no intention of telling Joe about the attack. But at different points in the evening, I found myself wanting to bring it up, at first maybe just an oblique, mysterious reference. Soon I was tempted to spill the whole story. It was strange. I hadn't felt that impulse since the days when I would tell anyone and everyone. *Don't do it*, I told myself. It was bad enough that I was this far outside my comfort zone, impulsively spending an evening with a stranger. I didn't need to make it worse by engaging in a true confession at the first opportunity.

But, on the other hand, there was Joe. He had this aura about him that made me feel that he had all the answers. He would have made a good therapist. If he had been one I had seen in the past, I probably would have stuck it out.

We sat in the dark wood-paneled restaurant illuminated by little table lamps, sipping beer long after we had finished dinner. Joe asked a lot of questions, which struck me as true interest, not just polite conversation. He listened intently to my responses—which only heightened the urge to tell him my secret—and shared some details about himself. But while Joe seemed skilled in inquiring about topics without being rude, I was reluctant to ask too many questions. I mostly listened. When he described himself as boring, I did smile a little. I found him comfortingly normal. I was fascinated with normal.

Joe was from upstate New York, born to older parents who had given up on the idea of children until they were surprised by Joe. "They were more than surprised. Flabbergasted, really. But thrilled," he added quickly. A sister followed a year later, and the two were doted on by their parents and several aunts who lived nearby. But Joe apparently was the special child. "Maybe because I was first? I don't know. But I got everything I ever wanted, and was constantly the center of attention. How I didn't turn out spoiled is a mystery. Genetics, I suppose."

Joe grew up and went into accounting, following his father's career path. "A little piece of me is still rebellious. A throwback to my college days." He gave a wry grin. "But now I need to look the corporate part whether I want to or not." Joe worked in the accounting department of a fairly large company where his promotion to a position just below the chief financial officer had been announced that very morning.

"It's a big deal. Well, to me. And just at my office. So, I guess it really isn't such a big deal," Joe said, reddening again. I felt compelled to help him.

"Are you kidding? It's a great achievement and you should be proud." I saluted him with my half-empty glass. He smiled gratefully.

"So why aren't you celebrating with a girlfriend? Or maybe there's a wife somewhere?" I raised my brows whimsically.

"Neither at the moment. Well, I never had a wife. Not yet, anyway. I did have a girlfriend until about eight months ago. It just didn't develop into what either of us wanted. Sort of death of a relationship by mutual agreement."

I nodded. "That's pretty much the story of my ex-boyfriend." I took another sip of beer. Something else out of character for me. I didn't even like beer.

"You know, we seem to have things in common," I blurted out.

"Yeah? How so?"

"Well, we both have recently failed relationships," I ticked off the items on my fingers. "We both moved to Maryland for our jobs—well, I moved here because I liked the area and found a job—and we live in the same apartment building. So I guess we have the same taste in apartments."

"But we do have very different careers. I work in a place that's mostly men, and all they talk about are sports. You work in a very creative environment. We wouldn't know creative if we tripped over it."

Not for the first time that night, I surprised myself by laughing. The capacity he had to make me laugh put me uncharacteristically off guard. Then without thinking, I proceeded to launch into the one topic I had sworn off. Before I knew it, I was relating all the familiar details: the attack, the kidnapping, the rape, the subsequent trial—all of it. The old reactions set in, too. I crossed my arms and hugged myself to try to control the tremors.

Joe didn't seem to notice me shaking. He was even more absorbed than before, breaking eye contact only to hold up two fingers for the waitress to bring more drinks. Unlike nearly everyone else who had heard the account, he did not appear to be planning his escape. As I talked, I had the fleeting thought that he was actually interested.

Maybe it was the unexpected attention to my story, but something else was different. For the first time ever, I talked about how I felt, rather than just relating a narrative of the events.

"I don't know if you—as a man, I mean—can understand this, but everything can change in a second. He does this to you and many guys may think, what's the big thing, really? But it is. It's a total violation. I can't adequately describe it. Afterward, you can never think of yourself the same way."

I stopped, certain that I had crossed some invisible line. Joe was looking at me, nodding. I wasn't sure if that meant he understood or whether he was just being agreeable. But he appeared riveted and that gave me the courage to continue.

"Actually, I'm not sure what was worse, the actual crime, or the way the so-called justice system . . . I get so angry even now, thinking about it. It just wasn't fair." To my horror, tears sprang to my eyes. I dipped my head and tried to laugh it off. "We're supposed to be celebrating. Let's talk about something else."

"No, no, please. If you're okay, I'd really like to hear it all."

"Seriously?" I found a rumpled tissue in my purse and wiped away the mascara from my face before I could bring myself to look at Joe. I saw nothing but sincerity in his face. "Okay," I agreed.

I finished the tale but tried to race through the rest, editing out certain parts. But at every turn, Joe slowed me down. He would stop me and ask a question, then thoughtfully consider my answer. He seemed especially intrigued with the trial and its outcome.

Finally, I was done. I leaned back against the booth, exhausted. Joe was staring at me. "Are you telling me," he demanded, "that after all you went through, all the humiliation of a trial, and after the jury found him guilty—after all that, the judge just let him go?"

I nodded. I tried to busy myself by running my glass in wet circles on the table.

"The judge let him go free . . ." Joe repeated, astonished.

I kept my eyes lowered and picked up my disintegrating cocktail napkin, then let it fall into small bits on the table. I was really regretting opening up this whole discussion.

"I didn't go to trial for payback. Well, I guess I wanted some justice. Every victim does. But the main reason was that I thought it was my duty. Everyone kept warning me about future victims. Don't forget, they said, there are bound to be other women." I gave a tortured laugh. "I was stupid enough to believe that I could stop him."

Joe was quiet. "Do you think about it a lot?" he said finally. "I mean, after all this time, is it something always in the back of your mind? That's probably insensitive. I'm sorry."

I waved away his apology. "Not that long ago, I would have said I never think about it except on the anniversary of the attack. But a more truthful statement is that I think about it every time I close my eyes."

I was suddenly deeply embarrassed. What possessed me to start nattering about this? I looked past him and caught sight of a clock on the wall behind him. "Do you realize we've been sitting here for hours?"

Joe glanced over his shoulder to see for himself. "Wow, it's past midnight." He turned back. "I might have commandeered your evening, but I'm glad things worked out. It's been a great ending to one of the best days I've had in a long time."

"Lucky for us I happened to pull into the parking lot at that exact moment."

"Yes, lucky." He looked sheepish. "Actually, I was sort of hanging out waiting for you to come home."

"Are you kidding? I left the office late. How long were you waiting?"

"Just an hour or two." He laughed at my expression. "It's not like I had your number and could call you or anything. Why not give it to me? So I'll have it the next time."

I was tempted to ask how he was so sure there would be a next time, but I simply pulled a business card from my purse and wrote my home telephone number on the back. I handed it to him and marveled at how quickly he had managed to overcome all my carefully built defenses. Or maybe I was just ready to cave in.

I probably wouldn't hear from him for a few days because he was going out of town, Joe said when he dropped me off at my apartment. By then it was early Saturday morning, and he was heading out in a few hours to visit his mother in New York. The previous evening he had mentioned that his father died a few years ago and his mother was not in the best of health. "I've been promising her I would be there, but I had to put off the trip a couple of times because of the job."

"That's good that you're visiting your mother. But you really don't have to explain yourself."

"I didn't want you to think that I'm the kind of guy who stalks people in the parking lot, takes them out for pizza, and then doesn't call."

Actually, I didn't mind at all. I would have the luxury of mulling over the evening and how I felt—which was, in short, a little scared. I needed time alone to consider if I wanted this to continue, and I wasn't sure I wanted to discuss it with anyone. Once the workweek resumed, I even waited a few days before discussing it with Suzy. I could have predicted her reaction anyway.

"What exactly is so bad about spending time with this man? He seems like a very nice guy, right?" Suzy glanced at me for confirmation, then refocused her attention on her computer screen. Once again, she was working like a madwoman. I was perched on the edge of her desk, unconcerned about my own growing pile of work.

"I really don't understand your hesitation." She was unperturbed by my hovering, even though I was now peering over her shoulder. That would have annoyed me. "I know, I know, you want to be independent. But you might be passing up a perfectly good relationship. And remember: the beginning is critical. Don't be too standoffish, but don't get too close, too fast. If you share too much in the beginning, you might not ever hear from him again. I don't care what he says to the contrary."

"This isn't high school." I laughed but felt pangs of guilt. I thought about my jabbering about the attack. I had shared way too much already.

"I don't care how old you get, the rules don't change. In nursing homes they probably pass notes and talk about who kissed who."

After nearly two weeks, when I had neither heard from Joe nor run into him, I was starting to think Suzy was right. Joe must have decided that the evening we spent together at La Taverna was a big mistake. I tried to shrug it off. After all, I had spent days wondering if getting involved with someone again was a huge lapse in judgment.

The problem was, I missed him.

All the more reason to let it go. I had to be firm. I decided to focus on my work, both my job and the painting I had started working on in my little studio. But I couldn't help wondering whether Joe was going to great lengths to make sure that we didn't bump into each other. I noticed his car in the parking lot every morning in its usual space and I pictured him waiting in his apartment, peering out the peephole to make sure I had gone before he ventured out. But we couldn't steer clear of each other forever. I dreaded the next encounter, which would be both inevitable and awkward.

I can't rearrange my life, I thought with exasperation. I resolved two things: to forget about my neighbor and, for Pete's sake, not to cry about it.

It was a Sunday afternoon in early August, so hot that heat seemed to float in waves from the street. But I was oblivious to the weather, spending the day in my studio with the air conditioning set on high. I was engrossed in my latest painting, a scene of a sailboat pulled up on a shoreline, and thinking of nothing else when Joe knocked at my door.

Through the peephole I saw him standing close to the opposite wall so that I could get a full view of him and the large bouquet of flowers he held.

I hesitated. For one thing, I was wearing paint-splattered sweatpants and a kerchief tied to keep my unruly hair out of my face. Not exactly my best look. After a breath I pulled open the door and then just stood there. I felt a little silly. I couldn't think of a thing to say.

Joe cleared his throat. "Before you say anything," he started.

"I didn't," I mumbled.

"Good point." He looked down at the flowers as if he had forgotten about them. "These are for you."

I bent my head to examine the blossoms. The gracious thing would have been to invite him in, but my mind was racing as I attempted to adjust to this unexpected turn of events. When it came to Joe, I seemed to have difficulty keeping up with developments.

"Here's the thing." Joe looked miserable. "I went to visit my mother. Well, you knew that. My mom has been in poor health, but I had no idea . . . I don't think her doctor even realized how bad she was. Anyway, when I got there I found out she had been hospitalized. She wouldn't let anyone call me before I came. Then three days later she died. After it was all over, I went to call you and . . . well, I lost your number. I know it sounds like a totally lame excuse, but the fact is, I must have forgotten or lost that business card with your telephone number. I had to take a few weeks off from work for the funeral and to take care of her affairs, so there was no way to get in touch . . ."

Joe finished his explanation, but I still stood there frozen, the back of my hand to my mouth. That was when it struck me what it was about him, what I hadn't been able to put my finger on before. He was authentic. The genuine article, nothing fake about him. It's not often that you meet someone so true, I realized, let alone have the chance to invite them into your life.

I reached out a hand and allowed my fingertips to brush his face very lightly. Then, self-conscious, I moved back and held the door open.

"Won't you come in?" I started to say. But I didn't quite get it out before I was enveloped, then nearly crushed along with the flowers in an embrace.

CHAPTER FIVE

April 1998: a state park in Maryland

It had stopped raining, but the air was damp and chilly, the kind of weather that got into your bones. Not what you would expect for April in rural Maryland, which, being south of the Mason-Dixon Line, was normally mild and lovely in springtime. Instead it was the kind of night that made Michael Grimaldi, squinting to see as he drove down one dark road after another, wish he were watching TV instead of poking around some wet field and examining a corpse. It probably would turn out to be some old geezer who had suffered a heart attack during an ill-timed camping trip.

This wasn't Grimaldi's typical reaction to a call to investigate a possible homicide. Ordinarily, he lived for this. The beginning of it all was his favorite part: the analysis of the scene, the gathering of clues, and the unshakable belief that he could piece it together and catch the bad guy. It was why he loved being part of the Maryland State Police's crime unit and why he had worked like a dog to get on the team. He didn't know what his problem was. Cranky, he supposed. A sore throat, evidence that he was probably developing a cold, didn't help.

Considering that at seven thirty it was pitch black, it was no surprise that Grimaldi nearly missed the entrance to Nanotanchee State Park. The park, which was tucked away in a fairly secluded area of the eastern shore of the Chesapeake, was where Grimaldi, along with the forensics team, first responders, and other necessary personnel, had been dispatched. Once he had turned in and traveled more than a half a mile down the access road, he could make out the glow of the bright halogen lights that the crime team must have already set up. It was easy to find after that. Just follow the ever-brightening glow.

Grimaldi pulled his state-issued car, a high-mileage Ford, among the haphazard grouping of state police and fire vehicles. Once he reached the yellow police tape that marked off the scene and had signed the log at the makeshift entrance, he spotted a trooper he knew. Brewster was standing with a skinny young man who was shivering in thin jogging shorts and a tank top. *This must be the responding officer*, Grimaldi thought, and the miserable-looking SOB with him had to be the one who made the 911 call. *Leave it to a runner to ignore the unseasonable weather and try to squeeze in a run after work.*

Grimaldi nodded hello to Brewster and jerked his head toward the runner, who hunched over with his hands tucked inside his armpits. "Do you have a blanket for this poor guy?"

Brewster shrugged. "I used the one in my car to cover the body. At least what was left of her." He cast a sidelong glance at the runner, who appeared to be on the verge of throwing up.

"I have one in my trunk." Grimaldi tossed his keys to the cop. "You know which car, right?" Not waiting for an answer, he turned to the runner. This case might be interesting after all. He felt himself switch gears. He wanted to get as much information as quickly as possible, but he was going to have to do a certain amount of sweet-talking to this guy.

"I already told the other officer the whole thing," he said when Grimaldi began to question him. "Which wasn't much. I was on the running path and the body was right there on the ground, next to one of the picnic tables. Not even under the table. It was like there was no attempt to hide it or anything." His teeth were chattering. "Um, when do you think I can go home?"

"So what you found was pretty decomposed, huh? Maybe the animals got to it?" Grimaldi tried to sound sympathetic.

The man licked his lips, which even in the shadows Grimaldi could see were badly cracked. "It wasn't that. It was—I mean, *she* was, like, beheaded."

Grimaldi's eyebrows shot up. "Really. Where was the head?"

The guy looked woozy again and reached out clutching air, but managed to grab Brewster, who had just walked up with the blanket.

"We haven't located the rest of the remains yet," Brewster said. "We have another trooper searching the vicinity, but it doesn't seem likely we'll find anything until daylight."

Just then all three of them turned at the shout that seemed to emanate from a pinging flashlight about fifty yards away in the darkness. It was the one-man search party, sounding the alert that he had found something.

"I stand corrected." Brewster turned to the runner. "Don't move. I'll be right back." The runner, now huddled in the blanket, nodded but did not look happy. Grimaldi wasn't happy either. He considered ordering Brewster to stay with the witness. Brewster, reading his thoughts, jingled a set of car keys at Grimaldi as they moved away. The guy wouldn't be going anywhere.

They reached the other trooper the same time that most of the forensics team did. The group looked at the disembodied head in the pool of light of their collective flashlights. The eyes were open, looking back at them.

After several long moments, someone gave a loud sigh and said to bring over one of the klieg lights so they could get started processing the scene. Brewster mumbled that he would go back to baby-sit the witness. Grimaldi nodded absently. He put on latex gloves and squatted down to shine his flashlight methodically over the head, which was resting on a pile of weeds. A flattened, dirty carton that had once held chocolate milk lay partially under the matted hair. He resisted the temptation to move it. Touching anything in a crime scene—even a piece of garbage—wasn't proper procedure. But it just seemed so disrespectful to the deceased.

Generally, Grimaldi had no difficulty separating himself from the gruesome crimes he worked on. He usually was able to focus solely on piecing together what happened and trying to get into the mind of the perpetrator. But every once in a while, he found himself wondering whether the victim was looking down on them crawling about the scene like ants on a pile of sand. He shook his head and stood up, stepping back to allow the forensics team to do their work. Indulging in that kind of sensitivity wasn't going to solve the murder.

Grimaldi walked back to the picnic table and pulled back the blanket to examine the body. The autopsy would show for sure, but he was willing to bet that the beheading occurred postmortem. Maybe the killer was one of these sickos who got off on dismembering corpses.

He looked over the body for any other signs of dismemberment. Nothing was visible because the body was fully clothed, which in itself was rather unusual. In so many of these kinds of cases, the killer was also a sexual predator. Still, the clothes were in disarray, so she still might have been sexually assaulted. The medical examiner would check for that, too.

Grimaldi was about to pull the blanket back up when he noticed the right arm, half-hidden under the body. It appeared that lines, fairly deep lines, had been carved into the flesh of the underside of the victim's forearm. They seemed to form some sort of pattern—a bloodless pattern, so the perpetrator must have used his knife after killing her. Grimaldi looked closer and realized it was more than a pattern. These were letters.

Gingerly, he picked up the arm between his latexed thumb and forefinger, and read the word: NOTHING.

What the hell was that supposed to mean? That she no longer meant anything to some pissed-off husband or boyfriend? Or that simply by being female, she was as worthless as that old milk carton?

Lifting his head, Grimaldi called the photographer over. "Hey! Did you get this?" He laid the arm down with the word facing up. The photographer came over and peered at it, his eyes widening. He pulled the camera to his face and started shooting.

Grimaldi stood a few paces back and surveyed the scene. They would have to wait for dawn to look, probably fruitlessly, for other clues, and even longer for all the evidence collected to be processed, for the results of the autopsy, and for the time and cause of death. But there was one thing that was abundantly clear. The murder hadn't happened in the state park. The body had been dumped. There was no blood, except what was on the victim and her clothes. Even assuming it had been lying out in the open for hours, during the steady rain that had fallen earlier, that much blood wouldn't have simply washed away. The killer probably had dropped the body in this secluded place the previous night or in the early morning hours. He'd had all the time in the world, with little chance anyone would see him. Sure, they would check convenience stores and gas stations in the area to see if anything suspicious was caught on a security camera, but the park entrance was not on a well-traveled road. They would have a hard time making a connection between the murderer and a motorist passing a gas station miles away.

The only reason this body was discovered at this point was because a die-hard jogger just happened to come by. . . .

Unless this was one of those killers who toyed with the police and liked to be at the scene of the crime? Grimaldi's head swiveled back to where Brewster was holding the witness. The man was still there, still huddled in the blanket.

Chances were slim that this runner was anything other than what he claimed to be. For one thing, homicides didn't tend to get themselves resolved so easily. *But just to be on the safe side,* Grimaldi thought, *we'll impound his vehicle to check for hair, fibers, and blood.*

He started walking back to the runner. *Yes,* he reminded himself, *solving a crime is all a matter of being methodical, and keeping your eyes open. And maybe a lucky break every now and then.*

CHAPTER SIX

April 1987: the university

Less than a week after my attack, the affair was wrapping up, at least as far as other people were concerned. As for me, I couldn't say that there was any resolution or that life was back to normal. Not yet, anyway. I had been released from medical care, my parents had returned home after their mad rush to the university to be by my side, and I was adamant that I needed to return to my regular class schedule. I had become convinced that this would help me, insisting to my friends that it was absolutely necessary to attend class. I had already missed so much school, I told them, I was in danger of losing the entire semester.

It was exhausting, trying to pretend everything was fine. It required much more energy than I seemed to be able to muster. My friends contended that it was too soon, that I needed to give myself a break, that I wasn't allowing myself the proper time to heal. "I have to do this," I kept repeating in a hollow voice. "I'm okay. Really."

I was fooling no one. Yet one by one, my friends gave up or grudgingly conceded. "Don't worry," I would repeat with a frozen smile. "I'll get back into the swing of things." I used that phrase a lot because I thought it sounded upbeat.

I knew they were concerned about me, that they all meant well. Still, I was relieved when one friend or the other, whoever had her shift in staying with me, would reluctantly end the conversation or leave my apartment. I wasn't crazy about being alone, but I seemed to deal with it all better by myself. In one stroke of luck, my roommate, Judith, was leaving me alone. She hadn't made a single appearance since I had returned to the apartment. I assumed she was staying with her boyfriend, Sal. Even though I considered this a godsend, I wasn't about to take any chances when I was by myself. I would lock all the doors, sometimes even shoving the kitchen table under the doorknob to block it. Then I would usually head to the shower, spending as long as an hour there. I had this idea, a hope, really, that water would help the healing process. I made the water as hot as I could stand it and stood under the stream until the hot water tank ran out. Judith would probably have been furious, had she been home.

Despite the continued turmoil inside my head, physically I was slowly recovering. The sensitive tissue around my blackened eyes was turning ugly shades of purple and yellow. The multiple cuts and contusions on my body were still raw, though. He had sliced me, with my own knife, numerous times on my torso, arms, and neck. I was fortunate, as the emergency room doctor informed me, that my attacker had managed to miss the carotid artery. "A tiny nick there could have disastrous results," the doctor said offhandedly. I closed my eyes, sick at the thought.

It was strange that the cuts were almost surgical. It appeared that my attacker intentionally avoided my face and areas that could have caused someone to bleed out. His missing the carotid didn't seem to have been an accident. The way he had cut me was not some wild slashing, and there was no stabbing or plunging. He had even carved a word into the smooth skin of my forearm, but it was the crude but superficial lettering you might find on a school desk or tree trunk. The rest was like the purposeful but light crisscrossing a cook uses on a slab of meat before marinating it.

These wounds would heal, I knew. I was a little more concerned about my state of mind. Sometimes I thought I would polarize, turn into tiny particles and spin out in all directions into oblivion. I tried giving myself a stern talking-to. I remembered my mother telling my brother to stop making faces if he didn't want his face to remain permanently in its contorted position. *If you don't revert to a more normal life*, I warned myself, *the nightmare just might become your permanent reality.*

When I had gone screaming into the dark dormitory corridor that Sunday morning like a raving lunatic, I had finally caught a break.

At the point I broke free of my kidnapper and rapist, I unwittingly had chosen the precise moment when two members of a tiny segment of the college student population—the sliver that consisted of pious, churchgoing young people—were on their way to ten o'clock services at the local Methodist church. It was doubly fortunate because this pair of young, pimply teens, who were from not only the same small town but also the same strict congregation, were the only other human beings awake and mobile in the dorm at that hour on a Sunday morning.

Without even considering whether I might be seeking shelter from young men who could be more dangerous than my attacker, I ran full tilt straight into the arms of the smaller of the two. A pasty-looking slight boy, he was waiting for his taller friend to lock his dormitory room door, and happened to be closer. The slight student turned at the noise and opened his mouth. But before he could speak, I came crashing, literally, into his arms.

"Help me. Please," I croaked and promptly conceded to the dizzying blackness, slumping to the tile floor. I must not have blacked out for long. When I came to, the students had covered me with their jackets and were hovering with concerned expressions.

For a moment I was unsure what had happened. I stared back at their worried eyes and tried to remember. It was something bad, I knew that. Then it all came rushing back along with the panic.

"He might be coming. Is he coming? You have to stop him."

The short, pasty one looked scared. The tall student bowed his painfully thin frame in an attempt to calm me. He reached out his hand, then pulled it back, clearly afraid that he might accidentally touch me. "We called the police. They'll be here soon."

I jerked in a spasm, startling them.

"Here? Oh, God, I promise I will never do that again. That was so stupid. I'm so sorry. I was so stupid."

As logical as my thinking was during the attack, now that it was over I was falling apart. I covered my face with my hands and sobbed. The students exchanged glances, alarmed. They were having trouble keeping up with my wild swings. Eventually, my crying subsided into hiccups.

At length, the smaller student whispered to his friend, "Do you think we should try to find him?"

"No!"

My scream was piercing, nearly jolting the students from my side. "Please. Don't leave me," I begged. I licked my dry lips and concentrated on fighting the sobs that were rising again. "You said the police were coming, didn't you? Let them . . ." I wanted to add, emphatically, "He's a monster," but my throat was too dry.

"Okay, don't worry," the tall student said quickly, making ineffectual gestures in the air a few inches over me in a half-hearted fanning motion. It did have a strange calming effect, although I refused to let my eyes close, sending quick glances down the empty hallway. I was terrified my attacker would appear and make short work of all three of us.

By the time the police—or more accurately, campus security—arrived, my eyes were glazed. Shock had set in. I was shivering uncontrollably. A security guard, a young man with a crew cut, fired questions at me, but I was having trouble forming answers. My only clear thought was that he had military written all over him, which was comforting. The two nice students might not have much of a chance against my attacker, but this guy should be able to stand up to him.

I phoned my parents before I left the hospital. I had briefly considered trying to hide the event from my family, especially my mother, who was still reeling from the death of my grandmother, but a nurse persuaded me that telling them was necessary. My parents deserved to know, she said.

So I called, crying and shaking so much that it was difficult to get the words out. This was infuriating to me, because I badly wanted to present it calmly and not add to their worries. I briefly imagined convincing them that I could handle it. That didn't happen. They immediately left home, arriving at the university within a few hours, record time for my notoriously cautious-driving father.

My father examined my battered face, his own ashen. My mother cried.

"I'm sorry." I didn't know why I kept apologizing.

My parents stayed three days. I stayed with them in their hotel room, spending much of the time sleeping in one of the room's two huge king-sized beds.

While my mother and I stayed at the hotel, my father spent the better part of two days camped out in the anteroom of the university dean's office. He waited patiently even as every thirty minutes the dean's administrative assistant would announce in sonorous tones that the dean was not in and therefore it was a waste of time to stay. She was like a damn cuckoo clock, popping up every half hour on the button, my dad told us when he returned to the hotel in the evening. My father said that he would simply thank her politely and indicate that he would rather wait.

Near the end of a second day of fruitless waiting, my dad began to doubt his mission. He might have given up, he related later, if he hadn't caught the secretary sneaking into the dean's office with what looked suspiciously like a ham sandwich.

"The dean who supposedly wasn't in his office all that time. Trapped by the call of nature. Hunger got him," my father would crow. "His kidneys would have given out, too, except I'm sure he had an executive washroom."

My father seized the opportunity. He pushed past the startled assistant, and the dean had no choice but to invite him to sit down. Because he wasn't sure how long he had before he would be thrown out of the office, my dad wasted no time in getting to the point, which included two primary demands.

My father wanted the university to arrange for my case to be handled by the local district attorney's office instead of campus security. And he demanded that the university take its own action against my attacker. It had already been determined that the person under arrest was a current student. "You can't possibly allow this student to continue going to classes here alongside my daughter and all these other young women," my father told the stone-faced dean.

For the first sixty minutes of the meeting, the dean wouldn't budge from the university's position: that this was strictly a university police matter and it was moving through the proper channels via the office of campus security. Any action by the university could jeopardize a criminal case, if it came to that. The university must be like Solomon, the dean intoned, and remain on the sidelines.

Ultimately, my father prevailed. The dean eventually, and reluctantly, agreed to pursue some sort of measure, most likely a hearing to assess possible suspension or expulsion for the accused.

We not only knew my attacker was a student, but also that he was a resident of the dormitory where I had been held. We became aware of these details because a suspect had been arrested. It was a surprise to everyone that he was arrested that easily. When I escaped, literally running into the arms of the churchgoers that Sunday morning, the attacker inexplicably had not run away. Once the campus police arrived, they had me identify the room where I had been held. They whisked me away and then they banged on the door, armed and ready for a struggle. I learned later that the young man who answered meekly didn't try to resist arrest, when the police saw the bloodstained mattress.

They also discovered rope stuffed in a trash can in the nearby men's room, but they couldn't find the knife. If they could find that, everything could be wrapped up in short order, according to the confident young campus policeman, who took my statement.

"But we do have the perpetrator. That's like having the corpse in a murder case," he informed me, as I sat shaking and cowering, wrapped in a blanket someone had handed me. He tried his best to be restrained about it, but in his eyes was a glint of excitement. He probably dealt with a numbing amount of routine cases like public drunkenness or fistfights. I could see what he was thinking: here was a real crime. Sexual assault, kidnapping, aggravated assault, perhaps even attempted murder charges. It had to be exhilarating.

One practical result of the arrest was learning the identity of my assailant: Dennis Price, a senior majoring in accounting.

Dennis Price was released immediately on a few hundred dollars' bail. My parents complained bitterly that this was ridiculously low, that even a financially strapped student could raise that. This outrage was the final straw for my father. He reignited his campaign against the college, and then expanded it to the local district attorney's office. He made calls, argued incessantly with everyone, and called on state legislators or anyone in a position of power he could track down. He became a hopeless insomniac and lost twenty-five pounds, much to my mother's alarm.

At length, the university set the date for the hearing to assess Dennis Price's conduct as a student. The hearing, which would be separate from the criminal trial, would be held before the close of the spring semester. Despite this victory, my father continued, my mother informed me, to look worried and gray.

Throughout my father's war with the university and local authorities, I remained on the sidelines, a disinterested observer. I dutifully called home every other day, as my mother begged me to do, and listened dully to the latest developments. It was odd to be learning about my case from my parents, who were a couple of hundred miles away.

"Your father is thrilled that this hearing is going to take place," my mother said for the fifth time. "Isn't that good news?"

"Yeah. It is," I said automatically. I checked my watch. Five minutes had passed so I could allow myself another look outside. Even though I could see only a small area from the tiny casement window in my basement apartment, I nonetheless cocked the phone receiver between my ear and shoulder, and moved the curtain slightly to peer out. My mother's voice startled me.

"Quinn. I don't get the sense you're all that interested in this."

"Of course I'm interested. It involves me, doesn't it?"

She was silent for a moment. "I wish you would just come home. Forget school. You need to recover."

"Mom. I told you, I can't." This came out more sharply than I intended because I was tempted to do just that—pick up, go home, and curl up in the deepest part of the house. But the same stubborn thought kept reminding me that if I left the university, I would never return.

I sighed and started over. "Remember when I wasn't even in high school yet, and Frank was starting to look at colleges and I stole all his college catalogs? I must have spent hours poring over them. I couldn't wait to go to college." I swallowed. "I'm not giving up now."

I knew my mother was crying because the only thing I could hear was the sound of her blowing her nose.

Less than five years later, when my father died of a massive heart attack, I would begin to question my behavior during this post-attack period. If I had come home, if I just had gone to another school closer to home, my dad might have had less stress. He wouldn't have had to worry about trying to protect me from afar. At the time I wanted to tell him that he couldn't always shelter me. I wanted to say that I had to figure out on my own how, not only to survive, but survive the surviving. But he wouldn't have understood.

Then he was gone, and I wondered if I was the one who didn't understand. My father had been driven to an early grave. That was the phrase I once overheard my mother use, and I got the impression that I was the one who had driven him there. It was proof, as if I needed any, that my mother—just as I did— held me responsible for my father's death.

The first weeks after the attack were a blur of raw emotions. I swung between not caring about what had happened, and raging at the slightest provocation. I was floundering.

It was just as well that Judith seemed to continue to avoid me, having been conspicuously absent since my return to the apartment. The consensus among my friends was that she couldn't handle trauma, her own or others. I felt it had more to do with our low tolerance for each other. I figured Judith and I would probably part ways at the semester's end anyway.

One night as I lay sleepless, I heard a key slide into the lock. I went numb with terror. In an experiment to see if I could sleep without building a fortress, it was the first night I hadn't pushed the kitchen table against the door. I calmed down when I realized that it had to be Judith. I lay still, not breathing. Soon I heard the hushed sounds of someone creeping across the living room and the quiet closing of Judith's bedroom door. I lay there motionless for a long time. The stillness grew deeper, and eventually I slept.

When I rose the next morning, Judith was gone, along with most of her belongings.

By the end of my first week of returning to classes, I appeared on the surface to be functioning, but it was a thin veneer. *It's over. Get a grip*, I reminded myself. But it didn't feel like it was over. I couldn't shake the sense that I was in a two-act play and it was only intermission. It didn't help that I hadn't fully recovered physically, and I was self-conscious about the yellowing bruises and cuts that were visible even with long-sleeved shirts. There had been an article in the campus newspaper about what had happened, and I imagined that everyone who saw me could put it together. More than once, I caught others staring at me in class.

On Fridays that semester, I had a long break before my medieval history lecture. Before the attack—already I had bifurcated my life into before and after segments—I would spend the time studying in the library, or go to the student union building for coffee. Afterward, I wasn't sure I had the stomach for such public places that would be packed with students. At the same time, I couldn't face hiding out in my dark, dank apartment any longer.

On my first Friday back, I left my early class, falling into step among the group pouring out of the building, grateful for the anonymity of the crowd. Pausing on the pavement, I looked at the laughing, chatting students passing by, and impulsively headed to the student union, a large stone building that reminded me of a Swiss chalet.

Inside I tried to blend into another sea of student humanity. I joined the line in the cafeteria, but the smell of the food made my stomach rebel. I was considering some hot tea to settle it when I spotted red velvet cake in the dessert case. In a contradictory flip, suddenly I was starving. I added the cake to my tray.

Balancing the tray and my books, I picked my way among the wooden tables and chairs. I pretended that no one could tell that my face was still somewhat swollen and covered with a cascade of purple to yellow bruises, or that the whites of my eyes were a disconcerting blood red.

I chose one of the small tables in a corner. With my back to the room, I stared unseeing at an open textbook, and methodically chewed tiny bites of red velvet cake. It was too dry, but comfort food was comfort food.

I was just starting to relax, when a boy in ripped jeans and a sagging khaki jacket dropped his tray on my table with a deafening crash, dragged over a chair from another table, and slid it next to me.

The intrusion was not only horribly uncomfortable, but it instantly caused the soft tissue of my face to shift and flail. I looked directly at the offending student, who was no more than a boy despite his scraggly attempt at a beard. He didn't acknowledge my reaction. He didn't even seem to notice me. Scraping the chair back noisily, he dropped himself into it with the same recklessness with which he had dropped his food tray. I felt my heart, which had been pounding, begin to slow. This kid wasn't a threat, except possibly to his sandwich. As if on cue, he started attacking his food as if he hadn't eaten in a week.

I tried to turn back to my book, but I couldn't concentrate. I kept looking for any sudden moves in my direction. Soon I was openly staring at him, fascinated with his single-minded focus on eating. I watched him chew and swallow, chew and swallow, then rip off another bite. Dust particles drifted in the shaft of sunlight from the student union's high windows, basking him in a shower of dusty, golden light. It was so mesmerizing that I let my guard down, something I had sworn so recently that I would never do again. Less than a fortnight after the attack, only a few days back into my routine, I was caught flat-footed with someone hissing in my ear.

"So, on top of everything, you're a liar."

For the second time, my face convulsed. I jerked my head back, only to face Judith.

She had two bright spots across her cheekbones and was furious. With every word her decibel level rose. Soon she was screeching. I caught a glimpse of some people at a nearby table covering their ears.

"You're telling the police, you're telling everyone that you never saw him before in your life. You know what? You're a liar. You do know him. Because I introduced you. That's right, you met him before. He's my cousin, this guy whose life you're ruining. You two go out on a date and have an argument. Big deal! But trying to say that he's some kind of rapist? Let me tell you something. I'm not going to let you get away with ruining his life."

I felt my face grow flaming hot. I sensed, rather than saw, the stares from other tables. A rebuttal was pointless, though. For one thing, Judith was already gone.

Judith was moving fast toward the exit, despite the crowded tables. As she passed one of them, I saw her shove a stack of books that were sitting at the elbow of a student. Books went flying to the floor. Judith ignored the ensuing outcry and was out of the building before anyone could confront her.

I bit my bruised and cracked lip even though that made it hurt. The sandwich-eating student still sat next to me, his elbows propped and half a kaiser roll in front of his mouth. He had stopped chewing. He gaped at me, his open jaw revealing half-masticated food.

We stared at each other and then he swallowed hard. "Wow. Wild stuff, huh?" he said, then resumed eating, but I noticed his tone was admiring, probably the one he used when discussing Saturday's football game with his buddies.

All who thirst, let them come to the water.
And let all who have nothing, let them come to the Lord.
Without money, without price. Why should you pay the price,
Except for the Lord?

It helped to let the melody of one of the hymns from my grandmother's funeral, one I heard so many times as a child, to play in my head. It allowed me to gather what shreds of dignity I had remaining as I exited the cafeteria. The crowded room seemed to have already forgotten Judith's outburst, but embarrassment over it was compelling me to leave immediately.

I glided past faceless groups of students, my back as straight as possible and my chin high. I focused on two things—keeping the nausea at bay until I got out of the building, and listening to the hymn in my head without questioning why *that*, of all things, had popped in there.

Outside, I was ready to crumble. I stumbled toward the far side of the building and some granite-topped brick retaining walls there. The walls were barely visible amid the thick shrubbery. Leaning against the waist-high rough stone, I closed my eyes and waited for the sick feeling to dissipate. I was bone tired—so tired that my equilibrium seemed a little off. I had the gently swaying sensation that I was in a boat, a sailboat perhaps, rocking me gently to sleep.

That was it. I needed sleep, or at least someone to pet my hair and comfort me and say, why should you pay the price? You've already paid far too much. I was tempted to climb onto the wall to stretch out on the granite for a nap.

"Excuse me."

It was happening again. A female voice in my ear. But this one was hesitant and wavering, not like Judith's, with its barely controlled anger.

My eyelids fluttered open and I saw a tall, slim girl. The girl had haunted dark eyes with even darker shadows under them.

"I'm sorry—I followed you out here. . . . I have to ask you something. Are you the one they wrote about in the newspaper?" She lowered her voice, even though no one was in the vicinity. "The one who was attacked?"

I nodded. The girl's porcelain skin seemed to grow paler. She swallowed. "Can we talk?"

Again, I nodded and, by unspoken agreement, we both clambered on top of the wall. Cross-legged, we sat facing each other. Despite the relative warmth of the day, the girl clutched her jacket to herself, shivering as if in the middle of a blizzard.

She introduced herself as Deborah.

"When I first saw you inside the student union just now, I knew," she said, ducking her face closer to mine. "He asked you the time, didn't he?"

Startled, I didn't answer.

Deborah clutched my arm like her life depended on my answer. "When the guy who attacked you first approached you, did he ask you what time it was? Please just tell me." Still, I hesitated, then gave a brief nod of assent. She nodded back with sad satisfaction.

"The reason I knew is because that's how he approached me. He's done this before. Maybe a lot."

She pulled the sleeve of her windbreaker above her elbow and held out the delicate ivory of the underside of her forearm. There, already formed as thin scar tissue, was a word carved into her flesh: NOTHING. "Do you have something like this?"

Silently, I pushed up my own sleeve and showed her an identical carving. We examined each other's arms with wonder.

She's as scarred as I am, I thought. I looked at Deborah's face and saw her mouth was moving, that she was saying something, but I couldn't hear it over the roaring in my ears. I shook my head. I have to hear it, to witness it. I willed myself to be as still as the granite slab beneath us.

Deborah was describing how she had been on her way back to the dorm after her shift at the diner in town where she was working a couple of evenings a week. She was hurrying because she had to cram for an exam the following day. Like me, he hailed her with the question about the time.

"I was annoyed, but I did slow down to look at my watch. It was automatic," she said. "Stupid. Somebody asks you something and you don't want to be rude. Especially as a girl. You're taught to be nice. You know?"

I nodded. I understood.

Deborah told me how she had slowed but didn't quite come to a halt. But because it was after dark, she had maneuvered herself under a street lamp for a better look at her wristwatch. That's when he grabbed her, trapping her in that same relentless grip, hissing those same warnings not to scream, not to say anything or he would kill her right then and there with the gun he carried, the gun that Deborah failed to see but believed existed because of the vehemence of his threat. She believed she would die.

And like me, she was half-dragged to his dormitory room and held captive. No one so much as knocked on the door the entire time, she said.

"It all started on a Friday night. I didn't even hear voices in the hallway. Maybe most kids were away. But he took no chances because he kept me tied up, like a prisoner."

Deborah's story came out in breathless sentences. "He raped me a lot. Every once in a while he would leave, go take a shower or something. I never did see a gun. He had a knife, though. He constantly pressed it against my throat but he only cut me at the end. That's when he carved the word into my arm."

That's one small blessing, I thought. There was no reason to feel so guilty and stupid about his taking my knife. He already had one.

I glanced down at Deborah's forearm and then at her face. In the waning sun, her skin was translucent, stretching over her bones, waxy, like that of a corpse. I felt like I was looking into the casket of my deceased grandmother.

There was silence for a while.

"I don't know why it's so hard to talk about, even to you. You've been through it. You know how it is. I have to warn you, though, it doesn't get any easier. Every time I close my eyes . . . I relive all the degrading things he did to me."

Deborah covered her mouth delicately, gagging at the memory. "I can't sleep. I mean, I must sleep at some point. Little catnaps, I guess. It's been months. It feels like I haven't slept at all. I'm dying."

Hollow-eyed, cadaver-like, she did look as if she could slip at any moment from the world of the living.

"Did you report this?"

Deborah looked away. "Matt—my boyfriend—he didn't

want me to report it. He said to forget it. Just let it go." She started to cry, harsh sobs shaking her delicate frame.

I took her hand. It felt cold. Deborah used her other hand to try to cover her face.

As much of a mess as I was, it occurred to me that of the two of us I was the one in relative command of my senses. My case was being handled by law enforcement. I wasn't carrying it around as an awful secret. Maybe it would help Deborah to do something similar to hand over her burden. At least she might feel less guilty, like she was doing something to stop this dreadful cycle.

I cleared my throat. "There is something you could do. If you're willing, that is."

"What."

It came out as a statement rather than a question, but I thought I detected faint interest.

"I know your boyfriend was against it, but—let's just say his approach hasn't worked. Why not come with me to the authorities and report it now?"

Deborah looked panicked.

"You shouldn't do it for me," I continued hurriedly. "It's got to be for yourself. It was terrible, what happened to you. Look at you. It's destroying you, from the inside out. You'll never make it right unless you do something."

I tried to say this with conviction. By the look on Deborah's face, I could tell I wasn't convincing her, but she was going to trust me, probably against her better judgment. Over the next three frustrating hours, I saw the trust fade away. I couldn't blame her.

First, we made our way into town and the local district attorney's office, a tiny satellite office, as the main department was in the county seat, miles away. The D.A.'s office was my idea—in my thus far limited experience and from what my father had discovered in his incessant phone calls, I knew they would have to get involved in a rape case at some point. But in the small storefront space that consisted of a few empty desks and a dusty rubber plant in the corner, we didn't get past the matronly looking receptionist. She cut Deborah off before she could complete a second sentence, and dispatched us to the local police station. There, the police officer at the front desk listened a little longer, and then patiently explained that there was a protocol. If the alleged crime occurred on campus, the report would have to be made to whatever law enforcement agency was in charge.

That was how we ended up spending most of the afternoon waiting in the cramped, overheated offices that served as the headquarters of the campus police.

Slumped in the office's unforgiving wooden chairs, we stared at the institutional bile-green wall opposite us. The wall, badly scuffed along the bottom, was blank but for a cork bulletin board, and the bulletin board was empty except for a single sheet of paper. The paper was tacked up carelessly, as if someone had smacked it on the board in passing without coming to a complete halt. Yellowed with age, it had clearly been there for a while. I read it again, for about the hundredth time. The paper announced an office holiday party that had been held three years before. Attendees were to sign up to bring potluck dishes. There were lines for listing your name and what you were bringing, whether spinach dip or nachos or whatever. The lines were blank. Either no one attended the party or they didn't serve food after all. Stupid.

The decision to strong-arm Deborah to go to the police was also stupid. It was selfish. I stole another look at her profile. She looked tragic even from this vantage point. What was I doing? Just because we both ended up lost in the same ugly, foul swamp, didn't mean she wanted to be my traveling companion, taking the same route I was.

Deborah chose that moment to speak, but it was hard to tell if she was addressing me. "My boyfriend's going to kill me." Almost simultaneously, a door with a frosted pane of glass opened, and a short but fit man with equally short, sandy hair appeared. He was not someone I had seen in my previous dealings with campus security.

"Come on in, girls. Come in." The man's voice was much too loud for such small quarters.

Mr. Knox, as he curtly identified himself, waved us into his closet-sized office. The room was dominated by a large, heavily scarred metal desk and a stale locker room smell. Somehow he had also managed to squeeze in a bookcase, a visitor's chair, and a tall filing cabinet.

Deborah sat in the chair. There was nowhere else to sit, so I wiggled to the side of the massive desk and attempted to lean against the bookcase. But when I rested my arm on it, the whole unit rocked back and forth. I stood straight and tried not to touch anything.

Mr. Knox had seated himself behind the desk, where he now appeared a much larger person. "So. Tell me what this is about." His tone conveyed that our presence was preventing him from doing many more important things. I glanced at Deborah. She had reverted back to her catatonic state, a slack expression, hands limp in her lap.

I plunged into a halting introduction of our cases and their similarities. But I was unnerved and stuttering, having to backtrack at times, giving too much background. I looked at Deborah desperately. "You're going to have to explain it." It might have been my first coherent sentence.

Mr. Knox tapped his pen on the desk impatiently. As we waited for Deborah, her face had again taken on a waxy sheen. She seemed no more ready to spill out the details of her story than a department store mannequin, which by this time she strongly resembled. I was beginning to think that we probably had fewer than thirty seconds before we would be tossed out, when the tiniest, most timid voice possible emanated from Deborah's chair.

"All right. I'll tell you." Barely moving her lips, she managed a rational outline of the same events that she had told me earlier.

Mr. Knox listened without expression or comment. He didn't take notes either.

Deborah finished. For a moment none of us moved. Then Mr. Knox sat back and stretched his arms above his head. He could have been lounging on a deck chair.

"So when did this happen?" His loud voice boomed off the walls. His face twisted a bit as he said it. I looked at him, startled. Was he stifling a yawn?

"Almost ten weeks ago."

"Hmmm." Mr. Knox tilted the back of the swivel chair even further, to the point that he was nearly reclining, then suddenly popped up. We both jumped.

"Two months. Two months plus, really. That's a pretty long time not to report something." He leaned across the desk so that his face was close to Deborah's. "This is a very serious crime that you're talking about. What, did it slip your mind? And then when this event happens to this other girl here, then all of a sudden it's happened to you?"

The blood drained from my face. I couldn't bring myself to look at Deborah to see how she was reacting. Mr. Knox continued his rant, but with a tone that was measurably softer.

"How could we possibly pursue this? There's no evidence, no physical injuries. You didn't go to the hospital and have them examine you, right? So, we have nothing but your say-so."

"Wait." I shoved up my sleeve. "Show him your arm, Deborah."

We held out our arms with their twin scars. Mr. Knox stared at them in silence for a moment. When he looked up, his expression seemed almost sad. He shook his head.

"How do I know that you both didn't do this to yourselves? I'm sorry, girls—but no."

He rose, an imposing figure in the cramped room. The lighting from the floor lamp in the corner threw his face into relief and exposed the patchy blond stubble on his jaw. He snaked past us and held open the door to usher us out.

Despite the awkwardness of both the situation and the space, Deborah raced out of the office. She was already near the exit by the time I caught sight of her.

"Wait!" I dashed after her, but Deborah had scampered out of the building. The girl could move like a rabbit. Out of breath, I caught up with her two blocks away.

"Please," I gasped and lunged to grab her arm. Unexpectedly, Deborah stopped short and I nearly crashed into her.

"I'm so sorry. I had no idea he would be such a jerk."

Deborah, looking like a trapped animal, didn't respond. I touched her arm. "Let's sit down and think this through."

Impatient, Deborah shook me off. "What's the point? You saw what good it does to report it."

"Just because you got that kind of reaction from that neo-Nazi asshole doesn't mean the entire system is like that. They caught him. He's going on trial."

"So truth and justice will prevail, and the wicked will be punished," Deborah said, stone-faced again.

"I have to at least give it a chance. I wouldn't forgive myself if this were to happen again . . . " My voice trailed off. I hadn't meant it, but that sounded accusatory and superior. For a moment Deborah looked crushed. Then the waxy mask returned.

She looked at me. "You do what you have to do. But I think my boyfriend was right. He told me, 'I don't believe you, so how do you expect anyone else to?'"

Deborah turned. This time I let her walk away.

We split into different trajectories. More than occasionally over the years, I would wonder what became of Deborah. I hoped that she eventually left her obnoxious boyfriend, but she probably didn't.

I did see Deborah once more, not all that long after the afternoon we met Mr. Knox.

Our final shared experience was at a hearing of a special committee of university trustees. The hearing was to determine whether Dennis Price, accused of attacking several female students and awaiting trial in my case, should be permitted to continue matriculating as a student. The hearing fell between the first raw weeks following the attack and the nightmarish criminal trial. But the hearing was not nearly as traumatic as the events it was sandwiched between. Still, I found the experience overwhelming. The trustees were silhouettes at the opposite end of a long mahogany table, shadows against the brilliant light flowing in from the tall majestic windows at the far end of the room. The table itself was a shimmering pool, reflecting the dazzling crystal chandelier above it. The chandelier seemed unnecessary. There was much too much light coming from the windows, blinding the person being interrogated.

Despite the intimidating setting, the trustees were courteous and respectful. After about twenty minutes, they gently dismissed me. I would learn later that the committee decided to expel Dennis Price only weeks before he was to graduate. But at that moment of leaving the room half-blinded by the brilliant light, and with the participants careful to appear impartial, I had no sense what they intended to do or even if they believed me. I rose and left, carefully closing the double doors behind me. Turning back to the hallway, arms bent awkwardly behind me, I came face-to-face with Deborah. She was the next witness to give testimony at the hearing.

She's doing this, I thought, elated. Maybe Deborah couldn't bring criminal charges against Dennis Price, but she's found the courage to corroborate my experience.

Just as we had done on that golden afternoon, we looked silently each other. I can't say why I did it, but I bowed deeply from the waist, the ultimate sign of respect.

Deborah smiled a tiny, heartbreaking smile, and moved past me to enter the room.

CHAPTER SEVEN

Spring 1998: Maryland

Growing up, there was no question that I would become an artist. In school, my classmates spent a lot of time agonizing over career choices that seemed, even then, equal parts boring and inadequate. They would complain that it was unfair to ask a kid to make these kinds of decisions, to figure out at a young age what to do with your life. I would sympathize, but the fact was that I knew, instinctively, what I was supposed to do. My destiny was set.

My mother said that as young as three, when I could first hold a pencil or crayon, I was compelled to draw. I would even insist on it, she said, instead of napping or playing. It was a story my mother often told as proof of that destiny. "You would say, 'I have to draw. I just have to.'" She would shrug. "So we let you. We figured that's what you liked to do."

The inevitable angst of adolescence eventually took over. In high school I doubted my talent and dismissed the idea I had something resembling a calling. But I never entirely lost my affinity for art. I graduated from college with a graphics art degree and landed my first job as a graphic artist, secretly proud that I had fulfilled part of my dream. At least I was getting paid for it. So what that I wasn't quite the kind of artist that my family, especially my mother, had in mind. Not that they really understood the difference. I was quite sure they pictured me at work all day in a beret and a paint-splattered smock, in front of an easel and holding a palette.

After nearly a decade of working for design firms and agencies, I felt increasing dissatisfaction with my meager artistic output, in what I was accomplishing outside of my job. I had to face it, designing advertisements or marketing brochures wasn't the same as creating art. Not the self-expression I was starting to need, anyway. That's why, when I was hunting for a new place after my breakup with Alex, I jumped at this particular apartment with its large windows and the skylight in the side room, perfect for a little art studio. But the studio wasn't just a nice feature or even a place to create art; it represented the opportunity to have my own life.

With the introduction of Joe into the picture, every now and then I wondered if this new relationship would threaten my new independent lifestyle, which at that point was only shakily established. Joe seemed to instinctively understand this. He knew when to give me space and when to show up. After that time he mysteriously vanished because of his mother's death, he was careful to be there when I needed him. But even more than that, he gradually was becoming an increasingly central part of my life.

I tried to explain this to Suzy at work.

"If it's all so perfect, why don't you just marry him?" Suzy thought any relationship that wasn't heading inexorably toward the altar was pointless. And if it was heading toward marriage, the faster the better. She thought that I should be planning the wedding by this point.

"I kind of like things the way they are now."

I said this in a flippant way, but it was true. I was more content than I could remember having ever been. I was *happy*. It was like I had been an incomplete jigsaw puzzle and had thought I was getting along well enough, but now suddenly had found the missing pieces. Things were good. Maybe too good. Although everything was falling into place, I sometimes feared that some unseen force, a wrecking ball of nature, would inevitably demolish it. I would shake off these thoughts and tell myself to accept this period of calm. Don't go looking for trouble, as my grandmother always said.

I had gotten in the habit of coming home from work each evening and immediately changing into what I called my "real work" clothes for my painting, comfortable old sweatpants and a sweatshirt. Then I would spend at least an hour on my latest project, which had progressed from pen-and-ink drawings of scenes based on photographs I had taken, to watercolor, and more recently, oils. Sometimes, when I was finished, I would call Joe and we would share a late dinner. Other times I would lose track of time and keep working until past midnight.

On a late afternoon in April, I drove home in the golden sun that reflected the still-wet roadway following the rain showers that had finally cleared a few hours before. *This is good*, I thought. I could still take advantage of daylight for my painting before having to switch to the high-powered artificial lighting I had set up in the studio. This week I had been spending a lot of time on my painting, but no time with Joe. He was on a business trip on the West Coast, and wasn't due back until the end of the week.

I pulled into the parking lot of my apartment building and looked with a pang at the empty spot where Joe usually parked. I might have been jealously guarding my newfound independence, but it always felt a lot better when Joe was around.

I had just changed into my painting ensemble and was preparing my materials, when I noticed the blinking light on the answering machine I kept with the phone on a small side table. I moved over to depress the button. Maybe it was Joe, checking in between meetings. With the time zone difference and business dinners to attend each night, he hadn't been able to call that regularly in the evenings.

The message was static-filled and sounded as if the caller was trying to muffle his voice. "Hey," the voice croaked. It was followed by a couple of seconds of noises that could have been the phone on the other end being juggled. The voice resumed: "How about that news?"

The answering machine clicked off. What was that supposed to mean? I stared at it, as if the machine could resolve the mystery. Finally, I shrugged, deciding it was probably a misdialed number.

But now I was curious about what the "news" could be. The local news broadcast would be on, so I picked up the remote control to flick on the small television that I kept in the studio.

"Stay tuned for our news team's special visit to a neighborhood bakery that makes its own doughnuts. Yummy!" The newscaster wore a garish pea-green suit and was painfully thin. It was doubtful that she would ever allow even a morsel of a doughnut to cross her lips. "We'll be right back after this commercial break."

I went into the bathroom to clean my brushes. Over the running water, I could hear tinny music of television ads. When I heard the newscaster's voice return, stronger and with a clear note of urgency, I turned off the water and came back into the studio.

"We're taking you straight to the scene, where we're waiting for police officials to speak to the media," the Pea-Green Suit Woman was saying. The camera obligingly shifted to a scene in an auditorium, with newspeople milling about, cameras and video equipment being set up, and a stage empty but for a podium.

"We're waiting for authorities to come out and make an official statement about the case," said the anchorwoman's voice, now breathless. "If you're just joining us, police in Fairport have just announced the gruesome discovery of the headless body of a young woman, dumped in the woods at Nanotanchee State Park."

Nanotanchee. That was familiar. *Oh, yes, it's that park not far from here*, I thought distractedly. I had already turned my attention back to my painting, a scene from one of the local marinas. I considered it, and decided it needed more definition. I picked up my brush and got to work.

But an increase in the sound level made me glance involuntarily at the television screen. The scene of the auditorium had given way to a reporter standing outside. The female correspondent was in front of a wooded area, presumably Nanotanchee State Park. I watched the wind bend the branches behind the reporter, and play havoc with her hair. Her voice was coming through the TV louder than necessary as she shouted over the wind.

"Police believe the woman is twenty-one-year-old Nancy Pennypacker, the same woman who went missing two nights ago from an all-night diner here in Fairport. She had report-edly come to the diner with a group of friends and went outside for a cigarette. She never returned.

"As we have been reporting here on Channel 15, fam-ily, friends, and volunteers have been searching ceaselessly for Nancy," the reporter bellowed. The wind whipped her hair into her face. She retrieved strands from her mouth and shoved them behind her ear. "Now, she appears to have been found, discovered by a jogger who caught sight of the remains lying near a picnic area here." The reporter waved an arm behind her, "And, most unfortunately, she was found headless. A gruesome discovery indeed."

"Sarah, I'm sorry to interrupt." The anchor's voiceover broke through. The camera shifted abruptly back to the audito-rium, the stage now filled with officials. "The press conference is now under way." The voice faded and was replaced by the room's audio.

The camera closed in on the podium. There a burly man in uniform stood listening impassively to an indecipherable ques-tion shouted from the audience. He did not repeat the question before answering.

"No, we don't," he said without expression and pointed to the next reporter, who spoke with crisp precision into his microphone.

"Captain, have you determined a cause of death yet and whether the victim was sexually assaulted? Also, are there any clues you can share that might indicate anything important about the perpetrator?"

The policeman paused. The room of reporters held its collective breath. They had expected the captain to dispatch the questioner with similar efficiency, but he didn't. He must be preparing to say something big. Instinctively, they leaned forward as one. So did I. By this point, I had given up any pretense of painting and sat mesmerized in front of the television.

The captain pursed his lips. "We can't assume, even though the victim was decapitated, that this was the cause of death. The decapitation could have occurred postmortem. Cause of death is not yet determined, pending the results of the autopsy. That should also determine any sexual assault. The autopsy will be conducted this evening."

The room let out an audible, disappointed sigh, discernible even on television. The captain hadn't given them much.

"However." The policeman paused and adjusted his gold wire-framed glasses. "There is one aspect that I have the authority to share." He spoke slowly and with hesitation.

"This, um, aspect shall we say, is rather unusual so it may be helpful in identifying a potential suspect. I am telling you this because ordinarily we would not release this type of information in the course of an ongoing investigation." The captain looked pained at his breach of protocol. He sucked some air and spoke rapidly in a single breath. "There were markings carved into the arm of the victim. Those markings appear to be a word. And the word was *nothing*."

Silence prevailed for a moment while the media took in this new detail. Then as if with one breath, the room erupted into a babble of questions. "Do you mean there was something else about the word, or was that the word—*nothing*?" a female voice shouted above the fray.

"Yes." The captain's confusing response led to an even louder din.

I hugged my midsection. It felt like someone had just punched me in the gut. Even the breath seemed to have left me. I opened my mouth wide, trying to recover it.

The TV screen now focused on the police captain's face so tightly that I could see his skin pores and the red-rimmed eyes behind his glasses even through the graininess and pixels of television.

You should have done more, the fatherly face seemed to be saying directly to me. The reddened eyes were not so much accusing as sad. You could have stopped this, they said.

Hours later, the television was blank and silent, but I had every light in the apartment blazing. I paced the living room, halting every few minutes to stare at my arm in disbelief, rereading over and over my own tattoo of that hated word, *nothing*. Carved into my arm, inevitably, by the same person who had just murdered and beheaded a woman and left her remains in a state park. Like a rotting animal. It had to have been him. Dennis Price might not have been permitted to graduate from college, but he had clearly graduated to worse crimes.

I was sick, nauseated. But I wasn't able to throw up even though I had tried, thinking it would help me feel better. Eventually the shivering overtook me. I dragged the thick comforter from my bed and wrapped it about me awkwardly. The blanket made pacing difficult, yet I couldn't keep still. I expanded my perimeter beyond the living room, taking ever-widening rounds throughout the apartment. I had to keep kicking the comforter aside so I could shuffle across the floor. It was tiring and slow going, but somehow it felt better to be moving about.

I marched back and forth, trying to make sense of this development, a development that defied explanation. *Maybe it is all just a weird coincidence*, I thought desperately. But how could there possibly be two nuts out there carving the same word into the bodies of female victims?

My pacing halted near the phone. I looked at it and shuddered. That message, the one commenting about the news, no longer seemed like an accidental call or a wrong number. Now, it was even more disturbing.

I badly wanted to talk to Joe. He would be returning home the following night, but that seemed a million years away. I already had tried his hotel room several times and listened to the endless ringing, reluctant to hang up. It was still too early to reach him at the hotel. It wasn't even seven o'clock Pacific time, and it might be many more hours before he would return from entertaining clients.

I had, of course, tried calling Joe's cell phone but it predictably wasn't in service. Joe stubbornly refused to turn on his cell phone except for the rare occasions that he made a call, after which he turned it back off as quickly as possible. I often teased him that he was terrified of his phone; he always retorted that he was only terrified of unwanted roaming charges.

I pushed my arm tentatively from the comforter and slowly reached out and touched the phone. Maybe I could call the hotel operator and ask them to deliver a message to Joe. But even if they could reach him, that kind of message would just alarm him. *Don't you think calling him in a panic will have the same effect?* I berated myself.

Biting my lip, still eying the phone, I reconsidered my options. I could call Suzy. Or Mom.

My mother was probably not the best choice. Since my father's death, my mother's relationship with my brother Frank and me—and especially me—had changed. She was quite clear that she no longer wanted to play the usual parenting role now that we were grown and that she no longer had our father as her child-raising partner. "I'm through with the kid-raising part of my life. I don't have time to be worrying about you because it's my time now," she announced blithely when she signed up for the first in a long series of New Age workshops, all designed to bring inner balance and peace, at least according to my mother. Frank just laughed and said it was a phase. "It's a six-and-a-half year phase, I suppose," I hissed at him during one particular difficult Thanksgiving dinner.

My brother might dismiss it, but I felt abandoned and guilty. My mother was cutting me out of her life, and to me this was proof that she blamed me for my father's death.

No, my mother would likely not be happy to hear from me, and she definitely wouldn't be happy that I was bringing her my problems again. Not only problems, but the same problems. The trouble that wouldn't end. Still . . .

Impulsively shoving the blanket aside, I picked up the receiver and dialed. She answered, thankfully, on the second ring.

"Mom?" I was suddenly near tears.

"What's wrong?" My mother was instantly on high alert.

With a sharp intake of breath, I dove in, relating what I had seen and heard. I told her my fear that Dennis Price had surfaced again. How he had escalated from attacking women to killing them. And maybe, I blubbered, maybe he was stalking me. Maybe he was sending a message. I told her about the voice mail that had led me to turn on the local news.

My mother listened without comment until I had spun myself out. Finally all that was left was my breathing, which was perilously close to hyperventilation.

"Quinn, it's ten years later. A whole decade. Don't you think you're going overboard?"

"What?"

"This can't possibly be related to what happened to you."

"It is! Think about it! What about the word, the exact same word, carved into her arm? Don't you think that's significant?"

My mother sighed. "It's also possible that some other wacko happened to come up with the same calling card or whatever it is. Look. As bad as your attack was, you have to face the idea that this is different. A different state, a different crime."

I was sullen.

"Quinn, I know you're going to take this the wrong way, but I'll say it anyway. You need to hear it. Every crime isn't about you." She paused and when she spoke again it was with gentleness mixed with a certain amount of exasperation. "I thought you were making progress in getting on with your life, but I guess I was wrong."

I felt the blood alternately flood and drain from my face. This phone call was a huge mistake.

Stammering something, I ended the call. I became aware of a sharp sense of relief only after the phone was back in its cradle.

The relief was short-lived. I became angry, even livid. Turning sharply, I stumbled in the blanket at my feet. I kicked at the mess, cursing, and lost my balance, falling into a heap on the living room floor. Slumped there crying, I lacked the will to struggle back to my feet or the energy to resume my endless pacing.

Eventually I fell asleep.

CHAPTER EIGHT

Fall 1997: San Antonio, Texas

Billy O'Brien woke to dust floating effortlessly in the afternoon sun beaming around the edges of the ill-fitting shade. As usual, he had the sensation that his mouth was jam-packed with cotton balls.

Billy was lying flat on his back. He was fairly certain he was in a bed, but it could also have been a sofa or a floor. It was, after all, a motel room and they looked pretty much the same from every vantage point. He might not remember much, but he did remember that he was in a motel. Tentatively, he wiggled his fingers, feeling the wrinkled cotton of the bed sheets. *That's progress*, he thought. *I made it to the bed.*

Billy considered rubbing his eyes so he could open them properly. But his arms weighed a thousand pounds each and there was no way that he could lift his arms and bring his hands toward his head. He settled for blinking.

His next thought was that he needed a drink.

That propelled him to ignore the weight of his arms and raise himself on his elbows. There had been a bottle of Jack

Daniel's close by last night, he was sure of it.

He surveyed the shithole that only a month before had looked like any other motel room. Now it was covered in dirty laundry, newspapers, trash from take-out joints, and crumpled bits of paper from aborted attempts at letters to his wife.

"My God, it looks like a herd of cattle went through here," he said aloud. His throat hurt when he talked. Probably because it was so parched. The air conditioner rumbled loudly, but barely made a dent against the Texan heat. Outside, he knew from experience, it was likely 105 degrees.

Billy spotted it. There, on the cheap plastic-topped table that served as the dinette, was the bottle of Jack. Not much left. Maybe two fingers worth.

He struggled out of the tangle of sheets and staggered to the table. The ball of his foot dug into a shard of glass hidden amid all the litter on the floor. He yelped and cursed, falling into the orange plastic swivel chair near the table.

Pulling his foot toward him, he yanked out the piece of glass. The cut wasn't deep but the blood was already flowing. He limped a few feet to an old takeout bag from Burger King, retrieved some napkins, and pressed them to his foot. Returning to the swivel chair, he tried to walk on the outer edge of his foot but still managed to drip blood on the carpet.

"What the hell. They never come and clean this goddamn place anyway," The sound of his cracked voice was swallowed up by the air conditioner's rumble. His throat still hurt. *Dumb ass*, he chided himself. *Why keep talking out loud when there's no one to hear you?* Billy shrugged and unscrewed the cap of the Jack Daniel's, chugging the rest of the amber liquid.

The empty bottle banged down on the table, harder than he intended. "Now what?" he asked the bottle. The truth was, there were no answers. He was out of a job, out of money, out of a wife and kids, and, now, out of Jack. He would say he was out of luck, but he was pretty sure he had never had any.

In spite of everything that had happened to Billy—or maybe because of it—he still believed in luck even if he wasn't blessed with it. And he still believed in God. He had no choice but to believe. Faith was all that was left in this trashed motel room.

It was true that troubles had rained down on him in biblical proportions, starting with the day that he and his brother Jeff were in Jeff's garage, the bay door open to the afternoon sun. Everyone said this right before a terrible event happened, but it was true: It was just your ordinary day. That was before the dark-haired, bearded man appeared. He wore a raincoat despite the day's warmth, and was barely visible against the brightness of the open bay. Billy and Jeff had peered at him, both squinting, both realizing at the same moment that the man was holding a shotgun. *That* was not ordinary. Billy could clearly remember thinking, *This is weird*. There was that thought, and then before he could process another, the man was firing, blowing holes into Billy's brother.

Before the man turned to leave, he looked at Billy who was standing, shocked, over his brother's body. Billy dragged his gaze away from Jeff and returned the man's gaze and wondered if he was next. But the man only smiled, a thin perfunctory smile, as if he were a clerk confirming the satisfactory completion of a transaction. Billy half-expected the guy to wish him a nice day.

Reflecting on it later, Billy decided that smile had been a smirk, the same one he would see again often, during the trial a year later. The trial during which Billy was the star witness. The hit man—for the authorities were certain he was a hired gun for a small-time, self-important businessman—spent the entire proceedings grinning like a fool. In particular, he directed this unnerving smile toward Billy.

Billy and his parents showed up every day of the trial. They had total faith in the district attorney who proclaimed the case open and shut, and who earnestly assured the family that the facts of the case—the hard facts—would cause justice to prevail.

Billy had tried to hold on to this belief during the court proceedings, but he worried that so much of the case hinged on his own testimony. The defense team would seek to destroy him on the witness stand. He fretted over that. When the defense opted for a trial by judge, rather than a jury trial, Billy was relieved. At least that made it only a single person to whom Billy had to prove his credibility.

The trial, maybe because it was decided by a judge rather than jury, was not as difficult as he had expected. For one thing, the lead defense attorney was surprisingly easy on Billy during cross-examination. One could even say gentle. Billy could remember it all with perfect clarity years after the trial. *No wonder*, he told himself. *No wonder the defendant could do nothing but grin. The joke was on me.*

As soon as the prosecutor finished his closing argument, the judge held up a hand to the assistant district attorney and, over his vehement protests, called the defendant forth.

"You," the judge addressed the still-grinning hit man when he had been brought before the bench. "I'm going to give you my decision now. I have no desire to drag these proceedings out any further. We've wasted enough of the taxpayers' money." The prosecutor jumped up so abruptly to spit out his objections that he knocked his chair over. The judge shook his head.

"Enough," he glared at the prosecutor. "Okay then." The judge paused, glanced down at some papers and then looked up, not so much at the defendant as at the entire courtroom. "On the charge of first-degree murder. Not guilty. On the weapons charges, well, let's boil it down to carrying a concealed weapon. Guilty. You are hereby sentenced to one day in the county jail. Sentence is suspended." He banged his gavel once, hopped down from the dais from which he had presided, and was gone.

For Billy and his wife, those first weeks after the judge inexplicably set the murderer free were a jumble of frantic conferences with the police and the prosecutor's office. Eventually, the district attorney told them that the hit man had not only gotten off scot-free, but had publicly sworn revenge on Billy and his family. Not to worry, he said. The prosecutor's office, through a convoluted process of obtaining assistance from the federal witness protection program, was going to help them get back on their feet in a new area.

"You've got to be kidding me," Billy kept repeating to the cops, the D.A., his wife—anyone who would listen. "He threatens to kill little kids, and we're the ones who have to flee in the middle of the night? This is insane."

No one bothered to respond. Maybe they thought it was a rhetorical question. But it wasn't. He wanted an answer.

There followed months of tumult and confusion. The family took refuge in a series of motel rooms only slightly better than the one he now occupied. Their nomadic life continued for seven months—seven months of laundry hanging everywhere and the kids transferring from one school to the next—until they were brought here, this barren, godless place on the outskirts of San Antonio.

They spent almost a decade in Texas, with Billy finding employment as a mechanic and gas jockey in a service station. Mary waited tables in a Mexican restaurant. The kids adjusted and grew. They lived in a trailer, which Mary resented. It was cramped and it wasn't home. She missed her house. She missed her life.

As for Billy, he hated everything, starting with the hot Texan environment. He hated what had become of them. He hated that God was sending these tribulations as if he were Job. Most of all he hated himself. He blamed himself for them ending up this way.

Billy was a simple man at heart. Life had always been black and white. But the complicated turns his life had taken were beyond him. You kill someone in cold blood, therefore you get punished. You don't get off unscathed and then get to threaten to wipe out a whole family, for God's sake—those beautiful, innocent kids—and force them to live a lousy, dirt-poor life on the run. "We weren't the ones who did anything wrong," he would whisper to them in the beginning, gathering his son and daughter into his arms and pressing his lips into their unbelievably silky hair. "We did nothing wrong."

That was in the beginning. Billy, tired of being angry, tired of being disheartened, took to drinking heavily in the evenings after work. Soon, anytime he wasn't working or sleeping, he was drinking. Drinking took the place of speech. He didn't say much of anything to the kids or to Mary. He found he didn't have much to say.

My father was right, Billy would think. *I have turned into a bum.*

They hadn't heard from Billy's parents the entire time they had been in Texas, even though Billy had sent the address and phone number to his father, against the D.A.'s express command. And against his own better judgment, since he knew his father blamed him for his brother's death. For not stopping it. For not throwing himself in the path of the shotgun, Billy supposed.

Still, someone needs to know we're alive, he rationalized. In the end it didn't matter. They never called.

Mary began rousing him each morning with an ultimatum. "I mean it, Billy. It's the kids and me, or else it's the booze. You decide."

Billy knew she meant it. Finally he made the choice, telling himself it was better for the family if he left. And maybe without all of them around, he could think more clearly.

As soon as he moved out, he regretted it. He cursed himself for somehow finding a way to make his hideous condition even worse. He missed Mary; he missed his kids.

Billy couldn't stop drinking, but he also couldn't stop asking Mary to take him back. He called, he sent letters, he showed up at the door, the kids in the background silent and embarrassed. Mary held firm. He couldn't blame her. She was managing to take care of the kids on her own and with the small stipend the witness protection program still provided. What did she need him for?

Meanwhile he was drinking more, if that was possible. Sometimes he would stare at the bottle of whiskey and see a miniature of himself in there, thrashing around in the liquid, drowning in drink.

It had been six months since he had left the trailer and moved into this shitty motel room. It had been one day since he showed up at work still drunk from the night before, and his boss had gently told him to pack up and go home. "I can't keep you on anymore, Billy," he said.

"Can't keep a charity case, huh?" Billy stumbled for the door. But he couldn't blame him either. The man had been patient with Billy for a long time.

Billy moved some trash with his toe. Maybe he should start another heartfelt letter to Mary—

A harsh rap on the door startled him. It couldn't be the motel management already. He was paid up through the end of the week.

He moved to the window and peeked around the edge of the shade. Two men in suits. One raised his hand and rapped again, more insistently.

Billy went to the door and opened it slightly wider than a crack.

"Mr. O'Brien?"

Billy said nothing, but took the identification from the man who seemed to be taking the lead. An assistant district attorney from their old home county back in Pennsylvania.

He handed back the ID. "What do you want?"

Both men looked hesitant. "Can we come in?"

If they were horrified by the lack of housekeeping, they were polite enough not to say so. Billy offered no apologies. He did, however, throw himself back on the bed to allow the men to sit in the orange chairs with their ridiculous fake leather.

The spokesman cleared his throat. "Bill—may I call you Bill?—we're here because of the case in which you testified and consequently were forced to move here in order to, to . . ."

"Escape certain death?" Billy supplied helpfully.

"Well, I wasn't going to put it like that," the lawyer said. "All right, let me just tell it to you straight. You most definitely got a raw deal. Everyone knew the judge was on the take. Why else would he let an obvious killer walk, and leave you and your family out to dry? Unfortunately, there was never any way to prove it. Until now.

"I'm sure you remember the shooter's lead defense attorney," he continued.

Billy made a face.

"Well, he had some kind of wake-up call, a change of heart, or something," the man continued. "He decided to confess his part in bribing the judge." The lawyer paused, expecting a reaction from Billy. Getting none, he shrugged and continued.

"The fact that this guy came clean opened up an entire Pandora's box with regard to the judge. As it turns out, yours was not the only case where the defense was lining the judge's pocket. Any defendant with means would get the word that the judge was 'open' to quiet discussions outside of the courtroom. It apparently occurred quite often. The judge had a whole racket going. A bit ironic if you ask me. The judge didn't really demand all that much. A few thousand in the cases we know about for sure. In the case you testified in, for instance, it took just three thousand dollars for him to roll over."

"Three thousand pieces of silver," Billy said.

The two men nodded. Billy crossed his arms under his head and stared at the ceiling, thinking.

"So now we know. What happens to him now?"

"The judge? Nothing. He's dead."

"Dead." They might as well have punched Billy in the gut. He curled up on the bed. Not that he gave a rat's ass about the judge, but this whole affair was mutating like bacteria. Nothing about it was salvageable. He felt a sudden urge to crawl under the covers and try, for who knew how many times, to make the entire situation disappear.

"Yeah, when he got word that the defense lawyer had spilled his guts, the judge got out his trusty shotgun and blew his head off." The man shook his head. "Forget the judge, Mr. O'Brien. His death doesn't mean this is over. That's why we're here. There's something very important you can do for us."

Billy stared. Now he knew why they were here and what they wanted. It wasn't just to let him know about the judge. They wanted him to testify in a new trial.

"You've got to be kidding. Don't tell me you want me to go through this again. You want me to testify again, when you never even bothered to appeal the case to begin with? I don't know what you people were thinking, letting a murderer—my brother's murderer—walk free." Billy's breath was coming rapid and shallow, and he was starting to sweat. Damn. He felt like he might be having a heart attack.

The men exchanged glances, as if they were expecting Billy's objections. "It's a little complicated, but we have good news. Really good news," the spokesman lawyer said. "See, this is how it works. Normally, that is. Generally if you're accused of a crime like first-degree murder and then found not guilty, it can't be appealed and you can't be tried again. That would be double jeopardy. But this case is very unusual. It was trial by judge, not jury, and the judge was crooked. We have proof. He left a written confession about this case as well as a few others. All of this, the lawyer coming clean, the judge confessing, and so on, it happened over the last two years. We've pursued this case through the appeals process, all the way up to the Supreme Court. That's of the United States, by the way. The Supreme Court ruled in our favor, agreeing that this was not kosher. It means we've been cleared for another trial. But first we need to be sure that we have your cooperation. After all, you were the main witness in the case. And"—he cleared his throat—"for you, it's a do-over, a shot at redemption."

Billy was standing now, shaking. "You don't know. You don't have a clue how my life has been ruined by this." He moved over to the door, opened it. "Get out."

The two men exchanged glances again and, as if on cue, got up and headed toward the door. Billy sucked in sharp, raspy breaths. Partly out of the door and framed against the blast of heat and sunlight, the head attorney spoke one last time.

"You probably think no one got as raw a deal as you. That's understandable to feel that way. But hear me out one more minute about another case involving the same judge. In that case, the perpetrator was convicted but he walked out with a suspended sentence—after being found guilty of kidnapping and rape. Because it didn't involve murder, and the problem had to do with the sentencing, the decision was made to leave this one alone. So, here's a victim who didn't get justice and she never will. You see, someone is worse off than you."

The man gave Billy a jaunty salute. "Just something to think about," he said. He started to pull the door shut then reopened it for a second. "Also," he added, glancing at the bottles and trash, "you might want to think about tidying up here." The door closed with a quiet click.

CHAPTER NINE

Spring 1998: Maryland

When I woke, on the living room floor, still tangled in the blanket, my limbs were stiff from the odd angle in which I had slept. I sat up. The morning sun streamed in, competing with the table lamp that still burned from the previous night.

I'm late for work, came one thought, followed immediately by *I can't go to work.*

The phone rang. It was on the table that, from my vantage point seated on the floor, was very close to my head. I don't know how I wasn't startled. I merely looked at it as if the telephone were some kind of laboratory experiment.

After the requisite four rings, the answering machine clicked on. My disembodied voice suggested that the caller leave a message.

"Quinn?" It was Suzy, from work. Automatically I reached for the phone, then, without even knowing why, I let my arm drop. I couldn't talk, not even to Suzy.

"Quinn, if you're there, pick up." Suzy paused for a few beats. "Well, I guess you could be on your way in. It's just that—well, it's not like you not to show up and not to call. I mean promptness is not your top virtue, but you don't usually play hooky."

Suzy dropped her voice to a harsh whisper. "Listen, Helga hasn't even noticed, she's so busy with this new account. But you know her. It's just a matter of time. But what the heck. Screw her. I'm just worried about you. Call me." The last part came out as a hiss. The machine clicked off.

I struggled to my feet, feeling dizzy. I swayed for a moment over the now silent answering machine. I reached out and pressed the switch to turn it off. As if on cue, the phone began to ring.

This time I recoiled. The phone continued ringing incessantly. After the twentieth ring, I pulled the plug on the phone.

It could have been Suzy although she probably wouldn't try calling again that soon.

The phone call could be a wrong number or a charity asking for a donation. But it could also be—and I feared it would be—the mystery caller from the day before. Of course, it might have been Joe. However, this would be awfully early for him given the time difference. I knew Joe would eventually call, here or at the office. And when he would be unable to contact me in either location, he would call Suzy who would share her fears about me being a no-show.

Holing up in the apartment instead of going to work, and refusing to answer the phone, was stupid and unproductive. I knew I was being irrational but I couldn't make myself behave normally.

"Pull yourself together," I said aloud. But I was painfully aware of the damage within me, that I had been fooling myself all along. The beautiful, fragile facade I had constructed over the last ten years lay shattered.

Still foggy, I headed to the bedroom with the vague thought of pulling the Yellow Pages from the nightstand drawer and calling someone—anyone—for help. But the sight of the bed made everything seem suddenly overwhelming. Exhaustion overcame me. I took a detour for the mattress. Maybe resting would help me think clearly. Before I could refocus my thoughts, I slept.

This time I awoke with sunlight filtering into my windowless bedroom via the door that I had left open. The sun had moved to my apartment's side of the building, which meant it was late afternoon.

I shifted, wincing from my stiff neck, and checked the clock radio. Five thirty. The whole day was gone.

I turned my attention back to the ceiling. It was difficult to keep my eyes open. I felt drugged.

Although I argued with myself that it was pointless to continue to lie there swaddled in bedclothes, it was another thirty minutes before I rose. I moved slowly to the bathroom and clutched the sink, my thoughts bouncing. Finally I looked in the mirror. At least I didn't see in my face the debilitating fear of last night. That was a relief. Unfortunately, doubt and guilt had settled in as replacements. I looked haggard.

The loud knocking on the door was so startling that I jumped a few feet back from the sink. The pounding sounded again. My heart thumped along with it.

Racing silently in bare feet, I stopped short of the door by ten feet. The sound coming from the door couldn't be described as a knocking or a rapping. It was a desperate beating that had to be turning the person's fist into a bruised mess. The door, which was made of metal, by now probably had dents in it.

I could make out a voice. At first it was just beyond the pounding, then it increased in volume until it bordered on a howl.

"Quinn! Come on—open up."

It sounded like Joe. Although it was strange and sort of gurgling, it had to be Joe. I managed a wavering query. "Who is it?"

It was miraculous that he heard me at all, with all the noise he was making. But the knocking ended abruptly with my tentative question.

"Quinn? Thank God. Are you okay? Open the door."

The thought came: How silly I must seem. I continued anyway. "How do I know it's really you?" I could hear him sigh.

"Just look through the peephole."

I managed to get the locks undone with shaking fingers. Then Joe was there, gripping me, but he looked even more wobbly than I felt.

"Why didn't you answer your phone?" he demanded finally. "Did you unplug it? We were able to catch an earlier flight and I've been trying to reach you all day to let you know. I've been calling from airports, calling your office, here, everywhere. Then I got your friend Suzy at work, and when she said she wasn't able to reach you either . . ." He drew a breath and examined my face. Seeing no injury, he relaxed slightly. "I thought something had happened to you."

I looked at him aghast. The idea that he was in a near panic over some harm befalling me was a jolt.

"I'm sorry. I really am. I wasn't thinking straight. Look, um, why don't we sit . . ." I waved him in with a nervous flutter of the hands, and we perched on the edge of my sofa like strangers engaging in awkward small talk. I pressed my hands between my knees.

"I saw something on the news about a girl who was murdered," I started in a rush and then stopped.

Joe nodded, waiting. "Okay." He drew out the word.

"She was found not far from here. Her head was cut off."

Joe choked a little. "That's terrible. But why—"

I shook my head fiercely. "No, no, it's all about what he cut *on* her. He carved the same exact word on her arm as *this*." I shoved up my sleeve to reveal the scarred word.

"Good God." Joe was ashen.

I told him all that I had heard about the case, leaving out the part about the answering machine message about the "news." I worried it would sound nonsensical and paranoid. I also didn't mention my call to my mother or her reaction.

When I finished, Joe eased himself back among the cushions and sat motionless, staring at the window.

I watched him, anxious. He seemed angry. I wished he would drum his fingers or stroke his beard thoughtfully, like I had seen him do so many times. Anything but this angry stare.

"So." His voice was casual but his expression remained hard. "So, what's our game plan?"

"Game plan?" I was confused. "I've been sort of wandering around like a zombie and not really coming up with a game plan."

He actually laughed. Relieved, I leaned back against him, tentative at first. I could feel the tension drain from him. *Good,* I thought. *It wouldn't do to have both of us in a state.*

We sat in silence for a long while. I felt myself drifting to sleep (even as I wondered how I could possibly sleep more) when I became aware that Joe was poking my ribs.

"Hey," he said gently. "Wake up. We need to talk."

"Didn't we already talk?"

"No, I mean about going to the police. If they don't have any real leads in this murder, you may have the key. Right there on your arm."

All notion of sleep vanished. I struggled to my feet and resumed my pacing. "That's kind of a difficult decision. I'm not sure I can take something like that again." I halted my march directly in front of Joe. "And yet . . ."

"And yet what?"

I sank in the chair opposite him, now queasy. I pressed my head gingerly with my fingertips and willed my stomach to settle.

"It's just that I don't understand how the same thing—no, a far worse thing—could be allowed to happen. Why didn't they believe me?"

I stopped. Joe waited.

"At the time, I thought I was doing the right thing. Everyone told me I was. But there were things I could have done differently, different choices, I don't know . . . maybe I could have stopped this mess from turning into what it became. A bigger mess. Someone dead." My face was wet; I realized that I was crying. I wiped my cheeks with both hands and saw that Joe was looking at me, confused. It was no wonder. I sounded like a lunatic. Helpless, I buried my face in my hands.

Joe knelt in front of me and carefully pried my fingers from my face.

"Hey. Look at me." Stubbornly, I kept my eyes closed.

"I'm not sure I can totally understand your feelings, but I do know you can't blame yourself. It's not your fault. The whole system let you down."

I opened my eyes but averted my gaze. "I'm sure you're right," I said dully. Finally, I turned back to him. It wasn't fair to involve him in this any longer. As dependent on Joe as I seemed to have become, I needed to let him extricate himself. I took a deep breath.

"This is getting far more complicated than you bargained for. So I'll understand if you want to just forget about all this. Us, I mean." It sounded absurdly formal but it took tremendous effort on my part to keep from breaking down and sobbing. I held out an unsteady hand for him to shake. "You can just walk away, no hard feelings?"

Joe had a strange look on his face. For a second it seemed like he was struggling not to smile. He took my outstretched hand and held it for a long time without saying anything. Then he looked up.

"How about I go with you to the police station tomorrow instead?"

Suddenly, everything clicked in my head. The thought of having Joe beside me made the whole idea of approaching the authorities not only palatable, but the only possible course of action. And it meant that he was willing to go along for the ride.

I sat up straight. With as much dignity as I could muster, I wiped my cheek again with the back of my hand. "That would mean so much to me," I said solemnly. For the first time since the news report had seemed to unravel everything, I felt hope.

The next morning I woke at four thirty after a restless sleep. At least I had forgone the floor and had slept in a bed. But it had been after midnight by the time I could persuade Joe to leave. And that was only with the promise that I would call him first thing in the morning to coordinate our trip to the police station.

In the bathroom, I turned the shower faucet to as hot as I could stand it and let the steam and pelting water loosen my stiff muscles. That, and a pot of coffee, helped, but it was the knowledge that Joe was back home, that I wasn't on my own, that really helped me feel more human.

I sat at my little dinette table in the kitchen, watching the hands of the wall clock. I wondered if at six thirty I might be able to catch Helga, my notoriously workaholic boss, at the office. That might be a little early, even for her. I didn't want to call Joe yet—he was sure to be still asleep. I had just decided that seven o'clock would be a more reasonable time to call the office when the wall phone rang. Startled, I knocked my mug, spilling coffee over the table and onto my lap.

"I didn't wake you, did I?" Joe's voice was surprisingly chipper and crisp.

With the phone tucked under one ear, I tried to mop up the mess with a kitchen towel. "I've been up. As a matter of fact, I've already had coffee. Unfortunately now I'm wearing some of it." I laughed nervously.

"Oh, okay." He was businesslike and a little distracted. I had often heard him that way when he was calling from the office and others could hear his end of the conversation. I was puzzled.

"I just wanted to let you know," Joe was saying, "that I've been called into work. There's something I have to take care of and, unfortunately, it can't wait. But don't worry. I'll be at your place as soon as I can. Let's say eleven o'clock at the latest. We'll grab an early lunch and then go. Sound good?"

"Okay." I was disappointed, but hoped it didn't show.

"It's a deal then." He hesitated. "And I will be there. I just have to take care of this."

My disappointment shifted to anger. *If he didn't want to go with me, he should just say so*, I thought. But I kept my tone even.

"It's fine, really. I'm going to go now because I want to try to reach Helga first thing. She's probably already furious with me, so I imagine I'll have my own work crisis to deal with."

As soon as I heard the dial tone, I called my office. My boss wasn't in yet after all. Just Helga's smooth voice strongly suggesting that the caller leave a detailed message.

I left a brief apology about my absence the previous day, mumbled a reference to a family emergency, and then ended it with the assurance that I fully expected to be in the following day.

Replacing the receiver, I fanned myself with the dish towel. What I told Helga wasn't totally a lie, I rationalized. It was a lame excuse, though, and I didn't kid myself that it would probably be rejected out of hand. Helga didn't believe in the personal lives of employees.

I can't worry about Helga or work or anything else right now, I thought as I started cleaning up the kitchen and doing the dishes. I needed to prepare for my trip to the police station, a place I had hoped never to have to visit again. *This is more than a little ironic*, I addressed the iridescent soap bubbles in the coffeepot. I rinsed it over and over long after the water ran clear. The repetition was soothing.

In spite of my efforts not to dwell on it, I could feel the fear creeping in. Maybe Joe wouldn't be able to break away from whatever it was that called him in to work. I began praying, my lips moving silently as I sloshed water in the sink. I prayed that I would be able to get through this, that Joe would show up. Despite my brief stab at bravado the night before, I didn't think I had the courage to go to the police alone. And I couldn't put it off another day. If I spent one more day out of the office, Helga would fire me for sure.

I wiped down the table, the countertops, and even the walls in the kitchen, then wrung out the dishcloths and hung them neatly over the faucet to dry. I changed out of my coffee-stained clothes and went to the living room to wait. I sat on the sofa, very still, feet flat on the floor, hands folded in my lap. I closed my eyes and tried to calm myself.

If someone were to photograph me right now, I imagined, *it would probably be an image of complete serenity.* I may not be a quivering mess—for a change—but barely below the surface, I was a bundle of nerves. I was rapidly approaching the status of nervous wreck. I wished Joe would call.

The anniversary clock, the one that had been my grandmother's, that I kept in a curio cabinet in the living room, chimed the half hour. Normally, the chiming was just part of the normal background noise and I never noticed it. Now, as it chimed the hour and then the half hour again, the sound crashed through the apartment. I found myself watching, mesmerized, the endlessly revolving pendulum under the clock's glass dome.

The next hour chimed, and I forced myself to look elsewhere, anywhere but the clock. *No wonder they use swinging watches to hypnotize people,* I thought. Glancing down, I noticed that the cotton skirt I had changed into was wrinkled. I tried smoothing it with my hands, then considered dragging out the ironing board to press it. I decided the skirt was too short anyway.

I returned to the bedroom to change into something more conservative. Flipping through the hangers in the closet, I pulled out another skirt, one that didn't fit well and that I rarely wore because I thought it made me look dumpy. Better dumpy than not credible.

I went back to the living room. Soon I was worrying about my blouse. It wasn't exactly low cut, but maybe something with a high collar would be more appropriate. I made another round-trip through the closet, wondering if I should wear slacks instead of a skirt. Except that it might look like I was trying to appear mannish.

Oh, the hell with it, I thought angrily. I grabbed more hangers and threw them on the growing pile of clothes on the bed. I changed into black tailored trousers, a conservative white blouse, and a maroon blazer. I combed my hair again, pulling it back severely into a large hair clip.

I examined myself in the mirror. There. Now I looked like a parochial school student. I yanked on my cuffs to pull them below the blazer sleeves.

I plopped down again on the sofa and my eyes immediately moved back to the clock. It was past noon. I began to worry about Joe. The last thing I wanted to do was call him, especially if he was dealing with problems at work. He was now in a position of importance, I reminded myself.

It was difficult, but I forced myself to be still. I stared at the clock.

The clock chimed twelve thirty. *This thing is giving me a headache*, I thought.

By one o'clock I was standing in front of the anniversary clock with a surge of panic and the overwhelming sense that I was running out of time.

"Time to go," I announced to the clock, which didn't seem to care one way or the other. I picked up my purse and marched out the door.

CHAPTER TEN

July 1988: a county courthouse, Pennsylvania

Later, when I could look at it more dispassionately, it was obvious that Dennis Price's legal team's tactics had been very predictable. I had seen the same motions and the same methods in countless television shows about courts and lawyers. And to be objective about it, that's what they were supposed to do. Price's expensive lawyers were hired specifically to get him acquitted if at all possible, and barring that, the absolute minimum of any sort of punishment. So they played their little games along the way. There was the endless procrastination, based on flimsy excuses. None of it made much sense to me at first, neophyte that I was, but I grew more familiar with the terms—motion, continuance—every time my parents and I received a letter or a phone call from the legal authorities. It all added up to delay.

In the end, Price's lawyers did their job. By the time the trial date was finally announced, they had managed to postpone it more than a full year. And it was to be held deep into summer, when college was out of session. That meant far less publicity. It also made it more likely that any students who might be called as witnesses would be home for the summer and unavailable to testify.

My parents were indignant.

"Whatever happened to a speedy trial?" my mother raged. "I thought we were entitled to that." She shredded a wad of tissues, letting them flutter to the floor. My father held the latest correspondence in his hand. He read and reread it, as if expecting to find some new piece of information.

"At least we didn't drive all the way out there only to find out that the trial date's been moved again." Distracted, my father appeared to be ignoring my mother's distress. He could have been addressing me, but if so, I didn't react. I was even more disconnected than either of them.

I sank deeper into the corner of the sofa. From this vantage point, I could stay hidden from my parents but still look out the living room window. I could see the front walk and the mailbox, barely visible among the vivid blue morning glories that crowded it every summer. Part of me wished that the throng of flowers and vines would prevent the mailman from delivering more messages from the legal system—and another part hoped that more notices announcing even more continuances would sprout in the mailbox like blossoms. More delays seemed possible. Maybe this thing could be put off so many times that everyone would just tire of it. I was tired of it. I was dreading having to testify. I knew, without having stepped into a courtroom, that it would go badly— maybe even be disastrous.

When at last the time for the trial came, my parents and I were not much improved from the collective state of anxiety we had worked ourselves into over the long wait. The only difference was our unspoken pact: we would keep our dignity even if our insides were gelatin. These shared fears, and the fact that my parents felt this as intensely as I did, should have brought me even closer to my mother and father. I should have been able to take shelter under the protection they were offering. But it didn't. I found myself withdrawing. I tried not to show that I was shriveling from their well-intentioned bright chatter as we drove to the county seat with its hundred-year-old courthouse, not far from the college campus. I spent most of the trip curled up in the backseat, watching telephone wires streak past the car window.

The night before the start of the trial, we checked into a small motel on the edge of town. At dinner we barely spoke. I drank glass after glass of water, finally having to excuse myself. On the way to the restroom, I glanced back at my parents sitting stiffly and looking frightened. When I caught sight of myself in the ladies' room mirror, I saw their look reflected in my expression. Three people, scared to death. I thought sadly that no matter how much they wanted to ward off the pain, to do something, as any parent would to protect their child, this time they just couldn't help me.

The following morning, dawn broke on a spotless blue sky. By nine o'clock, the sun was streaming in the large open windows of the courthouse. It was a glorious summer day, but I barely noticed the weather. Head down, I stumbled into the courtroom behind my parents. We filed into one of the rows of seats on the prosecutor's side.

Ten minutes before, in a small room off the courtroom, we had met the lawyer who would be prosecuting the case. I had thought it would be the same assistant district attorney, a woman, who had handled the preliminary hearing. Instead, here was a dark-haired man with very large, very white teeth.

He seemed young, even to me. He certainly had a penchant for smiling.

He introduced himself as Mr. Goderich and gave a little speech about how he had the case under control. I was nervous and distracted by his teeth, so that much of what he said didn't really register. But his mentioning "not to worry about the kidnapping charge" did penetrate—there was something about how it was dropped because it was a federal offense. I wanted to ask about that and my father even tried to interject his own questions, but Goderich said we all had to get into the courtroom.

We left meekly. Goderich gave a weak, unconvincing thumbs-up along with his toothy grin.

It turned out we had plenty of time. None of the principals—the judge, the attorneys, or even Goderich—had arrived. A bailiff stood near the door. A young woman with a notebook, who was most likely from the local newspaper, and some old men were scattered in the audience section. We waited. The senior citizens, who seemed to be well acquainted with each other, talked quietly.

After about twenty minutes, the defense team marched in, Dennis Price in tow. I found it more than unsettling to see Price, but it wasn't just that. I was aware of a certain shift in the courtroom. We later learned from the group of senior citizens, who sat at the table adjacent to us in the crowded luncheonette, that the defense attorneys were the attraction. "Yes, sir, whenever these lawyers are handling the defense, it's worth watching. They're entertaining. Doesn't matter much what the case is about," one of the old men, one with watery eyes and a baseball cap, confided to my father across the small space between our tables.

The defense attorneys were a father-and-son team, Sam McHugh, senior and junior. The son seated himself carefully at the defense table and began scribbling on a legal pad. Impeccably dressed in an expensive Italian suit, he was young and handsome, which was not diminished by a nose just a trifle too large.

His father was rounder and mild-looking, with unfashionable dark-framed glasses. He seemed a bit rumpled, although that might have been due to the juxtaposition with his elegant son.

I recognized the younger McHugh. I had been on the receiving end of his ruthless cross-examination during Price's preliminary hearing. Maybe the senior McHugh would handle the trial. If so, I hoped the going would be a little less brutal. I was heartened by the fact he looked like a friendly country lawyer, like Atticus Finch.

Any hope for mercy faded as soon as the elder Sam McHugh addressed the jury in his opening statement.

"Ladies and gentlemen." His voice was rich and sonorous. "During the course of this trial, you will hear a lot of imaginative opinion, a great deal of wild description, but not much in the way of provable facts. Pretty much none at all. Throughout, you're going to hear the allegations of a disturbed young lady. A young woman who is questionable in many regards. A young woman who is a liar. Plain and simple, she is a liar."

I heard my mother gasp. McHugh's tone had grown thunderous and he had transformed into a charismatic preacher. His lined face shone. He was speaking the truth as he discerned it, and he was magnanimous in helping the jury discern it, too.

Without warning, he switched back to his mild-mannered, avuncular demeanor. His voice was again soothing, and the courtroom along with the jury were spellbound.

"This is a case, ladies and gentlemen, not of hard facts or circumstantial evidence. It's not even a matter of he said, she said. That would be giving it far too much credibility. This is simply a case of one young woman's attempt to ruin a young man's life."

McHugh returned to his seat. I wept, holding a handful of tissues to my face. My shoulders shook. "Stop it," my father hissed. "That doesn't look good at all."

I blew my nose as quietly as possible. My father, and probably no one else in the courtroom could know the real reason I was crying. I was grieving over the realization that, barely ten minutes into the proceedings, the real person on trial was me.

The trial lasted nearly two days, much of it a blur. In the time I spent on the witness stand—which felt like the entire trial—I managed to develop a technique for keeping my composure. It was simple enough: avoid looking at anyone directly and instead study my surroundings. Even in my ignorance of legal matters, I sensed that this was probably not the best idea if I wanted to appear credible. I should probably have at least made eye contact with the jury once in a while. But between the embarrassing details I was forced to repeat, and the humiliating questions I was subjected to, it was impossible to so much as glance in their direction.

I also avoided, at all costs, looking at the defendant's table. The sole exception was when I was required to positively identify Dennis Price as my attacker. Even then I only reluctantly steered my face in his general direction, taking in the table rather than the people seated behind it.

For the majority of the trial, I focused my attention on the courtroom itself. There was plenty of time to appreciate the vaulted ceilings with gold stenciling on the perimeter and the wrought iron chandelier that rose dramatically above us. If not for the minor drama of the trial, the place could have been the interior of a pristine New England church. I let myself wonder about the trials and events that would have taken place here over the years.

But as much as I tried to disassociate myself, it was difficult to ignore the proceedings in front of me. Without wanting to, I found myself watching the prosecutor, Goderich, grin like a game show host as he tried to make the state's case, with awkward attempts to sidestep the McHughs' procedural traps. It was becoming painfully clear that Goderich didn't have much experience, at least with rape cases, which even I knew were difficult to prove. Goderich tried to introduce a basic piece of evidence to establish the crime—photos of me that the police took immediately after my attack—but it became just another point on which he was rebuffed. In a weary voice, the defense argued that if the state was unable to produce the photographer who took said photographs, they therefore should not be entered as evidence. Objection sustained.

As Goderich experienced more of these setbacks, he began to look stunned. His smile faded and he nervously pushed his glasses up his nose. I couldn't watch, so I turned my gaze elsewhere, anywhere—to the judge's bench with its intricate carvings, and the heavy wooden doors on either side of the bench.

Also present in the courtroom were the two churchgoing students, the ones who had helped me when I ran down the dormitory corridor that Sunday morning. They had shown up, bless their hearts, and unlike the police photographer, they were prepared to testify. But Goderich was unsuccessful in this effort as well. The younger McHugh voiced an objection that I didn't understand, but it didn't matter. It was also sustained. Goderich perspired freely and mopped his brow with a wrinkled handkerchief while everyone waited for him to make some kind of counter-argument.

"Mr. Goderich, do you or don't you have anything to say?" The judge, shuffling some papers, appeared to be bored. Goderich turned purplish red and called me to the witness stand.

I turned to face the room to be sworn in and caught sight of Goderich's frightened face. Blood rushed in my ears and I thought: *He's not here to represent me anyway. I'm on my own.* I steeled myself for the testimony and cross-examination that I had been dreading, and focused my gaze on the mural on the courtroom's rear wall.

Unfortunately, this calming technique fell apart during my time on the witness stand. I was no match for the elder McHugh, who was as skilled as a circus trainer guiding a lion meekly through her steps. Unlike Goderich, who had stood at the prosecutor's table and woodenly asked me questions, McHugh was jovial and casual, standing uncomfortably close during his lengthy questioning. He reeked of cologne that was probably expensive but made me gag.

"Isn't it true, Miss Carlisle—or should I say, *Ms.* Carlisle? You're probably one of those feminists, right?" He winked at me and turned to the jury, leaning against the partition that boxed in the witness chair. I tried not to choke on the scent.

"Ms. Carlisle." He took his time speaking, his deep tones reverberating. "You *say* that my client had a gun." He sounded contemptuous.

I reddened. Every word from him, even the way he said my name as if it were something distasteful, filled me with shame.

"Yes. One of the first things he said was that he had a gun."

"You *claim* he said that. But did you ever see a gun?"

"No, but I—"

"Just answer yes or no," McHugh snapped.

I was rattled. He was focusing on the weapon, which would only lead to a discussion about the knife—my knife—the one

I had threatened Price with but hadn't had the nerve to use. I frantically tried to think where this questioning was going, but it seemed impossible to even guess.

"We're waiting, Ms. Carlisle. Yes or no?"

Yes or no, what? I had lost track of the question. Confused, I glanced at the judge and then at Goderich. Both seemed to be avoiding me. I turned back to McHugh, whose eyes under his beetle-like brows pierced me.

"Did you or did you not see *a gun*?" McHugh nearly shouted the last words.

I blazed with humiliation. "No. No, I did not see a gun."

"Did you see a gun barrel?"

Miserable, I shook my head no.

"Ms. Carlisle, you're going to have to answer audibly," McHugh said impatiently. "Come on, you're a smart college girl. Don't you know how to comport yourself in a courtroom?"

I heard a nervous twitter. I looked around again. Goderich was studying his legal pad. My father had his forehead buried in his balled-up fists. My mother's seat was vacant. No one could help me. I would have to get through this somehow.

I sat up straighter, took a deep breath, and tried to answer calmly.

"No, I did not see a gun barrel."

After that, it was a blur of questions. Some questions were similar to others, only worded differently, often with a twist designed to trip me up. I attempted to keep up, trying also to keep as composed as I could. My parents whispered to me during the break that if I looked too detached, the jury might not find me believable. Goderich didn't mention this, or anything else for that matter. The case was lost, and we all knew it.

The only blessing was that McHugh had appeared to drop the line of questioning about the knife. I was relieved. I feared that if it came out that the knife that Price has used on me was my own, it would make me look somehow culpable.

Toward the end of my testimony, however, McHugh appeared to stop caring how, or even if, I answered. He pounded home the same points, becoming like a television evangelist delivering a sermon.

"Isn't it true," he bellowed, "that you picked *him* up? In other words, my client did not stop you on the street, but you hailed him and made suggestive statements. That's right, isn't it, that you made suggestive statements?"

"No," I answered dully, my head pounding.

McHugh marched to his side of the defense table, pretending to consult his notes. I stared at Goderich, who was sinking lower in his chair.

"So, Ms. Carlisle." McHugh was back, practically on top of the witness stand, his face close to mine. "Let's have it. The whole, unmitigated truth. You're a college student?"

"Yes."

"Yes, good. So a young coed at a university known as a party school. Do you attend a lot of parties, Ms. Carlisle?"

"Some. I wouldn't say a lot."

"Parties are a lot of fun, aren't they, Ms. Carlisle?"

I found my focal point on the far side of the room and waited for his punch line.

"I didn't hear your answer, Ms. Carlisle. Don't you find parties to be fun?"

I turned back to face him and let the answer flow from me.

"I just don't see how that question is the least bit relevant. I wasn't at a party. I was walking home from the bus station after returning from a funeral. My grandmother's funeral."

Before I even finished my sentence, I realized that I might as well have taken a match and set the courtroom on fire. The jury and the audience stared at me. "My God," I heard the court stenographer whisper. McHugh turned to the judge, his hands spread as if to say, *What can I do with a witness like this?*

The judge adjusted his glasses and coughed. He seemed to be stalling, but finally found his voice. "Strike that from the record," he ordered the stenographer. "Now, your job," he said to me, "is to answer the questions without any additional commentary. I hope we're clear. Mr. McHugh, do you think we can get this wrapped up?"

McHugh returned to the defense table. Unperturbed by the judge's attempt at an admonishment, he stood there for long minutes, oblivious to the rest of us who waited silently for his next word. He took his time, rocking back and forth and pursing his lips as he studied some notes. At last he put the papers back on the table and returned to the witness stand.

"Let's go back for a minute to the matter of the knife," he said.

I caught my breath.

"Now, Ms. Carlisle, you say that you received these injuries from a knife—a weapon that has not been recovered, I might add. So we do not have the weapon in evidence, correct?"

"Um, I guess." I was on very uncertain ground.

"You guess? Come on, Ms. Carlisle. Okay, perhaps you can definitively answer this: When did you first see this alleged knife?"

"When? Ah, it must have been, I guess it was when we were struggling. On the path."

"But exactly at what point did you see it? For instance, did you see my client pull the knife from his pocket?"

Again I hesitated. "No, he didn't pull it out of his pocket," I said finally.

McHugh sighed heavily. "Then, what exactly, Ms. Carlisle?"

I swallowed. "It fell out of my pocket."

If I had my wits about me, I might have gotten some satisfaction from momentarily shocking McHugh. He looked as if I had used a stun gun on him. He stared at me for a full fifteen seconds before speaking. When he did, he was crowing.

"So! It fell out of *your* pocket. It was your knife! Isn't that accurate, Ms. Carlisle? It was your own knife, correct?" I nodded reluctantly, again forgetting to say my response out loud. But McHugh didn't even notice. He was gearing up for a full-blown harangue.

"How are we to believe that my client is anything but *innocent*, when the knife that purportedly caused these injuries not only is nowhere to be found, but now the accuser, by her own *admission*, says that it was her own knife anyway? How do we know that she didn't do this all to herself? That the whole alleged incident wasn't a total fabrication?"

I listened, miserable. It sounded like the truth, this tirade. Mercifully, it was over with shortly, with McHugh gleefully ending the cross-examination. I was dismissed.

I didn't even return to my seat next to my parents, but walked straight to the exit in the back of the courtroom. Once safely in the hallway, I gave in to the spreading blackness. I dropped down hard on a bench. I wasn't sure if I passed out or was simply in shock, but the next thing I was aware of was my mother peering at my face and calling my name in a frightened voice.

I didn't return to the courtroom. My parents wouldn't allow it. "We're not going to participate in this charade anymore. It's a goddamned circus," my father told Goderich bitterly when they met later outside the courthouse.

Instead, we packed up and went home before the trial was over. As a result, we thankfully didn't hear the defense testimony including that of my former roommate Judith McCloud, who claimed to have introduced me to her cousin Dennis Price. She even swore that I went on at least one date with him, suggesting it was on the night of the attack.

We also missed the parade of character witnesses for the defendant. We were absent when the jury left to deliberate, and not in attendance when they returned after only a few hours with a guilty verdict for rape and aggravated assault— amazingly enough, considering how badly the trial had gone, with every step along the way seeming to point to an acquittal. But we weren't there to exult in the verdict. Neither were we there when the judge suspended the sentence, allowing Dennis Price to walk out of court unpunished, free to do as he wished.

CHAPTER ELEVEN

December 1997: San Antonio, Texas

Billy O'Brien hadn't slept well in months. It didn't even matter how much he drank. He might conk out, yes, but only to wake up a few hours later. It bugged the hell out of him that he no longer could anesthetize himself for more than two, three hours, tops.

This was the way it was ever since those guys had shown up at his motel room. He hadn't had a peaceful night's sleep since. Waking at three a.m. and thinking of the same damn stuff he thought he had successfully stuffed into a dusty corner of his mind.

It didn't matter if he poured an entire bottle of whiskey down his throat. Even his old friend Jack Daniel's, normally guaranteed to allow him to pass out, had failed him.

What good is it to have a drinking problem if you can't drown your sorrows? he asked himself. He halfheartedly kicked at the table leg of the cheap dinette set, but succeeded only in stubbing his toe.

It was five thirty in the morning and he had been sitting at this crappy table covered with trash and an overflowing ashtray all night. He lit yet another cigarette and drew in deeply, feeling it irritate his lungs. *What the hell.* It was the one of the few pleasures left in his life, along with drinking.

Unbidden, some of the phrases that the lawyer fellow had said flooded his mind. How this was a shot at redemption. The chance to rectify the whole situation was tempting. More than anything, he wanted to go back in time, to do things over, and to reunite with Mary and the kids.

Mary. That's what he wanted to fix, more than anything else. So what that he could never find a decent job down here, that they were forced by circumstances to move from family and friends and their jobs. They could still overcome all the desperation and hopelessness.

But Mary might not take him back. That was the thing. She had refused so many times that he was afraid that this would become just another situation where he would get his hopes up, only to have them dashed again. That was the thing.

Just like that, he was crying like a little kid. It was all too much, the years of falling into the endless chasm caused by the trial. That's how he pictured it. A pit deeper than anything on earth, deeper than the Grand Canyon. There was no way he had hit bottom yet. He worried there was no bottom.

It was that goddamn trial. The whole travesty of it, the injustice. The trial blew up his and Mary's lives with the force of an atomic bomb. They had been naïve, believing things would be resolved at the end of the trial. Why wouldn't they? A crime had occurred, his brother had been shot dead, he had seen the shooter. But this fundamental truth somehow got twisted into a falsehood, and from then on everything was wrong and warped. Billy had begun his free fall. After all this time, he doubted there was anything in the universe with the energy and power to stop his descent, set him down gently, and lead him back to sanity. Still, he needed to be led back to Mary, which is where he always began and ended.

It took a lot of nerve for those suits to show up at his door a few months ago. Those guys who, with straight faces no less, told him they were offering him an opportunity to fix everything, to un–screw up his screwed-up life. You could get your life back, they said. And, oh, by the way, tough luck on that ruining-your-life thing.

Billy felt the anger well up all over again just thinking about it. It was a goddamn joke.

He upended the bottle to pour more whiskey into his dirty glass. The bottle was empty, but he shook it to be sure.

He looked at the open, blank top of the bottle. Then, with a banshee yell that he didn't know he was even capable of, he grabbed the neck of the bottle and threw it across the room. It smashed against the far wall with such force that splinters of glass flew back on him.

Just like that, the anger drained from him. He was tired of it all, tired of thinking of the past and of the bleak future.

He sat as still as possible for as long as possible and tried not to think at all. But once again the lawyer's words jumped into his brain, especially that last little story, like a throwaway line, the story about the girl. The girl was a rape victim, and as if that wasn't bad enough, she also was victimized by the same crooked judge who had presided over Billy's brother's murder trial. The rape case had a similar outcome, the lawyer said, and that victim wasn't going to get another shot at justice. *Think how she feels*, the guy had said. *Or maybe he had just implied that I should consider someone other than myself*, Billy thought. *In any case, it's working. I can't help thinking of her.*

Billy needed to call Mary.

It wasn't like he had never tried to call his wife—he couldn't bear to think of her as his ex-wife—in the two years since she'd divorced him. Usually she simply refused to speak to him. She wasn't rude about it. She would say something gentle like, "Billy, you know it doesn't do any good to talk," and then would patiently listen to his frantic ramblings. Lately she was letting the answering machine screen her calls. He knew it. She couldn't be out that often. He would inevitably retreat into whining and pleading, begging her to pick up the phone, to call him back, anything. She never did.

God, he needed her. Right now what he needed especially was her advice. Maybe if he could just convince her of that. And it wasn't just flattery. He really was in a quandary and needed someone to help him think clearly. For one, there was this business of the girl, the rape victim. He was curious about her. Had she been able to get on with her life, like he seemed unable to do?

For Billy, it had happened so fast. One minute life was normal, the next Jeff was dead. Billy wondered again, for the millionth time, why his brother had to die on the cold, oil-stained garage floor. He didn't know if it was a case of mistaken identity (a theory his parents favored but that seemed so random and horrible to Billy), whether Jeff owed somebody a lot of money he couldn't pay back, or if, God forbid, he had gotten mixed up in some bad shit, like drugs.

Billy had repeatedly asked these same questions of the cops during the investigation. When they weren't saying smart-ass things like "We don't know—you tell us," they just clammed up. They had probably uncovered the reason or at least had a damn good hypothesis, but they weren't sharing. They would only say, don't worry, you'll find out all the details at the trial.

Only Billy didn't. Not at that carnival. When it was all said and done, the judge had acquitted the accused while barely blinking, and Billy was left light-headed. He pulled at the sleeves of those around him like a child, asking, "What just happened?" Finally his father had to lead him from the courtroom.

In the absence of any explanation, official or otherwise, Billy reached the conclusion that there must have been some kind of legal loophole, some trick of courtroom procedure, that had allowed this mysterious killer to go free. It had never occurred to him that the judge was taking bribes. He didn't have a clue, not until the moment the lawyers showed up at his motel.

Maybe in the end he could be convinced to play along with the authorities. Maybe. But he doubted it would bring justice for Jeff.

Billy sighed and leaned forward until his forehead smacked against the table. This was exactly why he needed to talk to Mary. For some reason, he found himself remembering her announcement that she was throwing him out—an announcement made without rancor but with unutterable sadness. She had told him that she felt like a complete failure, since she hadn't been able to even slow down his drinking, let alone stop it. So, she had asked, what good was she anyway?

He raised his head. He suddenly had the answer to Mary's question. She had been keeping everything in check. Without her, his drinking was far worse. He was a mess. He would not only tell her that, he would prove it to her.

He headed out the door and purposefully, if unsteadily, started walking toward the only pay phone in the vicinity, a scarred thing in the back of the truck stop diner down the road.

Crime and punishment. He mulled over those words as he trudged through the dusty strip along the highway. He would talk to Mary about crime and punishment and second chances and what to do. She would know. She was his compass. And, God willing, she would talk to him.

CHAPTER TWELVE

Spring through summer 1998: Maryland

By mid-afternoon, several hours after I had arrived at the Maryland State Police barracks, I was still sitting in the section of the large utilitarian lobby that served as the waiting area for the public. So far, it appeared that the public spent as little time as possible in this part of the building. I saw a few uniformed people pass by, but no one who looked like a civilian. One or two looked back at me curiously.

I was starting to question the wisdom of this venture. For one thing, it was boring, not much different from my experience in the morning, which I had frittered away waiting for Joe to return from his supposedly quick trip to the office. So far the only distinction was that instead of sitting on my living room sofa, I was seated on a numbingly uncomfortable plastic chair.

Once again I shifted in my seat. For some reason the setting brought back the wait in the campus security office ten years before, when I accompanied the shell-shocked Deborah to report her parallel incident. I shuddered. No sense revisiting that event.

Still, much like that earlier time, I found myself scanning my surroundings and repeatedly reading the public service announcement posters on the wall. As I stared at them until the words made no sense, I once again reminded myself to keep calm. But that hardly mattered anymore. After hours of waiting, I was so calm, I was nodding off.

When I first arrived at the state police barracks, I had been nervous and hesitant, and had spent a lot of time explaining and re-explaining why I was there. I was bounced from one official to the next. Finally, one took pity on me and informed me that the lead investigator, who was the person I needed to speak with, was out. It was unclear when Detective Sergeant Michael Grimaldi would return as he was busy tracking down leads in the investigation of the murder. It was after all, he said, a very important case, one of the biggest cases in the upper Chesapeake area in years. My heart sank. *What am I doing here*, I thought, even as I nodded confidently, as if I had an implicit understanding of police procedure. The officer made the strong suggestion that it would be best if I left.

"I think I'll wait," I replied.

"Suit yourself." He shrugged.

Since then I had sat alone in the back row of orange plastic chairs in a corner of the lobby. The florescent lighting was harsh and made me blink. The cinderblock walls I had spent hours staring at were painted a shade I decided was peach. It was a pretty feminine shade for police headquarters. I speculated that maybe they thought it would complement the orange chairs. Twisting around, I saw that the chairs were actually bolted to the wall. Apparently there was a concern that visitors would have the audacity to walk out of a police station with this ugly seating under their arms.

I slumped a little, searching for a comfortable spot. I wondered again why Joe had failed to show up. I closed my eyes. There was a burning behind my eyelids, probably from the harsh lighting and also because dwelling on the subject of Joe was becoming hurtful. He had pressured me to undertake this foolish endeavor, had promised to be by my side. It felt like a betrayal that he wasn't here. Maybe I couldn't trust him after all.

No, it's something perfectly rational, I argued with myself. *It's exactly what he said, that he was caught up in something at work.*

It was all giving me a headache. I leaned my head against the peach-colored cinderblock and tried to clear my mind. An old passage from the Book of Psalms popped into my head.

With the Lord there is mercy
and the fullness of redemption
Call to him in your trials, he will answer when you call.

I felt myself relaxing, then falling asleep.

"Miss Carlisle?"

"Quinn!"

The greetings came nearly simultaneously. My eyes popped open. I saw a man, powerfully built but of average height, with a bald head that was so shiny it was shocking. This could only be the state police detective, Grimaldi. Standing next to him, jockeying to move into my line of vision, was Joe.

Michael Grimaldi, the Maryland State Police's lead investigator on the state park homicide, had worked hard and fought harder to attain his detective sergeant rank. He had wanted to be a homicide investigator ever since he was a boy. When he joined the state police, he started as a trooper, but had set his eyes on detective work. He had reached that goal relatively quickly. Much to his annoyance, he also had to take on the role as a leader of the small team of detectives in his barracks. Grimaldi tended to ignore others, even colleagues. But they would misread his negative vibes and continually pestered him for ideas on their cases. Grimaldi supposed that it was a form of flattery, but it got on his nerves. He usually tossed them a bone—some half-baked idea—only because they wouldn't leave him alone otherwise.

With his fast-growing reputation, it wasn't unusual for Grimaldi to be called upon to investigate high-profile cases. It was this current high-profile case—a young, white female beheaded and dumped in a state park—that had him exhausted. His sleep was interrupted nearly a week ago with the phone call alerting him to the discovery of the body, and he hadn't slept much since. He had just staggered into headquarters, and had been hoping to spend a few minutes checking his messages before going home to catch some sleep. Finally.

Instead, the trooper at the front desk had pointed a bony finger toward the woman sitting in the waiting area. The waiting area that no one ever actually waited in. Most citizens who entered the state police barracks tended to arrive in handcuffs, rather than of their own volition.

"Name's Quinn Carlisle," the trooper said. "So she says." He added this sardonically. Grimaldi knew that was only because the guy was a smart ass. There really was no need for further information. She was there about the case, of course. The wing nuts were starting to surface.

In the seconds it took Grimaldi to cross over to the seating area, a man appeared out of nowhere and, before Grimaldi knew it, was standing alongside and calling the woman's name just as Grimaldi spoke. As the two men glared at each other, the woman's eyes fluttered open.

For a moment, no one seemed to know what to say. Grimaldi was in no mood for nonsense, so he took charge. "I'm Detective Sergeant Grimaldi. I understand you wanted to see me?"

The woman rose from the chair, a bit unsteady. Grimaldi watched her shoot a look at the other man and mouth the words, "Where have you been?"

Here we go, Grimaldi thought. *Domestic issues. Just what I need.* The woman turned back to him and closed her eyes for a long second before she spoke.

"I have some information that I believe may relate to the young woman who was found murdered."

Quinn Carlisle was fairly tall, a bit over Grimaldi's own five-ten frame, and she appeared to be trying to stand very erect as she made this pronouncement. *What the hell is her deal*, Grimaldi thought. He was starting to feel even more tired.

"Okay," he said, drawing out the word, when she failed to continue. Most likely he sounded impatient or sarcastic. He didn't care.

She looked around. "Is there somewhere we can discuss it? This is my friend, Joe Armstrong. He should be part of this discussion."

Grimaldi and Joe shook hands briefly. "This way." Grimaldi ushered them toward a metal door that led to a stairwell, and nodded for them to go up to the second floor.

I'll reserve judgment until they have their say, he told himself as he followed them up the stairs. But it didn't look promising.

Once they were seated in his spare, meticulously neat office, Grimaldi glanced again at Quinn. She was sitting ramrod straight on the edge of the stained visitor's chair. She looked scared, like a rabbit in the split second after it spots a predator. She wasn't bad looking though. In fact, she was pretty attractive. Grimaldi unconsciously flexed his muscles, and promptly became aware of the boyfriend stiffening in annoyance ever so slightly on his perch on the folding chair Grimaldi had dragged in the room. *Man, how do they know,* Grimaldi wondered.

"Okay, Quinn Carlisle," he said, trying to appear interested. "Let's have it."

"Ten years ago," she began, and hesitated.

They waited.

"Ten years ago," she started again. She turned to her boyfriend and murmured, "Maybe this is a mistake."

"All right," Grimaldi interrupted. He had to agree that this was indeed a mistake. "So what happened ten years ago?"

"Ten years ago I was attacked and abducted on a college campus in Pennsylvania, held hostage in a dorm room, and raped," she blurted out. She stopped again. Apparently she was incapable of adding to this brief narrative.

The investigator's face could be expressive when he wanted. Now it clearly said: So why are you telling me this? He was starting to lose patience, but tried to keep his tone mild.

"I'm sorry about that. What does it have to do with the case at hand?"

"Because of this," Quinn said, shoving up the sleeve of her blouse to reveal the white scar spelling out a word on her forearm.

A single eyebrow shot up. "I see." Grimaldi reached across the desk and took her arm, turning it slightly, examining it like a doctor. He retrieved a camera from the filing cabinet and took several photos of her arm from different angles. Then he pulled a legal pad from his desk drawer and uncapped a pen. "Perhaps you better go through the particulars. Did they catch your guy?"

Quinn recounted the events leading to Dennis Price's arrest and trial. She told how another student victim, Deborah, had come forward with the belated report of an identical crime against her, including an identical word carving, and how the authorities had dismissed Deborah's report, although their testimony before a university hearing had led to Price's expulsion from school. She told of the trial and Price's conviction, and the judge's decision to set Price free.

Grimaldi listened with his head cocked. He took few notes; the page was mostly blank. He asked a few questions, one of which was to ask for Quinn's contact information. Then he recapped the pen, slipped the pad back into the drawer, and locked it. He stood.

"Thank you for coming in. We'll check it out."

Frozen, Quinn and her boyfriend stared at him. "You'll check it out?" Joe repeated finally.

"Yup. We'll check it out."

"But you think this is significant," Joe persisted.

Oh, for God's sake, Grimaldi thought. A ten-year-old case, a different state, and no actual murder? It was a coincidence at best. Or she was fabricating the whole thing. True, there was too much faded scar tissue for the carved word in her arm to have been recent. But it was possible she was a cutter who had done this to herself, blaming it all on some imaginary perp in a big bullshit story.

In any event, he was not inclined to automatically believe accusers in rape cases. It was often difficult to tell what was truth and what was a lie. This was just one of the reasons why he preferred homicide.

Grimaldi glanced at the girl. She was sitting very still, her mouth tightly set. He guessed that she was not so comfortable with her boyfriend's persistence. Grimaldi waited for her to call him off, but she said nothing.

"Look." Grimaldi's tone did not invite argument. "We'll look into this angle. If we need further information from you, we'll let you know." He strode to the office door and held it open.

The two started to shuffle out.

On impulse, Grimaldi touched Quinn's arm as she passed.

"I was just curious. When you were assaulted, did you fight back? You know, did you try giving him a swift kick or something?"

Quinn flushed and glanced at Joe. *Bad move*, Grimaldi thought. *Sign of a liar.*

The telephone on Grimaldi's desk began to ring. He turned to answer it, losing interest in Quinn's answer. He let the door slam behind the couple and returned to his desk, thinking that what he needed was a hot shower, a few hours of sleep, and for people to quit hitting him with stupid shit. Then maybe he could make some progress with the investigation.

He sighed and picked up the phone.

Billy O'Brien cradled the phone on his shoulder and squinted at the small type on the business card. It was the business card the lawyer had left on the table on his way out the door. "Just in case you change your mind," he had said.

Tapping the numbers on the keypad, it occurred to Billy that, for the first time in years, he felt good about what he was doing. When the district attorney's office representatives had shown up and proposed that he testify in a retrial of his brother's murder, Billy would have bet money that he would never willingly go through that again. Yet here he was. He had not only changed his mind, but he was now convinced that it was absolutely the right thing to do. Mary had shown him that.

The lawyer's voice coming on the line snapped Billy back into attention. He began a halting explanation, wishing that he had bothered to plan what he was going to say. He sounded like a rambling fool.

But as soon as the lawyer caught on to the reason for the call, Billy didn't even have to finish.

"You're going to testify? That's great!" The lawyer was so excited, he was nearly shouting. He began speaking rapidly, something about travel arrangements to Pennsylvania, but Billy interrupted him.

"Listen, I'd like to ask a favor first. I'm not saying it's a condition of me testifying or anything like that," he added quickly. "It's just something I've been thinking a lot about."

The man hesitated a moment, for which Billy couldn't blame him. "If it's something I can do, I will," he responded.

Billy cleared his throat. "Remember you told me about that girl, someone else who ended up with a raw deal because of this judge? You said she wasn't going to get a chance for any kind of retrial. I was wondering if I could talk to her. It really seems like our situations are the same, you know? It would help me to talk to her about it, and who knows, maybe it would help her, too . . ." His voice trailed off. There was silence for a long moment. "Hello?" he asked uncertainly.

"There are some privacy issues." The man hesitated again, then seemed to reach a decision. "But maybe we could arrange to have you write to her via our office. It's possible she might agree to a phone conversation. We'll have to see, but I'll do what I can."

Billy wasn't quite sure why he felt such a compulsion to communicate with this rape victim who had, like him, also been victimized by this crooked judge. As he had told Mary, it was almost as if talking through their shared experience, it would unlock something for him and help him heal. Or maybe not. He just knew he had to try.

"That would be great," Billy answered. "And as for the retrial, I'm ready to do this whenever you are."

By the time Joe and I returned to my apartment, I was fuming. I had spent the drive back rehashing the meeting at the state police headquarters, growing angrier and glaring at traffic lights and other drivers.

"I can't believe he asked me why I didn't fight back. What does he think? That I should have put on my black belt moves?" I threw my handbag on the sofa and marched into the kitchen, rattling drinking glasses, and turning the faucet on full force.

"I think he was asking *if* you fought back; not why you didn't," Joe said mildly. He had seemed annoyed by Grimaldi's dismissive attitude at the police barracks, muttering to me that the policeman was an ass as we were leaving the building. During his ride home, Joe must have taken an opposite tack because he was now considerably calmer, and coolly objective in a way that was almost smug. I eyed him angrily as I gulped the water and smacked the glass down on a table.

"Whose side are you on, anyway?"

He simply shrugged, which only served to propel me into a rage. But even as the next words shot out of my mouth, I was regretting them.

"You know, it was your idea to go to the police in the first place. I was sweating it out, wondering whether you would even show up."

At that, Joe finally showed a flash of anger. "First of all, I am on your side. Of course I am. Second, I already explained about this problem at the office. And it was pretty important because the president of the firm personally called me about it. So I couldn't just say no. I took care of it as fast as I could and, let me remind you, I did show up."

We faced each other, glaring. Then I felt my anger melt away like an ice cube on a stovetop.

"I guess this is our first fight, huh?"

At my look of unexpected elation, Joe couldn't keep up the appearance of annoyance. He snorted, and then we were both laughing. "I think you could have taken Grimaldi," he said. "Easy."

"He was barely paying attention, so, yeah. It wouldn't even have been fair."

Joe gave me a brief, hard hug, then held me at arm's length. "Look, don't ever think that I don't support you in this. In fact, I was thinking that this whole scenario presents a great opportunity."

"An opportunity," I repeated, confused.

"Hear me out. You've been tortured for ten years by what happened to you." He paused. I realized he was waiting for confirmation, so I nodded reluctantly. "You've convinced others and maybe convinced yourself that it's okay, that you've recovered. But inside, you're tormented. Am I right?"

I caught my breath, then gave the barest of nods. With one statement—and Joe was probably just stating the obvious—all my shallow pride in having overcome this trauma, the idea that I had worked my way through it, disappeared.

"Now here's this crime, a murder. It has a weird echo of your attack. More than an echo. It's got to be the same guy. So you do the right thing. You report it to the proper authorities. The detective acts like we just ruined his day. But that's okay. Because now we're free to investigate it ourselves."

My mouth fell open. He couldn't be serious.

Joe continued, becoming more excited with his idea.

"We're going to find out whatever became of Dennis Price. If we're right and we find evidence that he was behind this murder, then we present our findings to the police and help bring him to justice. If we're wrong and he's been a fine, upstanding citizen, well, then you know that, and it's going to help you to resolve things. Either way, it's an opportunity to close the book."

Joe's voice had faded into a buzz that was filling my head. But within that buzzing, there was logic crystallizing. I knew he was right. What better way to rid myself of the demon? In my dreams, the demon was constantly there, constantly chasing me. Maybe I only had to confront him to be rid of this terrible burden, once and for all.

I sat for a long moment, eyes closed.

"I would love to feel at peace," I said finally, opening my eyes.

"Yes."

"I don't know what to do."

"I'll help you. We'll make calls, do some legwork. We don't have as many resources at our disposal as Detective Dimwit back there, but we'll make do. We'll hire a private detective if we have to."

At one time I believed there must be a secret to reassembling the pieces of a life. A trick I could conjure up, a technique I had only to learn. None of my clumsy ideas, nor any advice from friends, my parents, or therapists, had come close to this idea of Joe's. It could work.

I pinched the bridge of my nose and struggled to remain composed.

My voice was quiet. "When do we start?"

CHAPTER THIRTEEN

End of summer 1998: to Ohio

It was late in the afternoon by the time I convinced Joe to let me take a turn behind the wheel. I don't think he so much distrusted my driving, as much as he thought he needed to make things as easy as possible for me. "You just sit back and relax," he said, even as he hunched tensely over the steering wheel. Although I was grateful he was taking charge, we both knew that this trip was all Joe's idea, his strategy. I was beginning to have second thoughts about it, this wild idea of running off to Ohio to investigate my attacker, Dennis Price.

It was a flurry of arrangements, hurried messages to our respective employers, and packing, and then we had set out early, just at dawn. It was like an unspoken pact between us—if we delayed one minute more, we might lose our nerve.

We drove straight through the upper edge of Maryland and on through the rolling landscape of Pennsylvania, stopping only for gas. We had reached the western part of the state when we pulled into a rest stop and I offered to drive. Joe, looking drawn and tired, barely put up an argument. He was asleep before I pulled onto the highway.

I turned off the radio and concentrated tensely on the pavement lapping up beneath the car. After nearly an hour of driving, I felt a lot more comfortable maneuvering the large Buick. I relaxed behind the wheel and let my mind pore over our mission.

The strategy that we—well, mostly Joe—had worked out was to track down Judith, my college roommate and Dennis Price's cousin. I wasn't at all sure that Judith would agree to talk. I had tried to explain that to Joe. "Judith just plain never liked me. She wasn't crazy about me before the attack, and afterward it was outright hatred."

Joe was unconcerned and waved aside my fears. "A family connection is the best place to start," he had said.

How was he so sure about what to do? Had he been a cop in a previous life or something? I was a little taken aback by his confident manner, but I didn't have any better ideas. I continued to let him handle the majority of the planning.

I still couldn't quite believe I had agreed to do this in the first place, but since I had, it was probably much better that Joe was taking charge. The entire matter had become so personal for me. The more I tried to be objective about it, the more I realized it had developed into a knotted mess inside me. Worse, I had become self-centered about it, focusing only on how it had impacted me. It was *my* assault and rape, *my* hurt. In this cocoon, even knowing that Dennis Price had attacked at least one other student, there wasn't any room to consider that he had gone on to hurt others. It simply hadn't occurred to me.

That's why the similarities between the two Pennsylvania college assaults and the Maryland state park murder left me guilt-ridden. How could I be so profoundly selfish? I was the one, maybe the only one, who had had the chance to stop him. *You're being dramatic,* I told myself.

I risked a quick glance at Joe. He had awakened but was gazing out the passenger window. I was going to have to trust him, I realized. The plan was bold and maybe even crazy, but there was something about Joe's grand idea that was irresistible because it held out hope that this thing could be resolved once and for all.

Traffic began to thin out, which left me enough at ease to look at the scenery, such as the strips of brilliant autumn colors creeping into the hills that lined the road. I noticed a spot farther ahead, a larger patch of color. The patch shimmered, then in a startling way broke off from the hill. It grew larger as it approached us and I blinked once, twice. Impulsively, I put on my turn signal and pulled over to the wide shoulder of the road.

"Monarch butterflies." I tapped the windshield. We watched as waves of butterflies moved up and across the road, yet keeping in the herd as if magnetized.

"You know, there are millions of migratory monarch butterflies that fly every year from Canada, New England, and upstate New York. This must be one of their routes." I craned to see out the window. "I guess we happened to cross just at the right time."

"I wonder where they're headed," Joe mused.

"Oh, I know exactly where they go. They travel thousands of miles over North America, then they congregate on a few trees in a patch of forest near Mexico City. They turn the trees orange because there are so many of them. They winter there, and a lot of them die off, but their offspring know to fly back north. The great-great grandchildren of the migratory

butterflies know to start a new journey back to Mexico the following fall. And this is all with a brain the size of a grain of
sand."

Joe laughed. "How do you know this stuff? You sound like
a travel guide."

I looked over my shoulder to double-check the road and
pulled the car back onto the highway. "When I was a kid, every
year we went to Cape May, New Jersey. My parents liked to
take us after the summer season ended. Cape May is along one
of the big butterfly routes, so we were often there when the
butterflies were in town. That's how we referred to it. They were
'in town.' My brother and I were fascinated with the whole
thing and drove my dad nuts with questions. Eventually he got
tired of not knowing the answers, so he researched it."

I shifted, trying to relocate my comfortable driving position. "Everyone thinks of butterflies as flighty, but they have
purpose. They know they're supposed to get to Mexico. I like
that. I like that there's order and reason behind stuff that seems
random."

We were silent for a long while. I glanced over and saw
he was asleep again. I smiled. Either I had bored him to death
or he was totally comfortable with me. Our comfort level with
each other was genuine and, for me, surprising. After all, it
wasn't that long ago that I had thought I would never trust
anyone again.

Despite Joe's planning and his certainty that Judith would be
welcoming, even finding her was not a sure thing. After several attempts, I was able, the evening before we left, to confirm that Judith still lived in Columbus, Ohio. I tracked down
our mutual friend Eloise, who helpfully supplied a phone

number and address for Judith, as well as contact information for Judith's mother.

"I have to say that Judith's better than you at keeping in touch," Eloise chided me. "Though I don't think she called or sent a holiday card last year," she added, bemused.

"Maybe she moved."

"No way. Judith is so organized that if she moved, she would notify everyone in triplicate." She paused. "I'm surprised you haven't heard from her over the years."

"We didn't part on the best of terms."

"Well, never mind, I'm sure she'll be very glad to hear from you now." Despite the assurance, I could hear the doubt in her voice. Eloise was probably wondering about my sudden urge to get in touch with someone I had feuded with more than a decade before.

I ended the conversation—only after Eloise exacted my current contact information and a promise for more regular communication—and dialed Judith's number. An answering machine clicked on and I recognized Judith's stilted voice.

I was relieved that I didn't have to speak with her just yet, and also that this was evidence that this was still Judith's number. I hung up without leaving a message.

It was sunset when we reached the western edge of Pennsylvania and the end of the turnpike. We were waiting in line at the toll booths when I suggested that once we crossed into Ohio, we should stop for dinner and try calling Judith again. "It will be too late tonight by the time we get to Columbus," I said. "Maybe we can make arrangements to go over there tomorrow."

The rustic-looking truck stop diner had clunky pay phones, the likes of which I hadn't seen in years. I dialed Judith's number and heard the same answering machine message. Impulsively I tried the other number Eloise had given me, for Judith's family's home. A woman answered.

"Hello?" I repeated stupidly, losing my nerve.

"Who's calling?" the woman demanded, annoyed. Her voice was raspy, a smoker's voice. Judith had always been adamantly opposed to smoking.

"I'm trying to reach Judith. This is—I'm an old friend. I mean, I'm Judith's roommate from college. Well, one of them." That sounded completely dim-witted. This person was probably Judith's mother, who would of course know Judith's circle of friends and that a particular college roommate wasn't counted among them.

"I see." As the woman's voice became less aggressive, I breathed again.

"I'm Judy's aunt Sarah," the woman said. "I've been here a lot lately to help out Judy's mom. She's not doing too well. She either refuses to get out of bed, or she sits in a dark room, blinds drawn, watching a TV that's not even turned on."

I could hear the woman hesitate. "Look," she said finally, "I'm just going to tell you straight out. Judy's dead."

"What?" I clutched at the smooth metal of the pay phone. I felt dizzy. "Dead . . . how? When?"

"Almost a month ago. On a Tuesday. I don't know why that's important to me but it is. Judy was—wait, did you call her Judy or Judith?"

"She insisted on being called Judith. In college anyway."

"Interesting. The family calls her Judy. Well, three weeks ago she was found dead in the bathtub. The coroner's report said she was strangled."

"My God."

"I know." I heard the sharp intake and exhaling of breath as Aunt Sarah took a drag of a cigarette. The woman's remarkably calm discussion of her niece's murder was disconcerting. Maybe three weeks was enough time to get used to the idea.

"Apparently she was placed, well, arranged really, in the tub to make it look like she had drowned. I suppose the murderer didn't realize that there are some telltale signs, like ligature marks on the neck and burst blood vessels, that sort of thing, that give away the cause of death. Or maybe he just didn't care."

"Do they have any idea who—?"

"Who did it? They're still investigating of course, but the working assumption is that it's her husband, Sal. You probably remember him."

"Yes, of course. I knew Sal in college. But he didn't at all seem the type to do, you know, something like that."

"Hmmm." Aunt Sarah was noncommittal.

It was odd. She was surprisingly open to a stranger on the phone. On the other hand, Judith's mother sounded near catatonic, so maybe the aunt was desperate for someone to discuss this terrible turn of events. I wondered if this openness would extend to the subject of my college attack. Still, I hesitated. Even if this was the whole point of our journey, Judith being dead changed things. Or maybe her death was connected. Maybe Dennis Price was somehow involved.

"What I had wanted to talk with Judith, um, Judy about was . . . you might remember that one of Judith's college roommates was attacked and raped? Well, that was me."

Silence. I swallowed and continued.

"And the person who was arrested and convicted in the case was Judith's cousin Dennis, and—"

"Excuse me. Just who do you think you are?"

Aunt Sarah's tone took a dramatic shift. Her chatty demeanor was now clipped, scolding, and angry. But the change happened so quickly, I was still talking.

"And I just wondered if the police maybe have interviewed Dennis about—"

"I thought you were one of Judy's other roommates. But you're *her.*" The woman spat out the word. "You're the one who falsely accused Dennis. How dare you call here when we're mourning poor Judy and dredge up the past? How dare you?"

Oh my God. This is Dennis Price's mother. I could feel sweat running from every pore. The phone felt slick in my hand.

"I don't know who you think you are or what you think you're doing, but it takes nerve to imply that Dennis would somehow be connected. He loved Judy. You caused this family a bundle of trouble back then and now you show up trying to do it again?" Her voice had risen to a screech, a hairbreadth away from hysteria. She made a strangled sort of noise and slammed down the phone.

The muscles of my arm were cramping from my grip on the receiver. I stood listening to the dial tone, then very gently replaced the phone in its cradle and returned to Joe, who took one look at my face and wisely didn't ask questions.

The next morning we stood on the front porch of Judith and Sal's house, which was now occupied only by Sal. We stared at the blank front door, half-afraid to knock, unsure of what kind of reception we would get. Finally Joe rang the doorbell. I dug my fingernails into my palms and waited.

We needn't had been so nervous. Oddly, Sal didn't seem surprised to see me, someone who he had not laid eyes on since college, standing on his front step with a stranger.

At the same time, he didn't look particularly glad to see us. Just not surprised. It was as if Sal had been praying for someone to show up and listen to his troubles and, voilà, here we were.

Sal wordlessly ushered us into a messy living room, shoving piles of newspapers and unopened mail from a section of the sofa. As soon as we were seated, Sal began relating all that had happened with Judith, how he had arrived home to find her dead, and how his life was now in shambles.

The Sal of my memory was thin, slightly stooped, balding, and constantly complaining. The Sal I saw sprawled in a worn-looking recliner was fifty pounds heavier with not a strand of hair on his head. He seemed even more morose than he had been in college, which was not surprising considering the current state of his life. He had moved beyond complaining and had become downright whiny.

"I don't know why they have to torture me. The police, I mean," Sal said. It was a statement he had made in several variations over the previous forty-five minutes. We perched on our small area of the overstuffed sofa, nodding.

"They're here practically every damn day. It's the same questions over and over in slightly different ways. I keep telling them I didn't kill her. Repeat, I did not kill her. I would never do that to Judith. I loved her. You remember that, Quinn, don't you? But the cops, they keep saying, don't even think about skipping town. What do they think this is, the movies or something? Hey, I should have asked you guys before, do you want something to drink? A soda, beer, something?"

I took advantage of the brief moment he waited for our response to begin hurling the questions that I had traveled across several states to ask.

"Sal, do you have any idea who might have done this to Judith?"

Sal sighed. "I wish I knew. I've been racking my brain. There was no sign of forced entry, which I think is why the cops are focusing on me. Whoever it was, she let him in."

"Have you considered her cousin? Dennis Price?"

"Dennis? I can see why you might automatically suspect him, but still—"

"If it could be anyone in the world—without taking into account any preconceived ideas or biases or anything—who could it be? If you accept that it was someone who knew Judith, and you must know pretty much everyone Judith knew, what kind of list could you come up with? Who else could it be? After all," I added, leaning toward him, "you know it's not you."

Sal, for once, was silent.

"Well, he did come back to the area all of a sudden," he admitted finally. "Dennis. He had been gone, jeez, more than a year I'd say. Maybe longer. I don't know for sure but it might have had something to do with his dad."

"He went away because of his dad?"

Sal shrugged. "The family goes out of their way not to tell me anything, but I've wondered whether Dennis had a falling out with his father. Which would have been very weird, because his dad doted on Dennis, supported him no matter what." Sal looked at us. "But in the end it didn't matter, because his father died. Very sudden. All I know for sure is that Dennis didn't come to the funeral."

We tried to digest this information. I had the vague thought that I should be taking notes, but it seemed almost rude to pull out the notebook I had in my purse. I doubted I would forget any of this conversation anyway. Sal nodded sadly as if he heard me.

"Here's the thing with Judith's family. They're close knit, I guess you could say, but they definitely believe in thinking as a group. Just as an example, a few years ago someone in the family—Judith's mom maybe—decided that she should be called Judy. Silly, don't you think, renaming an adult with a kid's nickname? At least Judith thought so. She hated it but everyone started calling her Judy and acting like they always did. That's how the family is. Judith and I were married nine years and went out for years before that. But I was never really accepted into the family. They're loyal to each other to the extreme, and secretive. They don't like outsiders. Don't get me wrong," he added quickly. "It's nice that a family would be that tight."

"Was Judith surprised that Dennis left?"

She didn't say much to me about Dennis—she never did. She certainly didn't comment when he showed up recently. I didn't think he was in touch with her, but I guess he could have been. He could even have come here when I was at work or something. I would never have known one way or another."

Joe filled the brief, awkward silence. "Is there anyone in the family who might be willing to talk to us? Any kind of chink in the armor?"

"Well . . ." Sal looked even more dejected. "I did always get the impression that Judith's younger sister never totally went along with all this family-first shit. She might be receptive to talking. Her name is Ruth. They were very close, so Ruth is beside herself about Judith's death. If anyone is ready to break the family rules and speak out, it's probably her."

We were climbing in the car when Sal called us. He lumbered down his front walk, a little out of breath.

"There is one more thing you should know," he said. "About Dennis. You know how he suddenly showed up about a month or so ago? Well, it seems he's disappeared again. No one's seen him since Judith died."

On the way back to the motel, Joe and I fell into an argument, unable to agree on our next steps. The discussion extended through dinner and late into the evening. Joe wanted to pursue "the lead," as he put it. The obvious thing to do, he said, was to interview Judith's sister Ruth. He didn't see why there was even room for debate. But I couldn't face confronting another member of Judith's family. I was even beginning to balk at the whole investigation. Better to return to the ostrich-like comfort of my apartment and my art and my life, I told him, and leave the police work to the police.

"I want to try to forget Dennis Price, Judith, everything," I said wearily. "There's no point in trying to talk to Judith's sister. No matter how bitter this sister is, she's not going to open up to us."

Joe was dogged. "I can't believe you would come this far, only to give up after talking to one person."

"Two, if you count the phone call with Judith's aunt. That was lots of fun."

Joe had an answer—or at least a platitude—to every objection. You never know until you try. The most they can say is no. I would regret missing this opportunity.

"I just don't get it," I said, exasperated. "Not only are we arguing every two minutes over this thing, but already we've done—*I've* done—way more than the average person. I think it's time to let it go." What I really wanted to know was why he couldn't see that this thing was becoming torturous for me.

But instead of another retort, my little outburst had an immediate and unwanted effect on Joe. Shock moved across his face. He reddened, then broke into a sweat. I stared at him. "What's wrong?" I asked, suddenly panicky.

Joe struggled to regain control. "I do owe you an explanation. I should have told you this before. I've thought so many times that I should tell you, but you've been carrying such a big burden. The thing is, I guess I have my own burden."

Then Joe told me about his sister. About how as a teenager she went jogging one day, a beautiful summer day, on the streets of their nice upstate New York neighborhood, and how she was abducted, ripped from their lives in broad daylight. Her beaten, sexually assaulted body was found in the woods three days later. Her assailant was never caught.

I listened, both sad and somehow already aware of this truth. This was why my story had resonated with Joe and why he was so committed to pushing me toward some kind of justice. After months of feeling like I finally had a partner, even a protector, in this whole mess, it turned out that Joe apparently had his own agenda. Maybe I was on my own after all.

We sat in silence for a long time.

"So I suppose your interest in my case really doesn't have a whole lot to do with me." I couldn't stop my voice from quavering.

"Quinn, listen to me." Joe grasped my hands. "What happened to my sister was long ago and, no, I don't think anyone in my family got over it. I'm not going to pretend that it didn't help fuel my interest in what happened to you, but it's not driving it. My primary interest is in helping you. Remember, I first heard about your attack when we first went out. And"—he smiled a little—"I couldn't have guessed then how I would feel about you now. It's about you, not my sister."

I listened, head down, and nodded. I didn't have the nerve to ask how, specifically, he felt about me.

The next morning I stood next to Joe in front of Ruth McCloud's door, at the address Sal had given us the day before. I may have appeared stoic, but inside I felt nervous and sick.

We stood silent, shoulder to shoulder, waiting for the lacquered red door with its shiny brass knocker to open. One minute, then two minutes passed. No one came.

Joe pressed the doorbell again. We waited. Nothing.

"Not a good sign," I muttered. "Let's get out of here." Relieved, I turned away. I was a step or two down the walk when the door flung open. Hot air blasted from inside the house like a wave.

Framed in the doorway was a young woman with a thin, sensitive face. She looked frightened and clutched a bulky sweater around her frail frame, despite the warm fall weather and the overwhelming heat inside the house.

"Can I help you?"

Ruth McCloud spoke the words with a perfectly flat affect. Despite the question, there was no curiosity in her voice.

Joe launched into his rehearsed explanation. As he spoke, he grabbed my arm and nudged me forward, human proof of our mission. Ruth's face was impassive, even when Joe referred to me as the person who had accused Dennis Price of kidnapping and rape.

As Ruth remained motionless, Joe began to falter and then his voice trailed off. We waited awkwardly for some kind of response from Ruth. I thought her eyes seemed glassy and wondered if she was on medication.

The moments had stretched to a painful length when Ruth made a nearly imperceptible movement with her head and moved to the side of the door. "Come in," she mumbled a beat too late.

We stepped inside and were assaulted by the heat. Sweat immediately began to trickle under my clothes. A bit unsteadily, Ruth led us to the dining room. An electric space heater glowed perilously close to the single chair that had been pulled away from the table where an empty teacup sat. Ruth made a weak effort to appear hospitable.

"I was just about to have some hot tea. Can I get you any?"

I wanted to request the iced version but I had the distinct impression that there wasn't anything iced in this house. "No, thank you," I said. I glanced at Joe. He was busy scanning our surroundings.

They were beautiful; something out of a magazine. We sat at a table of rich cherry wood, with silver candlesticks and a centerpiece arrangement of white roses, spoiled by the fact that all the flowers had wilted. A valuable-looking Oriental rug showed off gleaming hardwood floors. The living room we had passed en route to the dining room displayed similar wealth. Whatever Ruth's problems, money wasn't one of them.

I perched on the edge of the upholstered seat, worried about dripping perspiration onto something expensive. Nervously, I grinned at Ruth, who looked blankly back at me. Turning from her, I pulled tissues from my purse and surreptitiously dabbed my face. When I looked up again, Ruth was hunched over her teacup, holding it with both hands, apparently forgetting that the cup was empty. Joe, his face glistening, shot me a look and rolled up the sleeves of his shirt.

"I hate to ask this," I ventured, "but is it possible to turn down the heat a little?"

This time there was a reaction from Ruth; only a small flicker of the eyes, but it was something. Then the blankness returned. Ignoring the space heater blasting by her chair, Ruth rose and moved to the wall thermostat. It was impossible to tell if she shifted the tiny lever a notch, or just faked it. We watched as she disappeared briefly into the adjoining living room and returned with a worn-looking afghan, which she arranged around her shoulders as she took her seat again.

"Sorry," she muttered. "Lately I can't seem to get warm."

I nodded, trying to think of how to start the discussion. But Ruth surprised us by offering the opening gambit.

"So you're Judith's college roommate, the one who caused so much uproar in the family."

"I thought the family called her Judy." I bit my tongue. I had to let go of this name thing.

That flicker again. "I suppose they do," Ruth said in the same flat tone. "I don't."

I began openly mopping my face with the damp wad of tissues. "I'm sure I did cause an uproar, but maybe you can understand why. From my perspective, I mean. But that's not why we're here now. We have reason to believe that your cousin Dennis might have been involved in another, um, incident. The murder in Maryland that Joe mentioned as the reason we're here. That's why we're wondering if you could explain, I don't know, what went on, or things . . ." I swiped my upper lip. "For one thing, I never understood why Judith reacted so *aggressively* to the fact that your cousin was arrested in my case. He really did do those things."

Ruth's eyebrows raised. It was the most visible reaction we had seen from her.

"Oh, I believe you. I can't say I did at the time, but I was very young then. I'm seven years younger than Judith. Also, I was only hearing the story from members of my family. But I believe you now." Ruth adjusted the afghan even tighter around her throat. I wondered how she stood it.

"You want to know what was going on with my family? I'll tell you." Ruth's face was very white, her eyes luminous black marbles. At the same time, she appeared almost amused, like she was letting us in on a practical joke.

"When the family got word that Dennis was arrested, we were shattered. The entire extended family, that is. But we're what a lot of people call 'close-knit.' That's what my parents, my aunts and uncles constantly say: we're a close-knit family. Like it's some kind of badge of honor. We're knitted together, all right—we're tangled up hopelessly in knots. They're all a bunch of sick people."

Ruth's face was finally registering emotion, an odd combination of anger and fear. "My grandfather was very successful. He started a manufacturing company and it made him very wealthy. He kept the money in the family but he made everyone pay for it, one way or another, manipulating us all. His two sons—one of them was Dennis's father—went into the business, but it wasn't like they had their way paved for them. It was more like my grandfather set traps, like having them manage a difficult, no-win project, and then publicly humiliating them when they failed.

"My mother, my grandparents' only daughter, didn't experience that because my grandfather doted on her. On the other hand, she wasn't allowed to go to college or be part of the family business. She wasn't expected to do anything but get married and have children. The God-mandated role for women, my grandfather always said."

When Judith went to college, in defiance of this tradition, their grandfather was livid, Ruth said. "My parents paid for school, of course, but it didn't matter. My grandfather never spoke to Judith again. Cut her completely out of his will. She said she didn't care—education was that important to her. I guess I was fortunate in that my grandfather died before I went to college. I'd like to think I would have had Judith's convictions, but I don't know. I kind of like the money I get from my trust fund."

Ruth clutched her blanket. "I'm cold," she announced and rose to adjust the thermostat.

Joe and I exchanged glances.

Ruth stopped short as she shuffled back to her seat. "And who are you again?" she addressed Joe. "I'm afraid I forgot already."

"I'm the boyfriend." Joe flushed.

Ruth nodded and resumed her story.

"Like I was saying, my grandfather thought he could control the family. On the surface we looked incredibly close. A big family who did everything together—dinners, picnics, parties, vacations, birthday celebrations, everything. But it was a sham. No one was having fun. Everyone was busy thinking and doing exactly what my grandfather expected."

Ruth paused and stared past us. "Now that I look back, the family had no different reaction to your case than we did to anything else. Everyone was in complete agreement on everything. Everyone thought as one. If the command was to be incensed, then we all were equally incensed.

"It didn't help that Dennis had the family wrapped around his finger. A lot of them thought he could do no wrong. Well, I can tell you that all of his cousins didn't think that way, but we had to keep our mouths shut. Maybe if Dennis had had a tough older brother, that would have kept him in line. But he was an only child, a son, which of course the family puts a big premium on. As a result, his parents spoiled him rotten."

She leaned toward us and said in an intense whisper, "He was just more rotten than his parents realized. Rotten to the core."

This appeared to be what Ruth had been leading up to, what we had been waiting for. My mouth began to form the question: why?

"Because," Ruth answered as if I had asked aloud, "he wasn't what he made himself out to be. He was a big lie. We all went along with the charade, even when news about your attack tore a hole in our fake family universe. For one thing, Dennis's father would have done anything—I mean *anything*—to protect his son. To protect the giant lie that his son was. But we knew the truth better than anybody, us cousins. Because—"

Ruth stopped abruptly and looked past us as if something outside had caught her attention. I glanced behind us at the tall windows. Heavy curtains were drawn across them, blocking any view.

I turned back to Ruth. "Because?" I repeated gently.

"Because Dennis had been raping us for years. With me, starting when I was eleven years old."

Her voice dropped to softer and softer levels as she said this, until she finished the last words in a whisper. All three of us slowed our breathing. I wanted to reach across the table and touch the hands that had emerged from the blanket and were now squeezing and twisting it desperately. Ruth must have sensed that I might move to comfort her. She shoved her hands under the afghan.

"You know, it's funny," she began again, barely audible above the roar of the space heater. "I should be righteously angry that he would do that to me, a little girl, and for so long. You would think that I would be so filled with rage that I would have jumped at the chance to see him brought to justice. I should have at least applauded it or something. But, no, I joined the family chorus. Like everyone else, I called you a liar and a bitch, and pretended that you were the one who deserved to be on trial and that you should go to jail for fabricating this story. We all said that."

She lowered her eyes. "I am sorry for that," she whispered. "I had no right."

Impulsively I rose and went around the table to kneel next to her. I put my sweaty palm on her shoulder. Even through the layers, I could feel her bones, like those of a fragile creature.

I waited a few moments to allow her time to compose herself. "You said 'us.' Who else was involved?"

Ruth didn't look at me as she answered. "I have seven first cousins. Five of them are female. I'm sure about three of them. A few of us have even discussed it with each other. Like, for instance, my cousin Linda and I were just talking about Dennis. I guess Judith's death brought it all back."

"Linda! That's weird . . ." I sat down hard on the floor, nearly toppling over. I looked up to see Ruth and Joe both staring at me. "Linda was the name he called me during the attack." I shook my head. "Okay, so there are three cousins, plus you."

"Well, there was Judith, too."

"But Judith always defended him."

"I know. But I know it happened to her because there were times when it happened to us together. At some point, I guess Judith went into denial. Maybe that's how she got through it. Denial is a very strong thing, so that's why I'm not really sure exactly how many family members were his victims. Or, for that matter, how many there were outside the family." She looked down at me. "After all, there was you."

Not knowing how to respond, I nodded.

Ruth was now shivering uncontrollably, her teeth chattering. "I have to say, it is an immensely freeing experience to finally admit it. To put words to it after all this time."

"How long did it go on?"

She hesitated so long that I thought I had misunderstood her last statement. "For me," she said finally, "it was off and on for twelve years. Then it stopped a few years ago when Dennis's father got the idea, for whatever reason, that Dennis needed to start over in a new location and learn how to make his own way in life. So my uncle tried setting him up with his own business, but Dennis wasn't exactly cooperative. They started fighting, Unexpectedly, Dennis's father had a stroke and died. Dennis took it pretty bad. Maybe he panicked, thinking he was without his protector, the Great White Father. Anyway, one day Dennis just took off. Disappeared. His mother claimed that even she didn't know where he was, although I believe she did. Then just as suddenly, he showed up again about six weeks ago. I didn't see him, but Judith did. Before you know it, Judith's dead and he's gone again."

"Do you believe Dennis had something to do with her death?"

"I don't know for sure. Is he capable of it? Absolutely." She blinked at us.

I looked at Joe, trying to convey with my expression that I had exhausted my questions and emotional reserve. This was becoming too much. Joe caught on and moved smoothly into the interviewer role.

"Just so we're clear, you don't think Sal is responsible?"

"No. He would never hurt Judith."

"But if you have suspicions about Dennis, why don't you go to the police?"

Ruth's eyes flashed anger, then just as fast, emptied again.

"As bad and as degrading as Dennis treated me, he was far worse with Judith. He kicked her around like a rag doll. That's why Judith clung to Sal. Sal's primary role was to be her protector. Most of the time that worked, but not always, unfortunately. Dennis is physically bigger than Sal and definitely more intimidating. Sal would never admit it, but there were times Dennis terrorized them both. Dennis got away with it the same way he got away with everything: his father would fix things. Even now with his father gone, I don't doubt Dennis's mother—and the whole family, really—would jump all over any attempt to accuse Dennis of anything."

I thought about my phone call with Dennis's mother and nodded.

"So you think that it would do any good at all for me to go to the police with unsubstantiated allegations? I would go to the authorities and he would find out in a heartbeat. He always does."

She started weeping as she spoke, not bothering to cover her face.

I tentatively reached out a hand again to comfort her, but she snarled at me, the tears gone. "You think the family would just sit by and allow me to accuse Dennis of murdering Judith? What do you think would happen to me? The same thing that happened to Judith, that's what."

I could see that beneath the anger was naked fear. This woman was trapped in this beautiful house by Dennis Price and the family she had the bad luck to be born into. I looked at Joe. *Let's get out of here,* we silently telegraphed to each other.

I had made a move to rise from my spot on the carpet, when Ruth suddenly bent her face close to mine. Startled, I leaned back.

"You may not be the liar everyone said, but you must be pretty damn stupid if you think I'm going to help you nail Dennis."

With that, Ruth returned to the same catatonic stupor we first saw her in when she answered the door. She rose and glided past me like a sleepwalker, and retreated into the recesses of the house.

CHAPTER FOURTEEN

Fall 1998: Maryland

Back at the office, it should have been an ordinary day, like any other workday. But it wasn't. For one thing, I had been sitting at my desk for more than an hour, still in my raincoat and staring at a blank computer screen.

While it was my first day back from our fact-finding mission to Ohio, it wasn't as if I had been out for an extended period. We had traveled over the long Labor Day weekend, so Joe and I had only missed a few days of work. But it felt like I had been gone for weeks.

From Joe's point of view, the trip had been more than a journey to Ohio. It was a quest, and in his mind, highly successful, although there was more to discover. On the return trip, he was happy and excited about the information we had uncovered, and was already talking about further investigation. What Joe really wanted to do, I mused, was to present to the police a solved case—maybe several of them—all wrapped up in a neat package. That way he could prove that one could get justice after all. Who needed the police?

I hadn't told Joe yet, but if he wanted to go on another mission to Ohio, he would have to go without me. Our little adventure, along with our earlier efforts to convince the police about the Dennis Price connection, had come close to unraveling me.

I was much better off in the blissful ignorance in which I had wallowed for the previous ten years. The Dennis Price–bogeymen types who had peopled my dreams all these years were bad enough, but at least I was usually able to shake free of them come morning. But ever since I had learned about the state park victim, I hadn't had a moment's peace. I was caught on some kind of mental treadmill, spending hours in endless and unproductive thought. I began to daydream of alternate endings to the attack, endings where I used my knife and killed my attacker (it would be self-defense, wouldn't it?) and ones where I took the reins of the disastrous trial and brilliantly prosecuted Dennis Price myself.

I shared these fantasies with no one, not even Joe. With Joe, the discussion always seemed to gravitate to logistics, or the practicalities of what we should do next. Until the previous weekend, I had thought that Joe's approach might be the healthier route, for my psyche anyway. But now it was different. Dennis Price was no longer the villain of my dreams. He was even more real than when I had faced him ten years ago.

Maybe I was paranoid, or maybe it was because we had just spent days talking to people about Dennis Price, but I couldn't help thinking that he might have something to do with the phone message that had greeted me at work that morning.

I had automatically picked up the phone to check my voice mail as soon as I arrived at my office. This was my standard routine as soon as I dropped my handbag on my desk. There was only one message, and it was disturbing. I slammed down the phone and took a step away from the desk. I couldn't have heard it correctly. I picked up the phone and redialed. The announcement preceding the message noted that it had entered the voice mail system on Sunday at 2:27 a.m. I listened again.

It's just a wrong number, I told myself desperately. It was a coincidence. But I knew that it was neither of those things. It was payback. Dennis Price apparently was fixated on making people pay.

I looked around as if I had just woken up. Everything seemed normal. The morning sun streamed through the oversized windows. From my desk I had a view of the park-like grounds and, there in the distance, was the pond with its small, ornamental footbridge. We referred to it as the duck pond, but while it held huge golden-orange carp, I had never seen any ducks. *Maybe I would feel better if I got some fresh air,* I thought. I tried to envision myself walking out of the building and down to the pond. But it was no use. I seemed to be hardening into stone at my desk.

"So."

The word hissed from behind me. It was Helga. With some effort I twisted in my chair to face my boss. Always redoubtable, now outright forbidding, Helga stood over me with her arms folded across her massive bust. She was extraordinarily proud of her breasts. They were so large and out of proportion to the rest of her body, which was as slim as a teenage boy's, that it seemed a safe bet that she had gotten breast implants. True or not, she managed to use them as a form of intimidation.

"Thank you so much for joining us. Finally." Helga's voice had an unpleasant edge, but a brilliant smile was plastered on her face. Her even white teeth were another of what she considered among her best features. She displayed them as often as possible, rarely with any humor.

Helga eyed my coat and dropped the grin. "It appears that you continue to show a serious lack of commitment. Do you think you can get rid of the outerwear? Or did you just arrive now?" She made an elaborate show of checking her wristwatch. "At nearly ten o'clock?"

I murmured something polite but unintelligible. Helga ignored me anyway.

"I thought you should be aware of a certain fact," she crowed. Her grin was back, wider than a lottery winner's. "Company policy is that an absence of more than three days requires a doctor's note." She paused for effect. "I could demand a doctor's note right now."

I peered at her. This was a typical Helga bluff. It would probably kill her to know this but her antics, intended to upset and irritate me, were having the opposite effect. They were pulling me back from the abyss and planting me on solid ground.

"I was out only two days," I pointed out. "I left you phone messages. Monday was a holiday and the office was closed."

Helga's face twisted. She pulled herself very erect—never a good sign as it generally meant wrath would rain down in short order. At the last moment, I was saved when a movement outside my door distracted Helga. She wheeled around to confront Suzy, who was peeking around the door. Suzy's normally confident demeanor, which generally led one to believe she could take on a street gang if she chose to, tended to vanish in the presence of our boss. Around Helga, Suzy was timid and unsure. But then Helga had that effect on people, particularly her employees. I often wondered why Suzy and I, the only graphic design artists at the tiny agency, put up with her.

Helga looked with disdain at Suzy, who moved sheepishly into the office but stayed near the door. Suzy made an attempt to hold Helga's gaze, but failing, looked down at her hands, pretending to examine her nails.

Helga snorted in a most unladylike manner. "We will meet at eleven o'clock, at which point I will deal with you people." She turned back to point a bony finger in my direction. "Perhaps at that point you'll be willing to share with us about your untimely absence."

Suzy shriveled against the wall and Helga swept out. As was our custom, we remained still for three full minutes, Suzy monitoring her watch. We had learned from long experience that Helga was not above taking a position outside the door and eavesdropping after her apparent departure. Once she caught Suzy whispering that Helga was a bitch, and swooped back into the room in full-scale fury.

The minutes passed and we nodded at each other. Suzy pulled the stool from my drafting table over to the desk and perched on it. "Why in the world do we put up with her?" she asked.

"Good question," I countered. "Why don't we just quit?"

"That was a rhetorical question. Len and I can't afford for me not to work, not with the kids. And there's not a lot of demand around here for our skill set, in case you haven't noticed." She gave me a pleading look. "Don't get any ideas of leaving me to deal with Helga alone. Like that day you wouldn't take my call. That was bad . . . and unnecessary. You could have told me what was going on, considering I know all the background and everything."

"I know." I was uncomfortable, still embarrassed that I had childishly refused to talk to either Joe or Suzy when I first learned about the link between the state park victim and my attack, and managed to frighten both of them.

"Well," Suzy said grudgingly, "the excursion to Ohio must have been something. Quick, tell me what happened."

"It's a long story. The details will have to wait until lunchtime. Suffice to say that we got the lowdown. Actually, more than expected."

"That's what you set out to do, so that's good, right?"

"No, not good at all." I picked up my phone and began dialing. "I want you to listen to this phone message." I punched keys until I retrieved the message, and handed the receiver to Suzy. Her eyes widened as she listened. When she handed the phone back, her hand shaking.

"My God. That was him, wasn't it? The guy who attacked you." Suzy was pale.

I nodded. "It doesn't really sound like I remember, but I think he might be trying to disguise his voice. But what he says . . . 'You've been sticking your nose in business you shouldn't be.' The first person I made contact with in Ohio seems to have been his mother. She was not happy when she realized who I was. She probably called him."

"He sounds threatening. And—oh my God—he called here at work. How does he know where you work? You've got to go to the police with this, Quinn."

"You know what they'll say? That it's a nonspecific threat, which it is. Plus, the state police investigator we talked to would be livid that we went off to Ohio to do our own checking. And he would be right. I don't know what we were thinking." I cupped my hands over my face and tried to keep my voice even. "I let Joe talk me into this. It's because I feel guilty that I didn't stop this guy when I had the chance."

Suzy was shaking her head even before I finished. "You shouldn't feel guilty. You did everything you could."

"Let's say you had the opportunity to stop a killer and you didn't. Would you be able to live with yourself?" I was practically shouting. Helga be damned.

Suzy recoiled from my sudden burst of anger. "Where is this coming from? I'm on your side."

I let myself go limp. "I don't know," I mumbled. "I'm sorry. Sorry."

Suzy moved over and perched on the edge of my desk. "You know, you're not going to like this idea either, but I think you should consider telling Helga at least some of what's going on. Especially now that this creep is calling you here. It might even be necessary to save your job. Helga thinks you're just blowing off work."

"And you think she would understand."

Suzy bit her lip. "Point taken," she admitted. "At least consider it. It's your job on the line."

It was only mid-morning, and already I was exhausted. I was definitely too tired to explain that I was losing interest in my job altogether. There were bigger things to worry about. But I nodded politely.

"Look, you better get going before Helga shows up again." I waved weakly. "We'll talk more later."

Suzy reached out and touched the soft fabric of my coat. "Okay, but first you might want to take this off and stay a while." She gave me a quick hug around the shoulders before ducking out of the office.

Once he finally decided to follow up on the crazy story told by Quinn Carlisle the day she appeared at state police headquarters with her boyfriend and the faint etchings of a crude tattoo, Maryland Detective Sergeant Michael Grimaldi was able to find Dennis Price easily enough. It was embarrassingly easy. The truth was he had delayed—unnecessarily delayed—looking into her information.

After the woman and her boyfriend had left, Grimaldi had, as usual, written scrupulous notes of the conversation in his neat, tiny hand. He put the notes in his growing file folder labeled "State Park Murder," the shorthand label that the media had given his case.

Grimaldi had dutifully completed the notes even though his gut told him Quinn was full of shit, and he always followed his gut. So she had the same word on her forearm. So what? It bore no resemblance in style, if you could call it that, to the word on his victim. That was a deep cut done with a flourish. Quinn's was made of more tentative block letters. He knew that proper procedure would be to involve the FBI. It might be considered a little unusual to request handwriting analyses on both skin carvings, and it probably would be a bureaucratic mess with many delays, but it was necessary. It was why he had taken the precaution of getting some photos of Quinn's arm before they left.

Still, he argued with himself as he grudgingly added the task to his list, he had to at least consider the probability of the same guy showing up in a different state a decade later. It was just that the odds dictated that it was unlikely to be the same guy.

More importantly, there was something about Quinn he didn't quite trust. His ex-girlfriend would say—and often did say—that Supercop Michael Grimaldi didn't like women. He wasn't gay or anything—he liked to screw women—but he didn't care to spend much time with them other than that. He tried to be patient, but ultimately he found them annoying. Even with the female victims, he just couldn't relate. Take this girl who was raped, strangled, and beheaded, butchered like an animal. It was wrong that a human being's life was unnecessarily terminated, and he would work tirelessly for justice because he was a cop and that was his responsibility. But a living, breathing female victim or witness? They were the ones he had trouble with—trouble getting inside their heads, trouble understanding how they felt.

When you combine a police investigator who had, face it, misogynistic tendencies with a woman who shows up along with the typical crazies in the aftermath of a well-publicized murder case, what do you expect will happen? That was why Grimaldi was inclined to dismiss Quinn Carlisle. She was likely one of those citizenry who calls or shows up with what they believe to be rock-solid information that will lead to the killer, when there's (a) reward money involved, or (b) a lot of publicity and interest in the case. Like this one.

At first, Grimaldi's superiors attempted to string along the media—and, by extension, the public—with press conferences. The top brass at the state police, feeling heat from a public impatient to have this crime solved, considered press conferences a valuable tool, helping to uncover some heretofore hidden leads and possibly send a message of toughness to the perp himself. As for Grimaldi, he considered all interactions with the media to be a waste of his time.

But in most homicide cases, it probably made sense to go the press conference route. That's because in most cases, there would be a load of forensic evidence that the police could use to tantalize the public and, hopefully, the killer. Flushing him out just might work when you had backup evidence to spring the trap. In this case, however, other than the gruesome beheading and the atypical word carving, they didn't have much. The victim had been sexually assaulted, but the DNA evidence was "minimal," according to the coroner. Still, it might be enough— if they were lucky enough to find someone who matched it.

Thanks to the press conferences, Grimaldi was left to sort through a pile of shit leads. Most of the tips and leads he had already pursued to varying degrees. None had panned out.

After weeks of work, the only lead left untouched was the one Quinn Carlisle had given him. Grimaldi looked through his well-thumbed file once again, and thought about the visitors he had dismissed as among the looniest of the loony tunes.

Grimaldi turned and dug into the files in his desk drawer. He pulled out the notes from his interview with Quinn Carlisle and read through them carefully. Then in a burst of energy, he dragged open another desk drawer, pulled out a dog-eared telephone directory, and flipped through pages in an irritated flurry. There were three possibilities listed. Grimaldi spent a half hour trying to track them down. He learned that one Dennis Price was eighty-seven years old and very hard of hearing, and that "D. Price" was actually Danielle. The third Dennis Price had "ins" next to his name. Grimaldi looked at it a moment and then flipped to the business listings in the yellow pages section of the phone book.

"I can't believe it," Grimaldi said to his empty office. "He's a frigging insurance agent."

The following morning just after daylight, Grimaldi arrived at a seedy strip mall. The shopping center housed a series of somewhat shabby storefronts, including an insurance agency that boasted the name Dennis Price Insurance—Auto Home Life. Grimaldi figured he would stop in Price's office at about ten o'clock, which was hours away. First, he wanted to get the lay of the land. He would watch the shopkeepers opening their stores and hopefully catch a glimpse of Price entering his office. Grimaldi drove slowly past the glass-front stores, and parked in a far corner of the lot. The spot was remote but still allowed him a good view. He didn't want to tip off Price that he was anything but a customer. Assuming, of course, that this Dennis Price was Quinn Carlisle's Dennis Price. If it wasn't, he might have to buy a policy, Grimaldi thought.

This particular Dennis Price had a small placement ad in the yellow pages, complete with a badly reproduced photograph. About the only thing that could be determined was that the person in the photo was roughly in the right age range to be the Dennis Price in question. But who knew when it was taken, Grimaldi thought. It could have been thirty years ago. Grimaldi wouldn't be surprised to find an ancient insurance man with white hair and outdated clothes.

The previous afternoon, Grimaldi also had tried to contact the Pennsylvania county where Quinn's case had been tried, attempting to arrange for a mug shot and arrest record to be faxed to him, along with any other documents associated with the case. After being shunted from person to person and put endlessly on hold, he had given up in disgust.

Now he wished he had held out for some kind of information. A description, something. Well, he did have a vague description from Quinn, but she hadn't seen the guy in ten years.

No harm in checking it out, Grimaldi told himself as he scanned the trash-strewn parking lot. He wished he still smoked. His ex-girlfriend had pestered and nagged him half to death until he quit a year ago. Now she was gone and so were the cigarettes. He missed smoking a lot more than he did the girlfriend. But he was too stubborn to cave in and buy a pack.

He tapped the steering wheel and checked his watch again. Ten thirty-five. He wondered what time these bozos got around to opening up for business. He also wondered if this shopping center got any customers. This neighborhood didn't look like it had many residents who could afford to do a lot of shopping.

Grimaldi scanned the stores again and was startled to see fluorescent lights visible in the Dennis Price insurance agency. Jeez, how had Price gotten in there without him noticing? He felt a little panicked until it occurred to him that most of the vendors probably used the strip mall's rear entrances.

He forced himself to wait five more minutes, then drove in a wide circle around the lot. He parked reasonably close to Price's office as if he had just arrived, and pushed open the glass door at precisely ten minutes to eleven. Despite having staked out the place, and after ruminating about the man in question for hours, Grimaldi was surprised by the tableau before him.

Price was seated behind a desk, the kind with metal legs and fake wood-grain top. His scuffed shoes were propped up on the desk. A magazine lay open on his knees. His hands were cinched behind his skull, pushing his head downward, presumably to read the magazine. The position forced a second and even a third chin on his flabby neck. He didn't look up as Grimaldi moved deeper into the office.

The place was sparsely decorated with a few old wooden folding chairs that looked like they came from a church basement and a sagging potted plant in the corner. There was a large dented filing cabinet with a coffeemaker on top, the carafe so dark from coffee stains it was no longer transparent.

Grimaldi slipped into a chair at the front corner of Price's desk, very close to the soles of Price's shoes. He looked expectantly at Price and realized why the guy hadn't budged when the door had opened. He was asleep. Grimaldi was fascinated and impressed that the man was able to keep his head upright. Price also appeared to be sleeping with his eyes open. They weren't much more than cat slits, but were open enough to give the impression that he was lost in his reading or perhaps deep in thought instead of out cold. Perhaps most amazing of all was that he was able to kick back, assume the position, and fall sound asleep within an hour—maybe even a half hour—after opening up shop.

Grimaldi took the opportunity to study his subject. Quinn Carlisle's description of her attacker was that he was tall, with nearly black hair, and a sharp, hawkish nose. He was in his final semester of college ten years ago, which would now make him in his early thirties. Grimaldi had to admit that this guy fit that vague description. He did have the right nose and very dark hair, though it was now thinning in the front.

Unflinching, Grimaldi watched Price for a while but soon grew tired of the game. He could be here a long time. He picked up a heavy, ancient-looking directory that sat on Price's desk, and let it drop from the height of about six inches.

The book's sharp bang did the trick. It woke Price, but not in the startled, embarrassed way one would expect from a storekeeper caught sleeping on the job. Instead, Price very deliberately lowered his legs, sat up, and grinned. It was so coy that Grimaldi wondered if Price had been faking sleep. An odd way to do business, he thought.

"Please, please have a seat." Price yawned and motioned to the beat-up chair in which Grimaldi's ass was already firmly entrenched. Grimaldi stared at him impassively.

"So." Price repositioned himself for a better view of Grimaldi. "What can I do for you? Maybe you're interested in a nice auto-homeowner package?"

Price looked amused, which Grimaldi found irritating. Price's dark eyes were beady, and the lids were hooded even when he wasn't pretending to sleep. Those attributes, along with the beak nose put one in mind of a hawk or some other type of predatory bird. The image stopped at mid-torso, however. He may have once been fit, but Price had gone to seed. He was flabby, with a belly that spoke of too much beer and insufficient activity. But not so far gone, Grimaldi thought, that he wouldn't have the strength to overpower a frightened female.

Price stood and moved to the ancient, grimy coffeemaker. "Hey, how about some coffee?" he called over his shoulder. "I could use another cup."

At least he's friendly, Grimaldi thought. And chatty. He was carrying the whole conversation, not seeming to notice that Grimaldi had yet to say a word.

Price placed a stained cup in front of Grimaldi and settled back behind the desk. He slurped noisily from his mug.

"So how long have you been in business here?" Grimaldi decided it was time to try to act human, even making a show of looking around as if he hadn't noticed the office before.

Price slurped again. "Oh, about a year, more or less. I took this over from some old guy. He taught me everything he knew before he passed away." Price winked. "You know how those old farts are. But I'm not so sure I'm going to keep this up. It's deadly boring."

Nodding as if he were interested, Grimaldi casually pulled his badge and identification from his inside jacket pocket. He held them up far enough that Price had to lean forward to make them out. Grimaldi felt brief satisfaction in seeing what he thought was a flicker in those self-satisfied eyes.

"You heard of the Nancy Pennypacker case? The one where a girl's body was dumped unceremoniously in a state park not far from here?"

The raptor eyes looked at him unblinking.

"No? Guess you don't get the news much around here, huh? Well, I'm the lead investigator in that case."

Price took another gulp of coffee without taking his eyes off Grimaldi. "And what does this have to do with me?"

Grimaldi waited a good thirty seconds. Already he didn't like this guy. "There seems to be, shall we say, an odd coincidence between the Pennypacker murder and another case about ten years ago. That was the kidnapping and rape of a college student. Both victims happened to have the same word carved in their skin. In the old case, the accused was one Dennis Price."

Grimaldi paused for a reaction. None came. *What the hell*, Grimaldi thought. *Go for the bluff.*

"We have good information, court records and such, indicating that you're the same person."

"Impossible. That's impossible." Price spat out the words.

It was Grimaldi's turn to be coy. "Really. Why's that?"

Price's mouth snapped shut. When he spoke again, it was with a sly tone.

"Well, Detective . . . what was it, Greenwich? No? *Grimaldi*? Okay, Detective Grimaldi, it's like this. Quinn? She was my girlfriend back in college and there was this big misunderstanding that went way too far, but it all got worked out."

The aha moment, Grimaldi thought. This was the Dennis Price who was connected with Quinn Carlisle. And to top it off, he was lying about it, presuming that Grimaldi was a blooming idiot.

"There really shouldn't be any court records," Price was continuing, rather earnestly, "because everything was resolved. As for this new, unfortunate incident—well, I don't know what to tell you. Weird coincidence? Coincidences do happen, you know. But I had nothing to do with this. I'm just an insurance agent minding his own business. So I had a little trouble with a feisty girlfriend ten years ago, but this is completely different. It's a stretch, don't you think?"

Grimaldi listened as Price's words flowed over him like molasses. Maybe he had a point, Grimaldi conceded. Price may be connected to Quinn Carlisle, but there still was nothing to prove that he was linked to the state park murder. Price's babbling broke into his thoughts.

"I don't really know if I should say any more than that," he was saying. "You know, be talking without a lawyer or anything. Maybe you'd want to talk to him? My lawyer, I mean. I have his card here somewhere."

Price already had his desk drawer open, and with barely a glance, he pulled out a tattered business card. He offered it to Grimaldi, who accepted it gingerly, pinching the corner between his thumb and forefinger.

"Guess you're scraping the bottom of the barrel," Grimaldi said, tucking the business card in his jacket pocket.

"What do you mean?"

"The card. It's all yellow and shit. A little worse for the wear, isn't it? I guess you've had to give out a lot of them over the years."

Grimaldi made the statement in a mild enough tone, but Price's reaction was violent.

"I don't know who you think you are, but you need to leave. And I mean now. NOW!"

Grimaldi stared him down. Price glared back. Finally, Grimaldi pulled himself from the chair.

He was almost at the door when he turned, unable to resist. "Have a nice day." He gave Price a two-fingered salute.

The prick answered with one.

Grimaldi drove absently back to headquarters, trying to sort through his thoughts on Dennis Price. What a strange bird. Price had essentially admitted his role in the Quinn Carlisle case and apparently had a lawyer on retainer. So the Carlisle woman was right in that after ten years, it turns out he was working and living not far from Quinn. But that didn't prove anything, least of all—which Grimaldi kept returning to—that Price killed Nancy Pennypacker. But what about the word carved into both victims? Grimaldi ran a free hand through his buzz-cut hair.

He needed to go through due process. In addition to exploring handwriting analyses of the women's skin carvings—a long shot at best—he would call this yahoo's lawyer and argue with him for a while about Price giving up a DNA sample. Then Grimaldi would reconcile himself to the fact that a voluntary sample was never going to happen, and attempt to line up a warrant to force the issuance of a sample. Eventually and inevitably, he would be disappointed by the lack of a DNA match with the state park victim. Then Price would probably sue the state of Maryland for harassment and Grimaldi could kiss his career good-bye. It was all so predictable.

A traffic light, thankfully, allowed him to stop this non-productive train of thought. Feeling light-headed and a bit nauseated, he rolled down the window and breathed deeply, rubbing his temples. His head was pounding. Maybe the bastard poisoned him with that coffee. But he couldn't have drunk more than half a sip, certainly not enough to harm himself even if it had been laced with antifreeze. The coffee had been so rank that he had barely tasted it.

Damn these nut jobs, he thought. Why couldn't he just get a straight homicide, with simple, uncomplicated motives like anger, lust, or greed?

The light turned green and Grimaldi still sat there, staring. The kid in the pickup truck behind him leaned on his horn. Grimaldi lurched forward just as the traffic light was turning red again, the truck following close behind, the horn serenading him across the intersection. Grimaldi wondered if the driver would have acted the same way if he knew Grimaldi was a cop. *Probably*, he thought. *Dumb ass.*

CHAPTER FIFTEEN

Fall 1998: Maryland

I had actually managed to sleep through the night this time, although it had apparently been in a near upright position, supported by numerous pillows. When I woke, my book still open against my chest, I was stiff and aching. My head must have dropped to an unnatural position. I tried rolling my neck back and forth to loosen the muscles. The previous afternoon and evening were spent almost full-time in bed, as I alternated between watching television and reading, and I didn't remember drifting off.

I reached blindly for the television remote on the nightstand. Not that I would have been able to see it even if it was high noon. It was always pitch black in my windowless bedroom. Often when I woke, my clue that it was morning was the sliver of daylight showing around the edges of the door. From my position in bed I could make out a brightness around the door jamb, but with my stiff neck I didn't want to twist around to check the time on my clock radio. My guess was that it was about eight o'clock in the morning. But morning, noon, night—really, what did it matter? I had no pressing engagements or anyplace I had to be.

An odd phrase: no place I had to be. I tried it out loud. "Is there anyplace I have to be?" I considered this for a second. "Nope."

After a few minutes I decided it was stupid to just lay there guessing the time. It would be easier to turn on the television. I groped the buttons on the remote that was still poised in my hand and pressed one. The screen flickered and came to life with a scene of giddy people lounging around a coffee table. A morning talk show. It appeared to be near the close of the program. I had my answer from my newfound familiarity with daytime television. It was almost nine a.m.

Only a few days away from work and already I had a routine. First, waking up and lying there in a stupor. Inevitably, broadcast news. As if the news would bring some answers or resolution to my situation.

Each morning, also like clockwork, the phone would ring around the time I was due at the agency. Each day I let the answering machine click on. Inevitably, there would be a message from work, either Helga's or Suzy's voice blaring out of the little machine next to the phone. I would listen to the message, and when they hung up, I would press the delete button.

The first day I stayed home, I relented and called Suzy back. It was a less than comforting conversation. Of course I wanted to tell her everything, but the words wouldn't come. Not even when I was talking to Suzy, in whom I had confided so much. In the end I settled for telling her that I was just too frightened to return to work. Suzy seemed not to know what to say at first. Then came a torrent of words and conflicting advice.

"Have there been more of those crazy phone messages? If it's that bad, you've got to report it to the police. You need protection, you need something . . . I'm telling you this for your own good. You'd better get yourself in here because Helga's on the warpath. You need to tell her what's going on. You need to tell somebody."

To calm her, I downplayed it all. But when she tried to extract promises that I would follow her advice, I stuttered that I needed some time off and made up some excuse to get off the line. Suzy called every day after that, sometimes several times a day. I stopped answering the phone during business hours. I waited to hear the voice on the answering machine. If it was Joe, I would quickly grab the phone.

Helga made one perfunctory call each day. As frantic as Suzy's messages sounded, Helga's were increasingly angry.

On the third day, Helga's message was a haughty announcement that I was no longer an employee, since I had failed to appear for three consecutive days.

So that's that, I thought. When the answering machine clicked off, I pushed the button to unmute the TV and settled back among the pillows. I watched the flickering figures on the screen and the frequent breaks to commercials, letting the comforting programming soak in like a warm bath.

I had just been fired. I should have been upset, probably even distraught. But I didn't feel anything. I should probably also be concerned that my automatic reaction to everything lately was to burrow in my apartment. But in here lay safety, security. I no longer felt safe outside, not even in parts of the building outside my apartment. Not at Joe's, not in the hallway or stairwell. Maybe it wasn't the healthiest thing to become a recluse, but I was driven to it by self-preservation and naked fear.

It was a really bad time to be alone, but my solitary condition was my own fault.

As soon as we returned from our Ohio fact-finding mission, Joe had started lobbying to return. He wanted to dig deeper. "I know we can find more. We left too soon," he fretted. "I know the rest of Dennis Price's family was about ready to open up."

He went on in this vein for days. At first I didn't respond, figuring that a discussion about it would only lead to an argument. He didn't seem to notice my lack of enthusiasm as he began checking his calendar and speculating about when would be a good time to make the drive back to Ohio. Finally, I spoke up.

"You might think there's value in going down this road and talking to more family members, but I don't have the stomach for it."

Joe glanced up from the map he was studying. "What? You don't want to go?"

"No, I don't. I can't stand the thought of facing them."

Disappointed, Joe busied himself refolding the map carefully, his jaw tight.

I hesitated. "Why don't you just go without me? You could just as easily gather the information yourself. You're better at it, anyway."

To his credit, Joe made a strong effort to convince me to accompany him, even bringing up the disturbing phone message at work. "I'm not so sure it's a good idea for you to be on your own."

But I saw that he had brightened considerably at the suggestion, so I countered that the answering machine message must have been a mistake, a drunk misdialing. I said it with a lot more conviction than I was feeling. "I'll be all right," I told him. "I'll just keep a low profile."

That, at least, was the plan.

The day Joe set off for Ohio, I went to work and picked up another phone message. It was similar to the first one, again left in the middle of the night. The following day, another voice mail. The running theme in the messages was that I should "watch out."

I couldn't pretend to write these off as flukes, not after three of them. But I resisted the urge to tell Joe about it. I knew he would rush back and I would feel foolish. When he called, I tried hard not to sound distracted. I listened dutifully to the progress he was making and asked appropriate questions. *After all, he's doing this for me*, I thought. But I was already wondering whether I could make it until he returned.

I told myself not to dwell on it. At the agency, I turned all my attention to my projects, so that at least during the day I was distracted.

Still, it felt like endlessly holding your breath underwater, I thought as I left the office on the third day Joe was gone. It was early evening and I was leaving late, long after Helga, Suzy, and other workers who shared our building, had gone home. I tensed as I made my way to my car in the empty parking lot. The halogen lights made eerie circles in the darkness. I still felt nervous in these kinds of settings.

But when I reached the car, I didn't hurry to climb in. Instead, I stood staring at it for a full minute, trying to make sense of what I saw. The word NOTHING was scratched crudely into the paint on the driver's side door.

I felt myself go cold. This wasn't the anonymity of a phone message. This was real, and close. He could be right here, in the parking lot.

My head snapped up, my eyes searching the shadows of the lot. Then, fumbling with the car keys and the door locks, I got in the car and peeled off.

This was the incident that sent me scurrying to the safety of home, what caused me to hide out in my apartment. I drove that night in the most roundabout route I could devise, taking every side road I knew, constantly checking my rearview mirror. It was just blackness behind me, but I couldn't shake the fear that I was being followed.

Once I was finally back at the apartment building, I raced up the stairs and shakily opened my front door. I don't think I breathed again until I had slid all the locks and dead bolts into place.

Heart pounding, my blouse drenched in sweat, I leaned my head against the door. Almost instantly, I popped back up. I had better search the apartment. If this person was bold enough to go to my workplace and vandalize my car, he might also break into my home. And who was I kidding, anyway? The "he" in question could only be Dennis Price.

I went through all the rooms, checking under the furniture, opening my closet doors, even lifting up the throw pillows. With every step, I held my little canister of pepper spray like a brave, flickering candle. Finally satisfied that I was alone, I retreated to the bedroom, the most interior room in the apartment.

Since then I had barely moved.

Joe called frequently from the road. The only thing that saved me from having to explain why I wasn't at work was that he generally didn't call me there, because of Helga. He was in the habit of calling the apartment late in the day, when he assumed I would be home from the office. If he happened to call early in the morning, I would grab the phone as soon as I heard his voice on the answering machine and make some excuse, like that I was brushing my teeth and couldn't get to the phone in time.

If I couldn't tell Joe about the new phone messages, I definitely couldn't tell him about that awful word being scratched into my car, or about how I was practically hiding under my bed.

I wanted to tell him. Every time I heard his voice on the phone, I would promise myself I would get it all out and beg him to come home. But then I would start picturing him worried and upset, and how he would risk life and limb to get back to me as quickly as he could. If something happened to Joe, I couldn't take it. I had come to rely on him. *Look at yourself,* I thought. *He's gone for a few days and you're falling apart.* In the end, I simply listened to his updates and tried to sound encouraging, silently praying that I would be able to persevere.

But the situation was unsustainable. I couldn't hide in my bedroom forever. I knew I should have called Helga and told her the reason for my strange behavior. Maybe if I had begged, I could have kept my job. I should at least call have called Suzy and explained everything. *Maybe I should call one of my other friends*—although I hadn't been in touch with any of them since I started spending all my free time with Joe. There was also the matter of my never having explained about my attack to anyone in Maryland other than Joe and Suzy. Still, I could probably use all the friends I could rally around me.

While I could picture myself picking up the phone and dialing the familiar numbers—and I practiced opening statements in my head over and over—I remained frozen in front of the television, watching endless hours of programming that only seemed to deepen my inertia.

Why did I ever reopen this Pandora's box? I thought as I lay lethargically, watching commercial after commercial. I never should have gone to the police. That state police officer Grimaldi was right to be skeptical. How did I know it was

Dennis Price perpetrating crimes on others? All I had done was stir the hornet's nest.

But what about Judith? came the thought, growing and growing until it filled my head. I wished Dennis Price would just leave me alone. Tears burned my eyelids. Hadn't he done enough damage? But I knew the answer. I was the one who couldn't leave well enough alone.

I lay perfectly still and felt myself drifting into sleep. Amazing, considering it hadn't been long since I woke from a fifteen-hour nap. I tried to force myself to sit up but had to rest on the edge of the bed for a moment. I was dizzy. Eventually I made my way to the kitchen. I turned on the faucet to fill the teakettle, and suddenly felt an overpowering hunger. It had been at least a full day since I had last eaten.

I felt shaky as I started pulling food and dishes from the cupboards, but after I ate two bowls of Rice Krispies, I couldn't face any more food. I sipped my cup of tea, and pushed away the crackers and cheese I had set out.

I put the food back in the refrigerator and cleaned up the kitchen. Then I brought a bottle of water back to the safety of the bedroom. Back in bed, I tried deep breathing to restore my equilibrium. But the anxiety seemed to have taken hold. Staring unseeing at my dresser, I tried to think through the dilemma that I seemed only to make worse at every turn.

"Way too late to second-guess your decisions now," I told my reflection in the mirror over the dresser.

It was too late. Outing Dennis Price had set in motion a terrible process. Now I was being stalked. He knew where I worked. As a result I had run to my apartment, cut myself off from friends, avoided work, and lost my job. My boyfriend was trying to investigate a murder case on his own. And I was here. Alone.

All that was left to do was to hang on until Joe got back. He would be home soon and would help me figure things out. *Dear God, let him come home soon.*

It had been weeks since the state police investigator Michael Grimaldi had confronted Dennis Price in his run-down, third-rate insurance agency. After that visit, Grimaldi went from dismissing Price as any sort of lead worth pursuing to making him his primary suspect. Check that. His only suspect.

All the other trails had gone cold. That had helped to make Price his current obsession. That, and the fact that there wasn't a whiff of another lead.

The one thing Detective Sergeant Grimaldi hated was a case gone cold. He liked to wrap things up. More than the satisfaction of bringing criminals to justice, he liked to solve cases. And it could be that Price was the perpetrator in the state park murder. There was something about the guy that Grimaldi found creepy, something that led him to think he had to make sure to rule him out.

As a result, Grimaldi was now spending the bulk of his time on Price. Checking him out, digging into his background, researching his arrest record, talking to any relatives and acquaintances he could track down.

He had made some calls and eventually verified much of the information that Quinn Carlisle and her boyfriend had given him. But when he talked to the Price family, and the few people he could find who knew the family, Grimaldi felt they were holding something back. There seemed more to tell and, for whatever reason, they weren't willing to tell it. He hadn't leaned on them yet; that was on his to-do list.

He postponed contacting them again, not because he disliked that part of the job, but specifically because he savored it. He was saving the best for last. He enjoyed playing with people's heads, squeezing them for information until it just popped out, willingly or not.

Grimaldi bided his time, trying to arm himself with as many facts as possible. He had also been spending time attempting to wrangle a voluntary DNA sample from Dennis Price. This meant he was forced to deal with Price's attorney, who, as it turned out, was hired by and still seemed loyal to Dennis's deceased father.

No wonder Price was so cocksure, Grimaldi realized. The father—who had made sure his son would continue to have a shield of legal protection—had been by all accounts a real son of a bitch. The lawyer, a smarmy, vulgar guy named Pawlowski, wasn't much better.

Grimaldi met Pawlowski once, at a diner, to exchange paperwork. Grimaldi had no trouble picking out the lawyer even though it was their first meeting. Somehow Grimaldi recognized him immediately: overweight, thick lips, bad combover. His suit was expensive and most likely Italian, but his tie was stained. As he shouted across the table at Grimaldi—it was immediately evident that the man operated nonstop at a high decibel level—Pawlowski brushed the sleeve of his jacket through a pool of ketchup without noticing. His telephone manners weren't much of an improvement.

"What the hell?" Pawlowski had screeched in one of those calls. Grimaldi had been forced to shift the telephone receiver away from his eardrum. Pawlowski sputtered with outrage, despite the fact that this was at least their fifth discussion about the DNA sample. Grimaldi was getting pretty tired of it. Apparently Pawlowski was, too.

"Let me ask you this," the attorney seethed. "Do you always randomly pluck men from the general population just to see if you get a match in your case? Are you that desperate?"

Grimaldi sighed. "No. Meaning, no, we are not soliciting random samples. As I've explained—and I've explained it many times at this point—we have reason to believe that there may be a link between this murder and Mr. Price's previous conviction. We would like a DNA sample to rule him out. I would think that if Mr. Price had nothing to hide, and did not know or have contact with the victim as you claim, then there shouldn't be an issue with that."

"Only the teeny-weensy issue of the man's civil rights. How about that issue, huh, cowboy? As I keep telling you, unless you get a warrant, you can take your voluntary DNA sample and shove it where the sun don't shine."

Grimaldi didn't answer. Nothing would have made him happier than to follow proper police procedure and seek a warrant. But that had proved difficult. He had gone up his chain of command twice and the answer had been the same both times: not enough to convince a judge. The second time the answer had been a little testier. Grimaldi had been informed that he needed to convince the suspect to give a voluntary sample. It was almost as if Pawlowski was aware of this order, the way he had been taunting Grimaldi.

"Get up off your ass and go talk to the judge, you lazy bastard."

"I'll take that as a no?" Grimaldi kept his voice light.

This time Pawlowski's laugh was genuine. "You're damn right it's a no. Come on, why don't you amuse all of us? See if you can convince the judge. He'll throw you out of his courtroom. A ten-year-old case from another state? Where the victim obviously has a vendetta against my client? It's a little thin."

Grimaldi wasn't offended in the least. It had never bothered him when anyone—parents, superiors, teachers, friends, or girlfriends—gave him a tongue-lashing. He was born with thick skin and with the knowledge that he was, most of the time, absolutely right. He trusted his instincts and they rarely let him down. And if he was occasionally proven wrong, so what? This attitude tended to drive others nuts. But it had usually worked in Grimaldi's favor.

This particular case was one of the few times that he wasn't one hundred percent certain that he was correct. Despite the fact Grimaldi had become focused on the *possibility*, he wasn't completely sold on the idea that Price was the culprit. That was exactly why he needed that DNA sample. He needed an answer, one way or the other.

Elbows propped on the desk, hands formed into a small tent over his face, Grimaldi considered his case that had grown ice-cold. Gradually, he started to relax, even coming close to falling asleep. Then, he started so suddenly he almost fell off the swivel-back chair. He had been so focused on getting a DNA sample that he had missed the obvious. Price was guilty as hell.

Of course, that should have been clear the first hundred times that Pawlowski refused to produce a DNA sample, but Grimaldi had been willing to convince himself that Price was a long shot, and the family and their lawyer were actually insulted by the implication of a connection with a murder. Pawlowski had threatened more than once to sue the Maryland State Police and ruin Grimaldi personally, which Grimaldi had pretended to ignore.

But what if it was just all a big ploy? Grimaldi realized he could use the very heated protests, the threats of a lawsuit, to convince a judge of possible guilt. Maybe even enough to get a warrant for a DNA sample.

Grimaldi opened the desk drawer where he kept his Rolodex. He would approach the judge himself, forgetting to make another formal request of his superiors, which was sure to be rejected again. He could beg forgiveness later, after he was proven right.

He flipped through the Rolodex until he found the number of a judge he had dealt with several times in the past. Then he had another thought. If Price was guilty of this murder, maybe Quinn was right about a few other things, too, like her paranoia about Price.

No wonder the woman looked scared out of her wits, Grimaldi thought. He briefly considered trying to organize some kind of protection for Quinn Carlisle. But he knew he would never be able to convince his superiors of the value of spending taxpayers' dollars on that. His bosses were likely to say that she had accepted the risks when she had come forward with her tip.

Anyway, Grimaldi thought, *I'm breaking enough rules for one day.* He picked up the phone to try to nail down a warrant.

It was nightfall and Joe was finally expected home from Ohio. The week had felt as long as a month. Energized by the prospect of no longer having to rattle around the empty apartment, I had ventured from the safety of the bedroom. I sat on the edge of the sofa in the dark living room. It was dark because I had intentionally kept all the lights off. It was silly, really. If Dennis Price was in fact watching me and my apartment, I was holding out the hope that if he saw no lights on, he would conclude no one was home. It was a faint hope.

It didn't matter. It would all be over soon. Once Joe was home, I could look to him to figure a way out of this mess. I wouldn't have to continue doing this alone. I felt like such a wimp, but I wasn't cut out for this—I needed help.

Yet I had toughed it out and had actually made it to Friday, the day Joe planned to return, before I broke down and told him what was going on. That morning I couldn't bluff my way through another phone conversation. Everything spilled out: what had happened to my car in the parking lot at work, how I had fled home, hid out for days, and lost my job.

"I should have told you," I wept into the phone. "I should have told my boss even if she wouldn't have understood. I should have called the police. I should have . . ." I pulled out a tissue to blow my nose and almost missed what Joe was patiently repeating.

"You're doing the right thing. You're staying there with everything locked up. We'll work it out. Just stay safe and I'll be home as soon as I can." With that, he hung up. I knew he would be hurrying to check out of the motel and get back.

That was the morning. Now it was evening and even considering Joe's long drive, he should be arriving soon. I curled up in a corner of the sofa and looked around. The room was not unfriendly with its shadows—just quiet. Light streamed in from the street lamps through the tall windows.

I took some deep breaths and tried not think about Dennis Price or the stalking or what Joe might have found out in Ohio.

But what else is there to think about? I silently queried the dark lamp beside me. It sat impassive, a fat sentry under an umbrella.

"At least you're a good listener," I said aloud, just as the sound of the doorbell ripped the through the apartment.

Even though I was anxiously awaiting Joe and knew it had to be him, the sharp buzzing made me jump.

I crept to the door and peered through the fish-eye lens into the hallway. It was Joe. He wore a tired smile and was waving at the door expectantly, if not very energetically.

Stepping back, I began undoing the various chain locks and dead bolts. When I opened the door I tried to turn on a big smile, but it faded in the reflection of his faintly shocked expression. In his face in the relatively well-lit hallway, I saw how I must look. I glanced down at my threadbare sweatshirt and old sweatpants that were miles too big. Self-conscious, I shoved my hair behind my ears and stepped back. "It might not be stylish, but at least it's not a robe and fuzzy slippers." Again, I tried to smile.

Without hesitating he strode in and enveloped me, unfashionable outfit and all, in a bear hug that I thought might never end, even as I feared it would.

It was close to midnight. I was still basking in Joe's presence, all of the anxiety of the previous days gone. We sat close together on the sofa, knees touching as we talked. He had automatically turned on the table lamp when he came into the apartment, but when he saw me wincing, he switched it off. As a result, our only light came from the street lamps outside, which was soon joined by slivers of moonlight.

Joe was overflowing with adrenaline, the result of his frantic drive from Ohio. He peppered me with questions about my experience, then launched into a summary of what he had learned on his trip. He had only been able to give me the highlights in his phone calls, he said. When I admitted that I had barely been able to focus on what he said during those calls, he looked at me sharply. But then he rubbed my head with his knuckles and answered playfully, "You managed to sound pretty normal, believe it or not. I did have my suspicions, but that was probably due to my great powers of discernment."

I had to admit that Joe's time in Ohio had been productive. During the day, he would track down new Dennis Price contacts. Nights in the motel room, he spent thinking, strategizing, and making phone calls. He sketched out possible scenarios on scratch pads, complicated webs of what Dennis Price might have done, or might be planning to do. Joe tested some of his theories with a Price relative or family member—anyone who would talk to him. By the end of his stay, Joe had managed to contact an impressive twenty-three people.

"Wow," I murmured.

Joe couldn't help looking pleased with himself, but protested that the network was surprisingly easy to find. Between the background Ruth had provided and a follow-up call or two to Sal, one person led to another, and then another, and another.

"It turns out everyone knows this family, and most of them have an opinion or a piece of information to share. The hardest part was separating rumor from fact." Joe grinned. "I'm afraid I led some of them to believe that I was a private investigator. One person actually asked, 'What took you so long?'"

Dennis Price's more distant relatives were among the group Joe had contacted, along with neighbors, former employers, teachers, and acquaintances. Not necessarily friends. It didn't seem that anyone would own up to being Dennis's friend.

Much of what Joe had uncovered about Dennis Price filled in some of the blanks from our conversation with Ruth. Predictably, Dennis Price had been a troubled youth. His mother was said to have a history of mental illness. It was widely suspected that Dennis, her only child, was the victim of abuse, or had inherited the mental instability, or both. His father had been bombastic and loud, using his money to clean up the family's messes.

And, as was apparent from our visit to Ruth, the family was quite wealthy. Because of his grandfather's money, Dennis Price felt a strong sense of entitlement. He learned early that any problem could be resolved with the family money. His youthful difficulties—and there were many—ranged from setting his elementary school on fire when he was nine, to a brief expulsion from high school. It had been in high school that he was accused of assaulting, possibly sexually assaulting, a student as well as a female teacher. Those charges were dropped, if they were ever officially made. As with all his "complications," they miraculously disappeared the instant Dennis's father intervened.

"The older Dennis got, the more difficult his scrapes became, and it cost his father that much more to straighten things out," Joe related. No matter what the problem, his father was the cleaner.

"That's why it was quite the shocker when your case came along. Price didn't wriggle out of trouble in that one as easily as he usually did. Of course, no one back in Ohio, at least outside the family, knew anything about it at first. It was probably the reason Price was going to an out-of-state school to begin with; to keep a lid on scandals like this. And a case that was actually going to court?" Even though it was in Pennsylvania, people began to talk. Eventually it all came out. No one was surprised that it had happened or that Dennis had been accused. It never crossed their minds that it wasn't true. The only part that was unusual was the lack of a cover-up, or the failure to clean up the mess.

I stared at Joe. This scenario had never occurred to me. "I didn't know," I said finally.

Joe nodded. "How could you? But after all I heard, I'm only wondering why Price's father didn't make some kind of offer to your family to hush things up."

"He might have tried. I doubt my father would have given him the time of day." I studied my foot in the dim light. "That would explain a lot in terms of what happened at the university."

"They didn't want to cooperate?"

"Not at first. My parents had to camp out at the dean's office. Eventually my father prevailed."

"And you were the only one, I'm sure, whose case against Dennis Price went to court. You should be proud."

"Yeah. Well . . ." I let my voice trail away.

We sat quietly.

"Anyway . . ." Joe cleared his throat. "It took courage. But it's possible that the prosecution, and the bad way it ended, might have had the unwanted effect of making Price more confident. He came out of it all unscathed and he knew it. In his own mind, he was invincible."

Joe leaned toward me. Even in the bluish midnight light coming through the windows, I could see he looked serious.

"I'm going to be totally honest about everything I learned. But I don't want you to feel guilt over this. You didn't deserve the crime he committed."

I bit my lip to keep from crying. The old wound was splitting open again.

"But I did have the opportunity to stop him. Then maybe these victims would be alive today. Maybe Judith . . . I just didn't see any of this coming."

"Listen to yourself. What if you tried to use the knife on him that night? He would have turned it around and used it on you. You would be dead."

I flinched.

"You did what you could. You fought, you got away. Then you tried to bring him to justice. I call that doing a lot."

"Then why do I feel so guilty?" I asked him, miserable.

"Guilt belongs with the ones who are really guilty. Not you." Joe grabbed my hand and squeezed it. When I didn't respond, he let go. After a long silence, he continued with his narrative. I was tempted to close my ears. I even angled myself away from him on the sofa. But I found myself listening anyway. I had to.

After the close call in court, Joe said, Dennis Price became more brazen. He stopped trying to hide his bad-boy attitude and everyone was too polite, or too intimidated by the family, to do anything but keep a respectful distance.

Yet over the years, there were persistent rumors that revolved around unsolved crimes in the area.

"What kind of crimes?" My tone was wooden.

Joe hesitation was barely perceptible. "Sexual assaults, mostly. Occasionally it would get into the media and some reporter would try to make a connection, but the police would insist the crimes weren't related. They were sort of sporadic, sometimes coming as much as a month or two apart, other times separated by years. But they all seemed to happen within a fifty-mile radius of Price's community.

"People tend to believe what they're told," Joe said. "Then all it takes is for somebody to start speculating to string these events together. One person whispers to another person: Dennis had something to do with these crimes. Next thing you know, everyone seems to have heard it."

I had turned ashen.

"Not surprisingly, Dennis's immediate family was not quite so cavalier," Joe said. "They were determined to stop the rumors. Then, as Ruth and Sal told us, Dennis's father died suddenly and Dennis dropped out of sight. Everyone believed that his mother had to know where he was and probably helped him get a new start somewhere. One said he was starting a business, but no one seemed to know definitively where he went. And this apparently all came about around the time of the state park murder back here in Maryland."

Joe fell silent. I had been sitting stock-still, but now shuddered.

"How many?" I whispered.

Joe looked momentarily confused.

"How many . . . victims?"

He wrinkled his brow. "That's not really clear. There's no proof—only rumors. But it doesn't sound like it was in the double digits or anything." He looked at me. "I know. Big relief, huh?" He looked down. "Sorry."

I slumped back on the sofa and shut my eyes. It wasn't that Joe was being insensitive. I understood his excitement about collecting this information about Dennis Price. But Joe and I seemed to be going down divergent roads: mine a twisting path that seemed to only lead to more terror, and his a superhighway that he believed was hurtling us toward justice.

"I tried to reach Deborah the other day. The other victim at school? I called on the spur of the moment." After a long pause, I opened my eyes and looked at Joe.

"And?" he prodded gently.

"And I spoke with her mother. Deborah's dead too." I swallowed. "Suicide. She hanged herself a few years ago. It sounds like she never did get over what happened to her."

Joe searched for something to say. "I guess that one can't be pinned on Dennis Price," he said finally. "At least not directly."

"Yeah, I guess."

Joe reached across and snapped on the table lamp. He stood up, blinking in the light. I saw how exhausted and drained he was. His clothes, normally neat and pressed, were rumpled.

"Look, I do have to go to work in the morning—God, in a few hours," he said, glancing at his watch. "If you want, I can grab some stuff from my apartment and stay here with you. If you want me to."

"I would be very grateful."

Joe nodded. "Good. In fact, if you give me your key, I'll stop by your mailbox. I'll bet you haven't picked up your mail in a few days either."

Joe returned faster than I had expected. He must have raced to and from his apartment. I ushered him back in, his arms full of hastily packed bags and a plastic bag stuffed with envelopes and circulars.

"This mail pickup was just in time, at least as far as the post office is concerned," he said, dropping the bag on my kitchen table. "Your mailbox was overflowing."

I fingered through the bag a moment and sighed. "Let's get you settled first." I led the way to the bedroom to show him the closet space that I had just as quickly cleared for his stuff. For a moment I watched him unpack, then wandered back to the kitchen to sort through the mail. It seemed a daunting task for this late at night, but before I knew it I was creating separate, neat piles for bills and junk mail.

"What's this?" I muttered, ripping open the small envelope addressed in red ink block printing.

Joe emerged from the bedroom. "Hey, thanks for making room on short notice." He caught the look on my face. "What is it?"

I held out the folded piece of paper. "Apparently he not only knows where I work. He also knows where I live."

Joe put out his hand to take the letter but seemed unable to tear his eyes from mine. Finally he opened the page. It was filled with oversized childlike printing in red crayon that looked like it might have been created by a deranged first grader.

"You escaped before," it read. "Don't think it will happen again. I haven't forgotten. Remember you are worth NOTHING."

Joe let the letter drop as if it had burned his fingers. We stared at each other. Then the clear thought emerged, *At least Joe is here.* It might be the only thing that kept me from dying right then.

For long minutes, neither of us said anything. We stood there with the letter on the kitchen table between us. I frantically ran through scenarios of what could happen and what we could possibly do to change the course of events. But maybe there was no stopping it.

Joe finally started to speak, but I chose that moment to interrupt him. I knew what he was going to say.

"I can't go to the police about this."

Joe's eyes widened. "Why not? We've got to."

I turned away.

"Look." Joe drew a sharp breath. "I can understand it. You go the authorities and it backfires on you. But think about it. This—, this *pervert* keeps contacting you. It's pretty clear the police must have contacted him."

I wheeled around. With Joe's last statement, it all made sense. Of course. None of this was about Dennis Price tracking me down. It must have been some twist of fate that he happened to land in my part of the world—although it certainly wasn't surprising that he was continuing to harm women. I was still convinced that it was Dennis Price who killed the state park woman. But he was probably unaware that I was anywhere in the vicinity until I happened to alert him to that fact via the police. Price knew that I had blown the whistle on him again.

The thoughts clicked through my mind as Joe still tried to convince me. "The police bungled it before, but all that means is that they have to take us seriously now. They can't dismiss us like a couple of crackpots. Because now he's stalking you, and we have proof."

I looked down and shook my head. Joe firmly believed that the system would work. He wasn't naïve. He just hadn't had the same experiences I had. And I was equally convinced that there could only be perverted justice. Which was the equivalent of no justice.

"Don't you see? The police, the courts, all of them—if it's not their brilliant idea, forget it. A former victim with an ax to grind? It's laughable." Blood was rushing to my head. Dizzy, I sank into the kitchen chair.

"They aren't going to listen to us," I said hoarsely.

Joe drew another deep breath, a quieter sigh. "It's late and we're both exhausted." He held out a hand. "Let's talk about it in the morning."

I gave him my hand so he could pull me upright. In that upward movement, I felt a brief sense of hope, a tiny thought that maybe, just maybe, we would find a way out of this.

CHAPTER SIXTEEN

Fall 1998: Maryland

The next day did not bring the promised solution. I wasn't surprised. After the intensity of the previous evening, we were too tired to take on any more drama.

At breakfast we shared a pot of coffee, neither saying much beyond polite banalities. We tried to pretend it was an ordinary morning. There seemed an unspoken agreement to delay any serious discussion. Joe caught me staring, dejected, at the pile of mail I had shoved to the far end of the table. The threatening crayon note was tossed upside down on the stack.

"I'm heading out, but I can change my plans if you need me. Are you sure you don't want me to stay?" Joe casually slipped the offending letter in his pocket as he stood.

I nodded, although it was true that I felt calmer just having Joe around. I even felt better that he was taking the hateful note from the apartment.

It was well after Joe left for work when I discovered the other letter.

I was seated at the kitchen table with more coffee and my checkbook, finally ready to tackle the bills. *I might as well pay them while I still have some money,* I thought, *considering I have no immediate prospects for income.*

Methodically I began slitting open envelopes, laying out statements, checking each amount. I was in such a rhythm that I didn't even notice the return address on an oversized envelope from which I pulled out a sheaf of papers.

The stationery of the cover letter was official-looking, carrying an embossed gold and dark blue seal. The letter, stiff and formal, was from the special prosecutor's office in the Commonwealth of Pennsylvania.

"Enclosed," the cover letter read, "you'll find a letter from William O'Brien addressed to yourself. Eleven years ago, Mr. O'Brien was the eyewitness to a murder, that of his brother. Mr. O'Brien testified at the subsequent trial, presided over by Judge Francis X. Mahoney, the same judge who heard the case, *Commonwealth v. Dennis Price,* during this same approximate time period."

My palms started to sweat. I took a deep breath before continuing to read.

"The disposition of your case was somewhat similar to what occurred in the O'Brien murder trial case, and apparently in several other cases. In the case of Mr. O'Brien's brother, the defendant was, according to our investigation, apparently linked to organized crime. In spite of Mr. O'Brien's testimony, the defendant was found not guilty by a decision from the bench. Subsequent to the trial, the lives of Mr. O'Brien and his family were threatened. They were forced to enter a witness protection program and were moved to another state.

"This brings us to present day, and why we are contacting you. It seems that Judge Mahoney was involved in taking payments either to dismiss cases or to render a judgment in the defendant's favor. In an apparent act of remorse, Judge Mahoney has taken his own life. He left a note detailing his wrongdoings."

I gasped. I had to go back and read the letter twice more to absorb these developments.

The remaining paragraphs told of a special prosecutor who had been named to try to correct as many of Judge Mahoney's miscarriages of justice as possible. Sadly, the letter noted, circumstances prevented them from taking new action in *Commonwealth v. Dennis Price* because there had been a conviction in that case, even if the sentence had been suspended.

However, they did have an opportunity to do something about the capital murder O'Brien case. This fact led prosecutors to locate Mr. William O'Brien to try to persuade him to testify, again at his own peril, at the retrial of the defendant.

"Mr. O'Brien is understandably apprehensive because of the extremely negative results of his testimony in the first trial. As he debated his decision, he expressed a desire to communicate with others in similar cases, such as yourself. We felt that a written communication such as this, forwarded by us, would be the least obtrusive method of facilitating that communication. Please know that Mr. O'Brien is only familiar with basic aspects of your case, and is not aware of any personal details or your contact information. It seemed the best way to protect your privacy. If you are so inclined, you may write him back care of the address listed in this letter.

"We sincerely hope that this effort will assist Mr. O'Brien in reaching a positive decision in this matter. While we can understand your natural disinclination, we hope that you can find it in your heart to help him make what we think is the correct decision."

I laid the creamy thick stationery on the kitchen table and turned to the underlying pages. These were very different. They were handwritten on yellow lined pages that had been carelessly ripped from a legal pad.

"Dear Miss Carlisle," it began.

Let me make that "Dear Quinn." Hope you don't mind me calling you by your first name. For some reason, ever since I heard about you and your case, I've been thinking about your situation almost more than mine. In a strange way, I feel like I know you.

It's funny. A lot of people, including my ex-wife, told me that I may *think* I have the worst luck ever, but I need to look around at other people and consider how they overcome and rise above the bad things that happen to them. Normally I don't buy that. But the hand you were dealt? It really was worse than mine. Mine was bad, believe me. I saw my brother, my best friend, shot to death before my eyes. Well, I won't go into it. But from what little I know about your situation, you must have just about walked in the valley of the shadow of death. You must have thought that at least you would get some justice when that creep was convicted. But it didn't work out the way it was supposed to, did it? Mine didn't either.

All of this has got me thinking that we're kind of in the same boat. I wouldn't be surprised if we both feel the same way about a lot of things all these years later. But without even having met you, I'll bet you've handled it all way better than I did. I didn't handle it very well. It was when he was threatening to kill my family, my babies, that I fell apart. I had to pack up my family and run to the godforsaken place that I am now. Running like a coward, like the coward I was when I couldn't make a move to protect my brother.

When we came here, that wasn't the end of it. I proceeded to make matters worse. I just couldn't stop thinking about how everything turned bad. I started drinking a lot. Finally my wife couldn't stand it anymore and she threw me out. Can't say I blame her. I'm a poor excuse for a husband, a father, a man.

I'm now, sad to say, living in a crappy motel and calling my wife every five minutes asking her to take me back. She always says, sure, Billy, as soon as you stop drinking. Except I can't. God help me, but the second I stop, that's the moment I'll see clear as day the horrible person I have become. I would see I'm as ugly and twisted as the guy who shot my brother Jeff like it was nothing.

I probably would have gone on living this forever, but one day the lawyers knocked at my door. They wanted to know, hey, would you mind repeating this nightmare? They want to retry the case and they need me to testify again.

At first I told them to get lost, but finally I said I would think about it. And I did think about it and what they mentioned about you, someone who wouldn't get the same opportunity for justice. So I asked if I could get in touch with you. I thought it would help me sort things out. It has helped already. I'm not the type to write letters, but once I got started—wow. It's a big relief to say what I feel with someone who probably would understand.

In this letter, I was all set to ask your advice. I was going to say, if you were in my shoes, would you do it all over? Knowing that there's probably never going to be any justice for Jeff, not real justice, even if they convicted the bastard and he rotted in prison forever?

Then somehow, just by writing this and getting this all off my chest, I seem to have found some answers. I'm not going to pretend that I know exactly how you feel or what you would do. But it sure sounds like you're a woman of courage. And that has made me think that it's time for me to step up myself.

In trying to write this, I've done more clear thinking than I have in years. Here is what I found out. Shit happens and you get a couple of choices. Number one. You can fall apart and make mistakes that will only make it worse for you and the people you love. Or number two, you can decide not to let it ruin your life. You might even learn from it. Maybe even pull something good from it. You can do the right thing.

So I've decided. I'm going to be like you and choose number two.

You probably will never know how much of a help you have been to me. Just guessing, but you probably wouldn't take credit anyway. That's okay. But you helped me a lot. And for that I say thank you.

The signature was a large scrawl: *BILLY O'BRIEN*.

I don't know how long I sat there struggling with my emotions. The crazy note from the night before had been threatening and terrorizing, but it hadn't come as a shock. I was half-expecting something like that or worse, after the voice mails and the car vandalism. But this correspondence stunned me.

I never considered myself courageous, especially after the attack. A stronger person would have fought back. A more courageous person would have prevented Dennis Price from victimizing anyone else.

But here was someone who thought I was some kind of hero. I certainly didn't deserve the title, but I couldn't help feeling restored, even buoyant. For the first time in days, maybe in weeks, I smiled. This perfect stranger, whose experiences in some weird way paralleled mine, had managed to take all my guilt and self-pity and recriminations, and smoothed them out somehow. Maybe it was because he had plenty of recriminations for both of us.

Looking at Billy O'Brien's letter, I realized that I had been thinking about everything all wrong. I did do the right thing by trying to connect the murder in the state park to Dennis Price, no matter how the police or his family or Price himself reacted. Of course he was going to try to intimidate me to make me stop. Was I going to curl up into a ball and die? No way. Billy was getting his second chance and so would I.

I moved to the phone, ready to dial Joe, when it rang.

"I just wanted to see what you decided. About going to the police, I mean." Joe sounded hesitant. "Do you want me to call Grimaldi? Or would you rather I didn't?"

I probably startled Joe with my markedly different, serene demeanor.

"I was just about to call you. I've thought about it and you're absolutely right. We do need to go to the police, and I'm ready."

Later we would agree that the second visit to the state police headquarters had at least offered the comfort of familiarity. It was a repeat of the first visit, only this time Joe was there with me from the start.

There was the same dour-looking desk officer, the same antiseptic waiting area in the lobby, and just like the previous time, we were informed that Grimaldi was unavailable. Joe tried to explain that he had spoken to the detective about an hour before and that we had been invited to come in. The desk officer glared at us with red-rimmed, watery eyes.

"So I guess he's not here right now," Joe said helplessly.

The officer kept up his stare, so Joe gave up and led me to the waiting area. "They're so friendly," he muttered. Even Joe's unremitting stoicism seemed on the verge of cracking. It was odd and rude, we both agreed as we waited, that Grimaldi would ignore an appointment he had just made. "He's just a weird duck," Joe grumbled.

In the end, Grimaldi kept us waiting ninety minutes. I used the time to show Joe the correspondence from Billy O'Brien.

"Well, this is pretty amazing," Joe said finally, as he straightened the sheaf of papers and carefully replaced them in the envelope. "Best of all, it's leverage."

I looked at him, puzzled. "What do you mean?"

"Grimaldi acts like Dennis Price is innocent, like he's some kind of choir boy. But this shows that the trial was a joke. The judge was on the take. Maybe we can get our friend Grimaldi to see that there may be more to this whole thing than he thinks."

When Grimaldi finally walked up, we had long since stopped watching for him. I jumped as I realized someone was standing over us. Joe and I gaped at him, momentarily silenced.

"How can I help you?" Grimaldi said flatly without a flicker of recognition.

Joe gave a nervous chuckle. "Remember us? The kidnapping and rape case with the Dennis Price connection? I called earlier and we set up an appointment to talk about some further developments."

"Ah, yes." Grimaldi was stone-faced. If he was embarrassed, he didn't show it. I thought he was bluffing. He remembered us perfectly well. If he didn't, he would have to have total amnesia or be the world's worst investigator, and neither seemed the case. He must be playing games, but to what end, I didn't know.

"Well, I suppose we should talk then."

Grimaldi led us to his office. This time it felt more claustrophobic and it reeked of onions. He must have been practically living there. Greasy crumpled wrappers and fast food boxes overflowed from a small wastebasket shoved in a corner.

This seemed out of character for someone who otherwise appeared obsessively neat. But then again, the detective was downright disheveled compared to the military grooming he presented in our previous interview. There were dark smudges under his eyes and he looked like he hadn't shaved for a few mornings. When he took off his inexpensive sports jacket and hung it on the back of his chair, I spotted perspiration stains on his shirt.

We took the two chairs on the perimeter of Grimaldi's desk. Joe launched into a long-winded description of the trips to Ohio and what he had found. I found myself wishing he would leave out a few of the smaller details and just get to the point. *He's nervous*, I thought. Not in character for Joe either. This case was getting to everyone.

I glanced at Grimaldi. He sat, impassive, listening. Once again, he fiddled with a ballpoint pen but didn't take any notes.

Joe told of Judith's sudden, unexplained death, our meetings with Judith's husband and her sister, and all the other
information he had compiled on Dennis Price. Finally, he told
him about the voice mails, the vandalism to my car that had
forced me into hiding, and the threatening letter I had received
in the mail.

"So, you see, it's a pattern of threats, really. If nothing else,
this has got to be considered harassment or stalking or something." Joe's voice had become patient and slow, as if he were
explaining things to a small child.

Grimaldi tapped the pen on the desk. Throughout the
entire interview, he had neither looked at nor addressed me.
Even when I outright stared at him, he avoided my gaze.

Joe was about to launch into the description of the letter
from Billy O'Brien when Grimaldi rose abruptly.

"Okay. Thanks for coming in." He bustled around the desk
to usher us out.

Spots of color appeared on Joe's cheekbones. "But wait, I
have something else—"

"Oh, I think I've heard enough." Grimaldi was standing at
the door, much like the campus security officer giving Deborah
and me the bum's rush so long ago. "We'll be in touch if we
need you."

I stood, hesitantly waiting for Joe, but he wouldn't budge.

"Let's see." Joe's voice was frosty. "We do your job for
you. We follow up on viable leads. At our expense, of course.
And all you have to say is, 'thanks for coming in.' That's just
great."

Nervous, I glanced from Joe to Grimaldi. Joe was fuming.
He seemed on the brink of taking a swing at the detective.
Grimaldi, who had wandered back to his seat behind the desk,
didn't seem bothered by Joe's anger. Instead, he appeared so

detached that I had the distinct feeling he was bored. Horrified, I saw the beginning of a yawn.

Joe saw it too and stopped talking. After an uncomfortable silence, Grimaldi folded his arms across his chest and addressed Joe.

"I know you think I don't have any sympathy for your girlfriend here. Well, maybe I don't." I might as well have not been in the room.

"Let me be clear. My job is to investigate a murder. A very specific murder. I can't be concerned about all these stories and soap operas about people in Ohio. I can't follow up on any of these other alleged crimes, especially ones outside of the state of Maryland."

"We weren't asking you to do anything about—" Joe started to protest but Grimaldi raised a hand to stop him.

"Now I will tell you what I can do. Or what I'm willing to do, let's say. In fact, I've already done it. I checked out your Mr. Dennis Price. I have to say, the thread is pretty thin. Not much to go on. Nothing to indicate he's been anything but a model citizen since arriving in Maryland. Nonetheless, just on the off chance that you're right, I've been working on getting a DNA sample from him and comparing it with a DNA sample that we've been able to extract from our state park victim."

Grimaldi coughed politely into his fist. "Unfortunately," he said, "Mr. Price has not been cooperative. Nor have my superiors, the state's attorney office, nor the judges in this area, when you get right down to it. Everyone thinks that the connection is tenuous at best."

I blanched. "You're saying that the judge is taking his side in this?"

"I'm saying no such thing," Grimaldi barked. He had at last turned to address me, but it was with all the warmth of an attack dog. I shriveled against the chair.

Grimaldi turned back to Joe and began explaining things calmly, as if Joe were the one who had questioned the judicial system and deserved an explanation.

"I'm merely describing a process that frequently occurs. The authorities must move cautiously and only with reasonable justification. They don't want someone falsely accused. The state could be hit with a wrongful something-or-other lawsuit. Now it would be a lot easier if the suspect provided a sample voluntarily. But, according to Mr. Price's lawyer, his declining to provide a DNA sample has nothing to do with his guilt, and everything to do with his civil rights."

"It could also mean he's got something to hide." Joe sounded more like his normal, mild self.

"True." Grimaldi was surprisingly agreeable. "Unfortunately, it doesn't make much of a difference now. Mr. Price is nowhere to be found. I think he took off after I paid him a visit."

We gaped at him. "What?" I whispered.

"And you don't think that's a sign of guilt?" Joe asked, incredulous.

Grimaldi shrugged. "His lawyer claims he knows where Price is. He says he's within reach if needed. Just 'hidden from view' is how he put it. And of course, being that Price has not been arrested or is he even officially a suspect"—he shrugged again—"he's free to go where he pleases."

Grimaldi resumed tapping his pen on the desk, then spoke suddenly. "You're saying you got strange voice mails?"

He grunted at our response, then spent a long minute in deep thought. In an abrupt shift, he turned upbeat, even stretching his mouth in what passed as a smile. "Here's a possibility: Dennis Price could still be in the area but laying low. Maybe waiting to pounce."

"That's exactly what we're talking about." Joe leaned forward intently. "We're worried that he could—"

"Okay, okay, I get it. What I mean is, we could use this to our advantage. We could flush him out. If it is Price doing this stalking and threatening, sooner or later he'll emerge. We just have to be ready to catch him when he tries to commit a crime. Then we will have valid cause to check his DNA against the state park victim. It's a win-win, really."

Joe stared at him. "That's risky. Do you really think it's our best option?"

Grimaldi nodded enthusiastically.

A small, strangled noise escaped from my throat. I had trouble believing that Joe would seriously consider using me as bait. I tried to listen to them discuss strategy, but I was too distraught to make sense of their conversation. Before I knew it, they were wrapping up and arranging to continue their discussion in a few days. I think I made a weak-voiced protest that was drowned out by general chair scraping and manly backslaps. Then we were shepherded from the room amid Grimaldi's promises to be in touch.

Three days went by, then five, with no word from Grimaldi.

Joe had been relieved and almost giddy on the way home from the police station, rehashing the conversation and why the plan they had come up with made sense. In turn, I tried to convince him why I hated the idea. Eventually I gave up. I concentrated on not being resentful, reminding myself that Joe was acting in what he thought was my best interest. Still, as the week went on, I couldn't help but feel relieved that there was no communication from Grimaldi.

Meanwhile, Joe slid into despondency, then anger. At first he would merely glare at the phone each time he passed it. Then he began to voice his complaints aloud. I did my best to ignore it. Occasionally, just for some relief, I would go in the bedroom and take out the Billy O'Brien letter and try to recapture the serenity and strength I felt the first time I read it.

"I don't understand why he won't follow up. This is ridiculous." Joe pushed away his half-finished dinner.

"By 'he,' I suppose you mean Grimaldi," I commented mildly as I halfheartedly sawed my steak into small pieces I probably wouldn't eat. I looked up and waved my fork at Joe as he hopped up and wandered into the living room. "Come back," I called. "You need to eat."

"I'm not hungry. And, yes, I meant Grimaldi. I can't believe that guy."

I tucked a very small bite of food in my mouth and, chewing slowly, considered our situation. It was an eternal circle. I should be willing to—I should even want to—track down Dennis Price. But the fact was, I was just as glad to let Dennis Price remain "hidden from view." Billy O'Brien was wrong. I wasn't strong and brave; I was plain scared.

Still chewing, I picked up my water glass and tried to flush down the food. The lump in my throat wasn't helping.

Joe was staring. "What's the matter?"

I swallowed hard and carefully laid down my fork. "Personally, I'm not upset that we haven't heard from Grimaldi."

"Why?" He was genuinely surprised.

"Because, well, because I've done my duty. We have. Haven't we, by going to the police?" I looked at him, pleading. "I guess I was hoping that our information might help the police catch him and that I wouldn't have to do anything more."

"But Grimaldi said they would—"

I held up a hand. "I know what he said. But forgive me if I have a hard time believing that the police will swoop in before any harm comes to me. I don't have a lot of positive experiences to draw from."

Joe's look of guilt immediately made me feel bad. I sighed. "I appreciate everything you've done. I really do. But if it is Dennis Price who's stalking me, police or no police, I don't feel safe." I glanced down at my hands. They were shaking. "Look at me. I'm a mess."

Joe seemed to accept this fearfulness of mine. In the following days, he stopped speculating about Grimaldi and then, much to my relief, dropped the subject altogether. I was fine with pretending that everything was back to normal even if it wasn't.

About a week later, we sat eating chicken pot pie at the little drop-leaf table that I insisted on using for dinner because it felt more formal than the kitchen table. We were chatting about ordinary things, and I was considering how I generally never ate chicken pot pie and that I really needed to start going with Joe to do the grocery shopping so we would have palatable food in the house. *You just can't depend on men in a supermarket*, I was thinking when Joe mentioned quite casually that he had called Grimaldi that afternoon.

The announcement caused me to jolt involuntarily. Some gravy slopped off my plate, staining the placemat.

"What did he say?" I reached for a sip of water.

"Oh, he's full of charm, that guy," Joe said contemptuously as he gazed past me. I could tell from his expression that he was reliving the phone conversation. "He gave me some bullshit story about how his boss assigned him this other big case just after we visited him, so he's been working on that morning, noon, and night. Our case, apparently, has taken a backseat."

Joe picked up a piece of crusty bread and ripped off a chunk with his incisors. He chewed, breathing heavily.

I pushed my pot pie around my plate with my fork.

"I was thinking . . ." Joe stopped.

I stopped and put my fork down, afraid to say anything.

"I think," he said finally, "that Grimaldi is more interested than he lets on. But I agree with you that we can't depend on the police. Not even for protection. So"—he cleared his throat—"what if we defended ourselves?"

"What?"

"Well, it's obvious that this guy Price is circling you like a shark. So, if we can't convince the police to give us protection, we'll protect ourselves. I've been happy to be your bodyguard, and you've been willing to stay holed up here, but that's not enough. We've got to get you ready. You need self-defense training, firearms training, the works."

"Firearms . . . as in a gun?" I blanched.

"Yes, a gun. Maybe guns, plural. Price preys on the weak. He may be aware that I'm around, but he's probably willing to bide his time. I know it frightens you to think this, but sooner or later, he'll get his chance and strike. But the last thing he would suspect is that any of his victims would be locked and loaded." He looked at me hopefully. "What do you think?"

What I had been thinking was that it would be best to ignore the whole thing. That I had made a serious error getting involved in this mess to begin with. I looked at Joe. His proposal was overwhelming. Was he hoping that I would agree to self-defense training or vigilante justice? I wasn't sure.

But I couldn't deny his logic. I had to face the fact that there was no putting this genie back in the bottle.

I struggled for a few moments with what to say, then reached for his hand.

"What I think is that when it comes to Dennis Price, I can't seem to think clearly. Left to my own devices, I would hide out here forever or until he came and got me. So, thank God we have one good thinker among us."

Joe was trying not to look triumphant, but he could barely suppress his grin. I resumed my pretense of eating. I half-listened to a now elated Joe make plans for my protection and thought of the silky braided Chinese handcuffs we had as children: the harder you pulled to escape, the tighter they became.

Almost as soon as I agreed to Joe's crazy plan, I regretted the decision. This series of events kept twisting and turning into knots I felt I would never be able to undo. But not only did there seem no graceful way out, but I also kept coming back to the fact that without Joe, I was totally on my own, and I couldn't face that.

Over the following weeks, I dutifully followed his lead and accompanied him wherever he wanted me to go. I didn't have any better ideas. Any number of times I wanted to point out that we hadn't heard from the stalker in weeks, but I knew I was grasping at straws, pretending that everything was okay. There were times I was tempted to call a halt to all of it, but something always stopped me from questioning Joe's approach. There was something about his belief that the danger was real, and that we had a shot at beating it.

Joe found a self-defense class, taught by a martial arts instructor and attended by a group of pasty and scared-looking individuals. Joe drove me to classes two evenings a week. I desperately tried to memorize all the moves, but I was certain I would instantly forget them when they were most needed.

But when Joe started planning weekend trips to the shooting range at a gun-and-hunt club in the middle of nowhere, that's when I balked. No matter what kind of faith Joe—or

Billy O'Brien—had in me, this was going too far. I made several attempts to dissuade Joe from the shooting part of the training program, but he was focused only on his mission. Nothing could penetrate his single-mindedness.

"Are you absolutely sure this is necessary?" I complained for the third time during the long drive to the range. "I really can't see myself doing target practice, let alone using a gun in a real situation," I grumbled.

"You'll see" was all he said.

I followed Joe into the front office of the shooting range with my new gun, a .22-caliber pistol, feeling like a fraud. The lean, grizzled man sitting in the paneled office eyed us with suspicion. I cringed, waiting for him to jump up and confront me because he could tell at a glance that I didn't belong to his Second Amendment rights world.

"Can I help you folks?" he said roughly.

Joe explained that we wanted to go through some practice rounds. Without a word, the man stood up and led us on a long, circuitous route through the building, which was more complex than it appeared from the exterior. We reached our destination via a rear entrance that led to an outdoor patio shaded by a green plastic canopy. The deck overlooked a field with some scrubby trees and bushes in the distance. A target had been set up at the edge of the field at a distance I guessed was about thirty yards. This seemed to be the shooting range. It wasn't what I had pictured. I had imagined something in a dark basement with targets painted on silhouettes, like in the movies.

The shooting-range proprietor handed me a gun, a higher-caliber weapon than my own handgun, and waved an arm toward the target.

"Before you use your gun, try this one. It's a Glock. Think you can handle it? Just aim for the target, and no more than four shots. Okay?" He didn't wait for a response but moved to the side near where Joe was standing.

I looked at the target, then down at the gun. I lifted the weapon and started firing.

Wait—did I fire four times or five? I felt panicky. He specifically said only four shots. I looked at Joe and then at the man. Both were staring at me.

"Well. We know what you're getting for Christmas," the proprietor said.

I was confused, but Joe laughed.

"I don't know whether we should continue. I'm not very good at this." I looked around for some place to lay down the Glock, but there was nothing but the concrete slab we were standing on.

"Are you kidding? You just hit the bull's-eye." Joe moved over and gently extricated the gun from my grip.

I leaned over and whispered in his ear. "But I couldn't do that to a person. Not even him."

Although Joe nodded, I don't think he believed me. He turned to the proprietor. "She's taking martial arts as well," he said, as if this explained it anything.

But the man had lost interest in my anxiety. "Okay, next practice round," he grunted and began reloading the weapons. He paused and looked at me. "You'll get used to it. You might even start to like it."

The weeks went on. Joe continued to take me to martial arts classes. I completed the self-defense course, and on weekends we practiced at the shooting range. We were planning for an assault, and my apartment became like a bunker. Joe would come home every day with another idea, such as more dead bolts for the front door, or alarms for the windows, even though

I was on the top floor of the building. One day Joe brought home three pepper spray canisters for me. I looked at them, dubious, wondering if he thought I really needed this much in reinforcements.

While Joe was at the office, I tried to distract myself with my painting or housework. I became obsessive about cleaning the apartment, often spending hours vacuuming and polishing the furniture. I wrote a long letter back to Billy O'Brien, care of the same attorney who had forwarded his communication to me. I told him about Dennis Price and how he may be continuing to commit crimes, maybe even doing far worse than what he had done to me, and how he might be stalking me. I wrote that whatever Billy decided to do would be okay, because it wasn't fair that these horrible things should have to go on and on and on. But maybe, I said, things would work out one day for both of us.

I had Joe mail the letter and hoped that what I wrote was true.

November ended with a quiet Thanksgiving. My mother had called earlier in the month to say that she had plans to attend a special yoga camp in Arizona and wouldn't be able to have Thanksgiving dinner with me and my brother. That was fine with me, as I didn't want to leave the apartment anyway. During the phone call, I thought several times about confiding in my mother all that had happened. But she sounded so tired and distracted, that I held my tongue.

Joe and I spent our holiday eating a small roast chicken at our little drop-leaf table. I thanked God for Joe and for the fact that I was still okay. I suspected that one had something to do with the other—since Joe had moved in, the threatening phone calls and letters had stopped. This was not only comforting, but it gave me confidence in his strategy. He had had the right idea all along. I shouldn't have questioned him.

We bowed our heads over the dinner plates and I prayed that all our precautions would prove unnecessary. But if that was not to be, I prayed for the strength to get through the ordeal that was to come.

One day just before the start of winter, as I was concentrating on a new watercolor, I thought about Billy's letter. At first I tried to ignore the impulse to get it out and read it. I had read it so many times, I just about had it memorized. But after I had cleaned my brushes and pulled off my painting smock, I found myself retrieving my silk-covered keepsake box from the bedroom closet and carrying it to the kitchen. I spread the letter out on the table, just as I had done the first time.

When I finished, I sat back and stared at the wallpaper's familiar pattern. The letter always seemed to have a powerful effect on me, probably far more than Billy ever guessed. With every reading, I was able to find new nuggets of truth. Like the idea that there's no point in whining about being tossed around by some nameless forces of destruction. Or the notion that we all have a choice. You can choose what to do with what life deals you. You can roll up in a ball and die, or you can live in spite of it, and maybe become a better, stronger person because of it. And here was a crazy thought, you might even help others who are going through the same thing. It's your choice.

I looked back at the loose-leaf pages and sat back with such force against the wooden back of the kitchen chair that it gave a loud creak. Maybe it was time to apply some clarity to my thinking. Even though I had been doing nothing but mulling over this problem for months, I hadn't spent one minute thinking about it clearly.

When I first realized the similarities between the state park murder victim and what had happened to me, I had the

prepare in case it all started again. Joe kept up this commentary while shaving in the morning, in his calls from the office during the day, and while eating his dinner.

"How was your day at work?" I noted that he hadn't eaten much. I picked up the bowl of mashed potatoes and handed it to him. He set it down again without taking any.

"My day? It was fine. You know, I was thinking that Price may be waiting for a time when I'm not here. That's when he might act, because ultimately he's a coward." Joe threw me a look over the little table. "I'm serious. He's too chicken to go after men, or to go after women when men are around. Women are his prey. And ninety-nine percent of them aren't going to fight back. That's why you've got to fight back. It will give you leverage. You'll see."

I folded my arms in a deliberate motion. "If he's just waiting for you not to be here to pounce on me, then why doesn't he show up when you're at work? Why didn't he do something when you were in Ohio? Or before you started staying here?"

"He's not going to take the chance because somehow he knows our routine. He knows I'll be back at the end of the day. I don't know why he kept his distance when I was away. Unfortunately he's just biding his time, I think, waiting for me to take a business trip or something."

Joe dropped his head but not before I spotted sweat glistening on his upper lip. He quickly wiped it with his napkin.

"Joe, do you have to go on a business trip? If you do"—I paused and swallowed—"I understand. It's okay."

Joe wiped each of his fingers slowly on his napkin. "Yes. I do need to travel," he said finally. "My boss said I had better go if I want to keep my job." He looked up. "But it's not okay."

I opened my mouth to protest, but Joe talked over me. "It can't be justified. I've been trying to think of a way around it.

Maybe I can convince someone else from the office to go in my place."

"Joe." I stopped and looked at him. He was so tightly wound, he was ready to spin off like a runaway top. "You just said that Price probably wasn't going to act until he has an opportunity when you're not here. Not only do I think you're right about that, but I think I'm ready. I *am* ready. After all these weeks of preparation I should be. Anyway, I've been wondering how long we could keep up this imprisoned lifestyle."

"You're not in prison." Joe was defensive.

"In the sense that I'm terrified to go anywhere alone, I'm imprisoning myself. But that doesn't change things. Also," I leaned toward him, "I want to stop putting this burden on you. It's not fair to you to make you my full-time protector."

"Speak for yourself. I like the job of guarding your body." Joe tried a weak grin.

"You know what I mean."

We fell silent. I drew designs on the table with the handle of my fork. "Part of me," I said finally, "would just like to get the inevitable over with. We've done all the planning and training and preparation."

Our eyes swept over the apartment, and rested on the door with its array of locks, chains, and the large deadbolt that we had installed. I had gotten in the habit of checking that the key to the deadbolt, the lock that could only be opened by a key—even on the inside—was safely on its ribbon around my neck. I felt for the key as we talked.

The discussion seemed to help Joe, who appeared to breathe easier. I even managed to wrangle a promise that he would at least think seriously about going on the trip. Even if I hadn't quite convinced Joe, I had managed to more or less convince myself. I no longer felt terrified at the prospect of being left alone. After all, I was alone in the apartment all day, every day. I did need to consider the worst-case scenario, that what Joe expected to happen would happen, but preparation would give me the advantage of surprise. Joe was right that Dennis Price would not be expecting someone ready to fight back.

In an odd sort of fantasy, I almost hoped I would the chance to face off against him again. Only this time it would be different. I would have everything planned out. I would be in control.

Again I touched the key that hung near my collarbone. Joe was right about something else, too. Preparation meant survival. And, by God, I was going to survive.

Our usual tendency was to talk everything to death, but during the next two weeks Joe and I reached an unspoken agreement: don't discuss the business trip. Other than his anticlimactic, almost sheepish announcement that he was indeed going, and some curt communication of travel arrangements, the topic was studiously avoided. Joe did mention that a decision had been made to make it a longer trip—Sunday as a travel day, then four days of client meetings, before returning on Friday. I tried hard not to show my disappointment with this news.

As we floated through the days, acting like everything was fine, in my mind the pending trip began to take the form of a large mass of garbage, rotting in the middle of the living room. We tiptoed around it, pretending it didn't stink.

Joe waited until the last moment but he was the one to broach the topic. It was the morning of his departure and he was standing with his packed suitcase in the little foyer by my front door.

"I must be out of my mind to be doing this." Worry lines crisscrossed his brow.

"I'll be okay." I had been expecting some eleventh-hour doubts from Joe, so I had been steeling myself in the hope of sounding strong. Instead, it came out weak and pathetic. I made a face, trying to get him to smile, but he didn't bite. If anything, he looked more miserable.

"Here's the thing," I said impulsively. "Now that there's the possibility of actually facing him again, I'm thinking that maybe it was meant to be." I became confused at the alarm in Joe's face. "I mean, I think I can handle it," I added hastily.

"I never intended for you to have to take matters in your own hands. I was just trying to make sure you could defend yourself and I was hoping . . ." His voice trailed off.

"Hoping what?"

He addressed the floor. "Hoping that I would have the chance to take care of this problem for you. I wanted to flush him out, that's the honest truth. I thought I would be here to be able to do that." He gave his suitcase a kick. "I hate that I have to leave."

I was taken aback by his vehemence. I spoke rapidly before he could say anything more.

"Well, you have to go, and I have to stay. But I know one thing. I'm not going to sit here and let this whole thing, the fear and the guilt, take over and eat me alive. I'm going to do what I have to do."

Joe looked doubtful. I kissed him and gave him a gentle nudge toward the door before he could see that I was scared out of my wits. Still, he hesitated at the threshold before he finally, reluctantly moved, allowing me to shut the door.

The door clicked shut and I stared at it, a little shocked that it had actually happened. Joe's voice came through, muffled. "Go ahead and lock up. I'll listen for it."

I clicked the deadbolt in place, set the chains, turned the

last key, and then leaned my head against the cold metal of the door to listen to Joe's footsteps recede down the corridor. My heart sank with each step. I had to stop myself from undoing all the locks and running after him.

I closed my eyes. Something told me I might never see Joe again, and I was suddenly filled with overwhelming regret. I regretted not running after him, not saying I love you the previous night, not saying it a thousand times before.

I slumped to the floor. I couldn't think of what else I could do, so I tucked my head in my arms and began to pray.

Because Joe had been booked on one of the first flights of the day, he left so early that it could have counted as the middle of the night. Once he was gone, though, I couldn't even think about going back to bed.

I made a pot of coffee and lingered at the kitchen table, staring at my all-too-familiar wall. One cup of coffee after another grew cold before I remembered to drink. My thoughts ping-ponged.

If I hadn't been thinking clearly about Dennis Price before, I might not have been thinking straight about Joe either. I looked at my surroundings, and all I felt was Joe's absence. Ordinarily I didn't mind so much being alone. I knew he would return. But this was no ordinary day. This felt like emptiness, as though I might rattle around the apartment endlessly.

Even with this awful empty feeling, I couldn't stop the thought from creeping in—why would someone go to the lengths that Joe had these past months? It had to be more than just being a good Samaritan, or even the mirroring of his sister's disappearance. Maybe, I thought, dumbstruck, maybe it was because he loved me.

This hadn't occurred to me before and, in a way, it was more emotion than I could deal with at the moment. I moved my coffee mug in restless circles on the table, then pushed it away sharply. It slid right off the table and crashed on the floor. I stared at it. Mooning over Joe was ludicrous, I decided, and not only because I had waited until now, five minutes after he left, to reach this conclusion. The timing was bad. Terrible, in fact. This was the moment we had been preparing for, and it would make a lot more sense for me to focus on the possible appearance of Dennis Price than to sit around wondering whether my boyfriend loved me.

I stood. I would think about that later, but first things first.

I cleaned up the mess on the kitchen floor, then headed to the bathroom to shower. I hesitated, then went back to the kitchen and dragged a chair into the bathroom, wedging the top of it under the locked doorknob. "There. Try to get in now." I said aloud with far more bravado than I felt.

When the phone rang I was still in the locked and barricaded bathroom, drying my hair. The phone had probably been ringing for a while before I heard it over the noise of the hair dryer.

"Hello?" I was breathless by the time I grabbed the phone. I clutched my robe awkwardly around me. None of this seemed careful or cautious. It could be Dennis Price calling, for all I knew.

It was Joe.

"Are you okay? You sound a little harried."

"I'm fine. I was just in the bathroom, taking a shower." I cradled the phone on my shoulder, simultaneously trying to straighten my bathrobe and push my still-damp hair from my face. "Are you calling from the road? This is a little earlier than you planned to call. I really appreciate your checking in," I added hastily. "It's just, you know, I'm glad I got to the phone so that you wouldn't worry if I didn't answer." That's right, I cringed. Go ahead and criticize.

"It is earlier than what we planned. But my plane just landed and I thought I'd give you a call. My fault for not accounting for hygiene breaks in the planning process." He chuckled.

"Listen, Joe . . ." I hesitated, then lost my nerve. "Well. I'm glad you called . . ."

"That's good." Joe sounded bemused. "I'd better go," he added. "The next time I call will be at the appointed hour. So don't go out to the store or anything."

That was our standing joke. I laughed and, instantly, the awkwardness disappeared.

I had to admit it. Joe's unexpected call perked me up. I hung up and looked around the apartment like I had just awakened from a long nap. *I have to keep busy,* I thought. *Maybe even more than that—I have to keep watch.* I resolved to be as watchful as possible and make Joe proud. And if Dennis Price didn't make an appearance, and I was simply dead tired by the time Joe returned, that would make me happy.

I wandered from room to room, resisting the urge to get out the duster and mop. It wouldn't do to wear myself out. I settled on distracting myself with art. I went to the studio and stared at my latest project, an oil painting.

Ordinarily this time of year, early winter, was not the best time to try to use natural light. It was early afternoon and sunlight streamed through the studio's large skylight, thin and refracted. Even though it would be gone before long, the light was perfect at this moment for the scene I was paint-ing: a snowy road curving alongside a rock-studded creek. Bare branches formed a mosaic above the road, and interspersed among them were tufts of golden leaves still clinging to a few trees. I was basing this painting on photographs Joe and I had taken on a walk one frosty Saturday in late November, the one weekend we had taken a break from shooting practice. I had been excited by the discovery of the golden leaves.

"They're definitely not birch." I had clambered down the embankment for a better camera angle. "I've never seen this type of tree before."

"My guess is pin oak. Something that holds on to its leaves all winter."

Joe's words bounced against the rocks and water. We both stopped and listened to their reverberation. Then once again all was beautiful and still. Snow from an unexpected early snowfall that morning mounded on the large tree branches and a few of the rocks, in sharp contrast to the inky black water of the creek. The place was desolate, but there was something beautiful, almost elegant, about the gilded leaves. A remembrance of the last vestiges of autumn. I was drawn to them. They were hanging by a thread, and so was I.

Ordinarily, I had no problem losing myself in my work. But I was distracted and didn't accomplish much. Twice the phone rang, both times Joe checking in, right on schedule.

The day wound down with agonizing slowness, but I was dreading the approaching nightfall. Anything could happen then.

At about four o'clock, I put the painting aside. With the solstice so near, twilight was quick to take hold in late afternoon. Even with the skylight, there wasn't enough light, and it was pointless to try to work with lamps.

After I cleaned and stowed my equipment, I dragged myself into the living room. I was suddenly exhausted to the point that I couldn't keep my eyes open. If the idea was to stay up and wait this thing out, I hadn't planned very well, what with the little sleep I got the previous night, followed by the early start in the morning.

I was tempted to stretch out on the sofa but I knew that was dangerous. Instead I brewed a pot of coffee. I watched the brown liquid drip into the pot and reminded myself that it was no different from cramming for exams in college.

I brought the mug of coffee to the living room and settled on the sofa in front of the coffee table. I looked around expectantly. Now what?

It was a good night to read the Psalms. I went to the bookcase and pulled down the Bible that had been my father's. Tucking my legs under me, I flipped through the Bible and was a little startled that it naturally fell open to one of my favorites, Psalm 27.

The Lord is my light and my salvation; whom should I fear?
The Lord is my life's refuge; of whom should I be afraid?
When evildoers come at me to devour my flesh, my foes and
*   my enemies themselves stumble and fall.*
One thing I ask of the Lord; this I seek:
To dwell in the house of the Lord all the days of my life . . .
For he will hide me in his abode in the day of trouble.

I read and reread it within the golden circle of light from the table lamp.

Wait for the Lord with courage.
Be stout-hearted, and wait for the Lord.

I looked up and glanced beyond the circle of incandescent lamp light. It might as well have been midnight, as dark as it was outside. Near the shortest point of the year, darkness dropped with a thud. *No wonder everyone tries to counteract it with Christmas lights*, I thought. I moved to the windows to close the blinds, and as I reached for them I had the oddest feeling of exposure, like I was on stage. I shook my head and again started to close the blinds. This time I was stopped by a gripping fear.

Someone was out there watching.

As fast as I could, I snapped the blinds shut and pulled the drapes back over them. I hadn't seen anyone, but I knew I was being watched as definitively as if a face were floating on the other side of the glass four stories above the ground.

I hurried back to the sofa to wrap myself in an afghan I kept folded there. But even curling up into a corner of the sofa and huddling under the blanket couldn't stop me from shivering.

There was a high-pitched cry, a sort of keening sound, coming from somewhere. Startled, I realized it was coming from me. I wasn't handling this well. No matter how much security I had—locks on the door and alarms on the windows—at the first whiff of trouble I was falling apart.

I pulled myself into a tight ball but my legs began to cramp. Untangling them, I got up, moving from room to room. I switched on every lamp and light fixture in the place. There was no point in pretending no one was home.

I looked around at the now-bright apartment and, feeling a little calmer, went over and perched on the edge of the sofa. It wasn't even a question anymore—I would have to keep vigil. I couldn't risk sleeping. I focused on taking deep breaths and not bringing the coffee back up.

The ring of the phone was like an alarm going off. I lunged for the phone at the far end of the sofa, if only to avoid having to listen to a second offensive ring.

"Are you okay?" Joe sounded anxious in reaction to my shrill voice.

"Yes, yes, of course." I was breathing heavily and nearly shouting, not sounding at all like a woman who had things under control. It was ridiculous to even pretend.

In any case, Joe wasn't fooled. "Reality has come crashing down on you, hasn't it?"

"I'm hanging in there. Just a—a momentary lapse, I guess you would call it."

"Did anything happen?"

"Not really. Well, I thought someone was watching me from the parking lot, but I was wrong. It's ridiculous, really."

There was a long silence.

"This trip was a bad idea. You're more important. And I'm not trying to imply you're weak or anything," he added hastily. "Anyone in your position . . . well, it's just not a good time for you to be alone."

A sigh expelled before I could catch it. "What if he never stops?" I wished I could take back the words as soon as I said them.

Joe didn't answer. He was probably considering this possibility as well. I decided to switch tactics.

"Sooner or later, I'm going to have to fend for myself. That's the reality."

More silence.

"I guess I just have to grow up," I said finally, embarrassed.

At last Joe reacted, with a halfhearted laugh. "All right, you win. But you're going to have to put up with being locked up there for the time being and not leave the apartment under any circumstances. When I get back, we'll work our way up to something approaching freedom."

CHAPTER EIGHTEEN

Winter Solstice 1998: Maryland

At least in the beginning, it took little effort to stay awake. Fatigue was quickly replaced by fear after the scare at the window. I had convinced myself that it had simply been my imagination, but real or not, it kept me alert and bolt upright all that first night.

When daylight arrived on the second day of Joe's trip, the dawn seeping around the edges of curtains I had drawn as tightly as possible across the windows, I was still at my post on the sofa. I remained wrapped in my blanket like a sausage, still staring with bleary eyes at the open Bible on my lap.

The departure of night gave me the courage to rise and head to the bathroom to wash up. But I wasn't quite courageous enough to take a shower. I thought of all those suspense movies where the hapless female victim is invariably attacked while in the shower. I could wedge a chair under the doorknob, like I had the day before, but with my new perspective that seemed so insufficient that it was foolhardy. I stood on the threshold of the bathroom for a full five minutes, debating what to do. In the end I settled for washing my face and hands and changing my clothes. It didn't make me feel the slightest bit refreshed.

Padding back to the living room, I flipped on the television out of habit, then immediately muted the sound. Listlessly, I watched the silent images sliding across the screen. I shut it off and looked around. I was too keyed up. The thought of working on my painting, reading, or even housework, seemed out of the question.

I let the remote control drop with a clatter on the coffee table and marched over to the windows. I pulled back the drapes and yanked up the blinds. Dust particles floated on a shaft of sunlight.

Here it was—morning—and he hadn't shown. Hallelujah! But there was no glory in having survived. The only thing Dennis Price's failure to appear the night before meant was that he might show up that night. Or the next one. Maybe he knew exactly how long Joe would be away. Or that I would be afraid to sleep with Joe gone. Maybe he was trying to exhaust me.

But how could he know? *Except that he seemed to know everything*, I answered myself.

I sank down again on the sofa, still untidy with my blanket strewn across it. I needed to reason through this.

I chewed my fingernails, ripping them off with abandon. Maybe we were overthinking this, Joe and I. This all could be an unnecessary exercise. Or, I reminded myself as I bit a nail so deeply that I drew blood, maybe it was just wishful thinking.

The truth, I felt in my gut, was that Price was out there somewhere and he would eventually show up. He might even be audacious enough to attack during the day. My eyes swiveled to the tall windows. I wouldn't be surprised if he came in broad daylight. Anything was possible.

That meant, I realized, heart sinking, that I had to be watchful not just at night, but during the daylight hours, too.

Wait for the Lord with courage, I repeated the psalm I had read over and over the previous night. Be vigilant and stout-hearted and wait for the Lord.

I managed to get through the second day, thanks to those watchwords and regular phone calls from Joe. I lived for those calls, waiting by the phone, staring at it and willing it to ring.

Joe was as faithful as he could be to our prearranged schedule. When he was meeting with a client, however, schedules were out of his control and he had to wait for the meeting to break before phoning. He had warned me that this would probably happen, but each time it did, he sounded distressed, like he had failed me. I told him I understood, and I did. Still, it was difficult to keep my jangled nerves in check. It was harder still to keep that from being apparent, even in a long-distance call.

I floated through the long hours. Sometimes I tried painting. Usually I gave up after a short while. I often kept the television on, just for background noise. I spent most of my time wandering about the apartment.

There was one positive aspect, I suppose. My emotions had cooled significantly from their boiling cauldron state. Unfortunately, they had hardened into one single frozen mass of fear. More than once I thought about calling my mother, but we hadn't talked about anything serious since that conversation when I first realized that Dennis Price was still attacking women and my mother claimed I was imagining the connection. I hadn't explained how far Joe and I had taken things and never told her that we went to Ohio to check things out, let alone what we had discovered. Now I wasn't so much concerned that my mother would again dismiss my fears—I was sure that if I explained all that had transpired, she would believe it to be real—but at this point . . . well, what could she do? She would end up as terrorized as I was.

I didn't sleep. I wasn't even tempted to doze off, not even at night. I seemed to have crossed an invisible threshold where sleep was an impossibility. By the third day it was taking a toll. I caught a glimpse of myself in the bathroom mirror and was startled by the hollow-eyed, frightening zombie I saw.

During the whole preparation period, during all my classes and training and practice, I never questioned the hypothesis that Dennis Price was stalking me. But without Joe's steady presence, I began to wonder whether we had just been paranoid, whether the state police detective had been right, and we were wrong. But as the days and nights of waiting wore on, I again grew convinced that he *would* appear. It was practically carved in stone for me. Price would show up.

Joe never suffered any doubts about Dennis Price's eventual emergence. On the contrary, as the week went on, the more anxious he became, and the more willing he was to abandon his stoicism. By the third day, he was obviously restless and unhappy.

"I see no point in these endless meetings. It's bullshit if you ask me. I can't wait to get out of here." It wasn't the first time Joe had made these statements in this particular phone conversation. But I could barely process what he said. Exhaustion was setting in. I weaved as I stood by the wall phone in the kitchen, suddenly dizzy and nauseated. I sank in a chair. Joe's raised voice, now with a panicky edge, penetrated my fog. I realized he must have been waiting for an answer from me.

"Quinn! Are you there? Is something going on?"

"I'm here." After a moment I added dully, "Sorry. Haven't gotten much sleep."

"You probably haven't eaten either." He sounded accusatory.

"I ate." It took effort to mount even this pathetic protest.

Joe drew a long breath. "Look. You do have to be on alert, but you can't go on like this. If you're that sleep-deprived, how good are your reactions and thought processes going to be if something does happen?"

He waited a moment, but I couldn't form a coherent answer through the fog, so he went on. "Why don't you consider getting some sleep during the day?"

I finally mustered the energy to respond. But I was horrified to hear how slurred my words were. I sounded drunk.

"You don't think he's brazen enough to show up in daylight?" I propped an arm on the back of the chair for support.

"You have to weigh the odds," he said. "You're too weak right now to fight off a kitten. Think about at least taking a nap. You can restore some of your energy." He paused. "And for God's sake, eat something."

I managed, with difficulty, to get the phone back on its hook and to twist around to look at the wall clock. I held the chair for support like an old woman.

Squinting at the clock, I tried to organize my thoughts. Four o'clock. It must be four in the afternoon on—was it the third day? Joe was supposed to return Saturday. Could I hold out with no sleep for three more days? I realized the answer was no. I had once read that it was possible to go insane or even die from lack of sleep. Maybe this is what Dennis Price was trying to do, kill me through the exhaustion of waiting for him.

I stumbled toward the bedroom.

It was unlikely he would show up at four in the afternoon, I rationalized, unless he was coming for tea. I didn't even have the energy to smile at my weak joke. I set the alarm clock for ten and fell into bed with the sensation of falling onto a cloud.

I woke before the alarm. I was instantly awake in the dark room, aware that for some reason, I had jerked my foot up in a sudden movement. I felt pain, something had hurt my foot, something had caused me to yank it away from the bottom of the bed.

I sat up and stared, frozen, at the blanket, which I could see in spite of the dark, windowless room.

My bed was on fire.

For the first time in his career, possibly for the first time in his life, state police investigator Michael Grimaldi was experiencing self-doubts. It was this damn murder case. His superiors had written it off—he had no viable leads—and the public, with the attention span the size of a gnat, had lost interest. The media also no longer focused on the headless dead girl found in the state park, since there were no new angles to pursue and plenty of other sensational stories to cover. Ordinarily it would have suited Grimaldi just fine to have the media off his back. But the lack of public pressure was making it easy for those in the upper echelons of the state police, Grimaldi's bosses, to ignore the whole thing. Let it go, they told Grimaldi. They loaded him with other cases and special projects. Technically, he was still the lead investigator in the state park murder, but his superiors made it clear that they wanted him to spend no more time on it.

But Grimaldi couldn't let it go. He managed to find time to work the other cases and finish his assignments. Mostly on his own time, he continued to pursue the state park case. He told himself that it was because unsolved cases bothered him. Other cops may be okay with loose strings hanging all over the place, but he wasn't. It was like how he had to watch the end of every movie, no matter how bad the film.

What really plagued him was the fear that he was responsible for leaving it unsolved. He couldn't have pursued all the right leads; he must have missed some clues. Grimaldi wasn't used to things left this way. Since he was a boy, he had been certain that he would go into law enforcement, specifically criminal investigation. His gift for it translated into confidence, if not arrogance. But unlike his previous investigations, when he was sure-handed and trusted his instincts, this time he was left with the feeling, nagging and tugging at him, that he had let the bad guy slip away. Even worse: the bad guy in question had not disappeared, was not on the run or was being elusive in any way. Dennis Price was right there, tantalizingly close.

Grimaldi had developed an absolute certainty that Dennis Price was his state park perpetrator. Price may have committed other crimes, but they weren't Grimaldi's concern. He had this one case to solve.

Unfortunately, Grimaldi had no evidence to link Price to the murder, circumstantial or otherwise. Hell, he still lacked probable cause for a search warrant. He certainly had insufficient grounds to force a DNA sample, according to the various judges he had contacted. Grimaldi had, in a word, nothing.

He knew he should forget about Price and write off the case. The girl was dead. Nothing was going to bring her back. Not that the victim was his primary concern either. Grimaldi made it a practice to disassociate himself from all that.

He kept going back to the fact that a DNA sample in hand should have been enough evidence to turn over a decent case to the prosecutor's office and gain a conviction. Without it, he was sunk, and Price knew it. Which was why, as long as

Price had his high-powered defense team, Grimaldi was not going to have access to one molecule of Dennis Price's DNA.

In recent weeks, Grimaldi had been forced to give up badgering various members of the Maryland judiciary and state attorney's office. After several firmly worded warnings from his supervisor failed to stop him, Grimaldi was called into the office of the major who ran the state police command for a brief, rather unpleasant conversation. And mostly one-sided, Grimaldi recalled. The upshot was that Grimaldi wasn't going to be told again. He was still on the case—for the moment— but he was to leave Dennis Price alone. The major was not about to put up with any more phone calls from Price's lawyer.

So here he was, officially on, but actually off, the case. Politically expedient, he thought. Not that he gave a rat's ass about politics.

Grimaldi thought there had to be another way to resolve the case. He began researching other cold cases, especially ones that might bear a similarity, however remote, to his state park murder. Crimes in which crude tattoos were carved into the flesh of the victims. But he knew it was dangerous to focus on only one aspect, especially the aspect that happened to be the obsession of Quinn Carlisle.

To keep things quiet, he worked alone, in secret. It hadn't been difficult lately because his coworkers had learned to steer clear of him and his bad humor, especially with his fall from grace with the top brass. He started his search methodically, combing the crime databases for Maryland and Delaware. Nothing stood out. A few grisly crimes, but nothing that caused a jolt in his gut. That's what he was looking for.

He decided to expand his search to Pennsylvania, where Quinn Carlisle had been kidnapped and raped, and Ohio, Price's home state. This was more difficult as these two states were not yet computerized. Pennsylvania in particular, consisting of mile upon mile of hick towns and rural areas between the anchor cities of Philadelphia and Pittsburgh, was light-years away from having a centralized database. This forced Grimaldi to be more strategic, focusing on western Pennsylvania near the Ohio border, and tracking down the local police chief in certain cases in order to pick his brain. A few times he took a day off so he could drive up to a town and thumb through their files. It took weeks, but he managed to set up a network of state police barracks and some local police departments sympathetic to his mission. Once in a while, someone would remember or hear about a potentially important case and call him. It seemed that it would be just a matter of time before he would strike pay dirt.

His first break came in a call from a tough-sounding ex-cop from a Pittsburgh suburb. Grimaldi had contacted him the previous week, having been referred by another police chief from the same area. The man on the other end of the phone had once been a small-town police chief, he informed Grimaldi, but after retirement he had missed "the action," as he put it. He was sort of a consultant, he said. For Grimaldi's purposes, the guy was perfect: intrigued by the mystery, experienced in police work, and with plenty of time to look for a needle in a haystack. In fact, the eight-year-old case he had found was from a town nowhere near his. It had occurred in a small community in the northern part of the state once known for coal and now known, if it was for anything, for hunting.

The cop was excited about his find. So was Grimaldi, though he didn't let on. He listened, taking careful notes, cradling the phone with his shoulder and interrupting once or twice to ask questions.

Grimaldi considered asking him to make a copy of the file and mail it to him. That might be a lot to ask, but it never hurt to pose the question. "So this victim . . ." he asked to get the man back on track, "she looked younger than she actually was?"

Indeed she had. The dental hygienist had been thirty-one but could have passed for nineteen or twenty. Apparently she had made it her life's mission to find a husband, and she had been going about it in a dangerous way, frequenting rough bars. Friends said she had started picking up men, often strangers. No one had been shocked when she turned up dead.

It was assumed that the man who had strangled her had been among her list of one-night stands. But even though any number of people had seen her at her favorite bar the last night she was alive, no one could recall her leaving with anyone. In fact, the female bartender—who remembered the victim sitting alone the entire night at the bar—was ready to swear that the victim had left alone. She might have been a little tipsy, but she was fine. While she might have been fine then, she wasn't the following morning. That was when she was found in a dumpster.

Two elements of this seemingly run-of-the-mill case caused the gruff cop to call Grimaldi: the word *slut* was carved into the soft skin of the victim's chest, apparently postmortem, and the body was discovered minus hands.

The tip triggered in Grimaldi a fresh burst of frenetic energy. In every spare moment, he called his police contacts again. The effort began to pay off. After prodding from Grimaldi, most of the contacts started researching old files. A few became intrigued and really began to dig. Another case, in which a dead young woman's body was found with a crude sort of tattoo, surfaced in Ohio.

A gradual awareness grew in Grimaldi. How many more cases were there total, he wondered, if these cases had been uncovered through haphazard research and luck? These murders might have their own sensational aspect in the small communities where they had occurred, but that's where the news had stopped. The crimes wouldn't have made it to a crime database because they went back seven or eight years ago. There was no such thing, certainly in rural communities, as a shared law enforcement effort. No one was connecting the dots.

Neither case ended with anyone being charged. There weren't even any serious suspects. One eyewitness thought she saw the Ohio victim get in a van, but that was it. All Grimaldi had to connect the cases were the weird tattoos. And some dead women.

Since Quinn and Joe's last visit, Grimaldi had further checked into their suspicions about the death of Quinn's college roommate Judith. He was interested in the possibility that Sid, Judith's husband, might be innocent of her murder, and the possibility that Price could be responsible. Grimaldi called the authorities in the Columbus, Ohio, area. Had he been there in person, he would have been laughed out of the place, clear across state lines.

"The husband would say anything to get his ass out of this sling," the investigator there said dismissively. "Sure, blame it on—who? A cousin? That's rich. Hey, if you want DNA evidence, we've got a ton that implicates the husband. It's all over the place where she was found."

Grimaldi was taken aback. "Wasn't the body discovered in the bathroom of her home?"

"Yeah, that's right."

"It's just that—well, he's the husband."

"So?"

"So it stands to reason his DNA would be all over a bathroom he uses every day. What, did you find it in his toothbrush?"

"There wasn't any *third-party* DNA. You know what that means, asshole? It means there wasn't any third party." The investigator snorted in indignation. "Do you want a sample so you can compare to your stiff? Maybe you can solve your little mystery out there in the metro-pol-ee-tan area."

"I'm really doubtful that the husband in your case in Ohio is a viable suspect in the murder of a woman hundreds of miles away."

Grimaldi let the phone slam on his desk and wondered if he would regret pissing off a fellow cop and rejecting the offer to explore a lead, no matter how tenuous. He thought about it for a moment, then flicked his hand in the air. The guy's a half-wit, he told himself. It was amazing any cases were solved with the Einsteins they had running these departments.

He stared at his notes, and faced the fact that they were pretty damn pathetic. The only thing he had succeeded in doing was running himself in circles. He had collected a few cases with possibly similar M.O.'s, but that was it.

And there was nothing to tie these cases to Dennis Price. Unless you chose to believe that the common denominator in all of them was the crude carvings.

Certainly the two judges, the ones that Grimaldi had been pestering—before he was forbidden to do so—considered the tattoos a weak link for purposes of obtaining a DNA sample from Price.

Grimaldi sat at his desk, thinking he was tired of obsessing over this case. He had to face the fact that a miracle was probably going to be needed to solve this one.

Suddenly he sat up straight. Maybe he didn't need an actual miracle. Maybe he just needed to widen his net, go a little farther afield. If one of the other cases had DNA evidence and it pointed to Price, then Grimaldi would have much more of a leg to stand on. The other cases were in small, insular towns, with investigators who lacked access to technology. But perhaps they had collected DNA evidence on the victim. And perhaps their local authorities could be persuaded to test it in order to resurrect the search for the killer in their cold case, and maybe, just maybe, they would agree to order Dennis Price to provide a sample.

A lot of maybes, Grimaldi thought. He leaned forward and rested his hand on the phone, deciding whom he should call first. The phone rang under his hand. He picked up the receiver and growled into it to cover the fact that he had been startled.

It was Joe. Grimaldi grimaced. *This is all I need*, he thought, Quinn's eager-beaver boyfriend checking up on the case.

But Joe was merely informing Grimaldi of a business trip he was scheduled to take in early December. Would it be possible for the state police or even Grimaldi himself to keep an eye on Quinn? Joe was still very concerned about leaving her alone.

Grimaldi listened for any trace of frustration or edginess in Joe's voice. All he heard was mildness bordering on meekness.

This is a switch, he thought. Grimaldi resisted the temptation to lecture Joe about how he may be a public servant but he wasn't a babysitter, and scribbled down the dates that Joe would be away. He ended the call without promising anything.

As soon as he hung up, Grimaldi regretted not being more blunt. A statement of "we'll do what we can" was going to be taken by any member of the public as a commitment of a firm police presence. He should have been honest with the guy and told him that the state police would probably have his badge if they knew he was continuing to pursue this case, let alone provide personal protection for Quinn Carlisle.

He eyed the telephone, debating whether to call Joe back. It rang again.

"You are not going to believe this," the voice said without preamble.

"Okay," Grimaldi said slowly, straining to recognize the throaty voice. As the caller began speaking, Grimaldi pinned down the raspy sound as belonging to the state police investigator from Ohio, an older guy hanging on well past what should have been the end of his career. Grimaldi had run into a number of these types while working this case. It was making him rethink his retirement program.

At first the cop seemed to be babbling, but the more he talked, the more Grimaldi remembered their previous conversation. The man had confided that he was putting off retirement specifically to try to solve a string of loosely related murders that he hadn't been able to solve because of a lack of DNA evidence. The cop's name even came to him: Murphy.

"After you and me chitchatted," Murphy was saying, "I went back and looked at all them cases, all the evidence, everything." He paused. Grimaldi could hear him take a drag off his cigarette. "I found something this time that's pretty interesting. It seems we got some DNA evidence after all. The scrapings we took from one of the victim's fingernails." He paused again, clearly waiting for a response. Grimaldi kept silent.

"I think it must have been overlooked before," Murphy admitted. "No one does their job anymore, you know what I'm saying? Anyway, we're hoping this is a good, clean sample, not deteriorated or anything. So, we can look at the sample, right, see if it's a match to your guy."

There was more of a silence. Grimaldi cleared his throat. "I guess there's just one small problem."

"Problem?"

"I mean we haven't gotten any cooperation from the person of interest. I've been fighting with his lawyer for months."

Murphy made a guttural sound that could have been a laugh, but it deteriorated into a hacking cough. When he recovered, he was dismissive of Grimaldi's concerns.

"So? What you do is, you just keep an eye on him. And then when the knucklehead goes to the local diner, grab his spoon. Or pick up the gum he spits out on the pavement. Jeez. Use your head."

"I thought of all that already. Bosses say it would be entrapment." Grimaldi hesitated. "Maybe your department could request a warrant?" He wasn't holding out much hope, but what little he had was blown away by Murphy's long sigh.

"Look, kid," he said, his demeanor no longer jovial. "Just get done what you need to get done. You can ask forgiveness later."

The dial tone was almost welcome.

His office silent again, Grimaldi returned to his meditation. He propped his head on his fists, closing one eye and then the other, watching the phone seemingly move. The phone was the only thing to focus on, as his desktop was empty of even an errant fingerprint or speck of dust. He made sure of it by cleaning it every morning and every night before he left for the day.

He retrieved his bottle of surface cleaner and a roll of paper towels and methodically sprayed and wiped down the desktop. He visualized clearing his mind the same way.

It worked. It always worked for him. The clutter, the half-baked thoughts and all the noise were gone. For the moment, it didn't matter that his superiors were ready to eat him for lunch. He could forget the machinations of his case. It was all a bunch of dust mites, swept away. His mind's eye was filled only with a beautifully blank, blue-gray screen, like at the movies after the film has ended, the music has stopped, and the credits have all rolled. Then on that blank screen, he saw, like a new film starting, the resolution to the whole drama play out.

He pressed the sprayer without thinking, sending particles of liquid into the air. *That's it*, he thought: (a) the stalker was just biding his time, waiting for Joe to move out of the way, even temporarily, so that he could pounce on Quinn; (b) the stalker was most likely Dennis Price; and (c) Joe was leaving on a business trip.

When the couple had come to his office the last time, Grimaldi had suggested using Quinn as bait to draw out Price. But he had only said that to make the boyfriend think that he had a plan. So that Joe would leave him alone for five minutes.

As it turned out, it might be the perfect strategy. All Grimaldi had to do was exactly what Joe had asked him to do, watch over Quinn. He would, from a distance. And in that way, without tricks or DNA evidence, he would finally catch Dennis Price.

It wasn't until a few weeks later, literally the middle of the night, when Grimaldi was sitting in his car in the back of the apartment building parking lot, freezing his backside off, that he wondered how Quinn might feel about secretly being used as bait for someone who could well be a serial killer. It was so unusual for Grimaldi to consider a victim's point of view that considering Quinn's feelings came as a mild surprise.

"I guess you've got to have something to think about," he muttered, his breath showing in the street lamp light that filtered into the car's interior.

It was his third night of watching Quinn's apartment building. The blackness of night, which seemed to suck up everything beyond the weak circles of street lamps dotting the silent parking lot, seemed to grow deeper and darker as the winter solstice approached.

And it was cold. Unusual for Maryland, which didn't ordinarily see frigid temperatures until maybe January. Unseasonable, the weather forecasters called it. Grimaldi just called it cold. The previous two nights had been blustery and bone-chilling, which had made for miserable stakeouts. This night was calm, but the temperature was still in the teens. It was so frigid that Grimaldi, who had broken down and resumed smoking the first night of the stakeout, hadn't even wanted to crack the window open to light a cigarette. He could turn on the car heater for a while, but was reluctant to switch on the ignition. Someone would likely hear the engine turning over in the stillness of the night.

Grimaldi continued his watchful gaze on the apartment building, then saw small flakes beginning to stick to the windshield. Snow. Great.

Still staring straight ahead, he absently sipped from his paper coffee cup. He had picked it up at a convenience store hours before. He winced. The coffee was ice-cold.

"Damn," he said aloud with a sigh and instantly regretted breathing out so hard. His breath fogged up the windshield. Between that, and the way the snow was starting to accumulate, he wouldn't be able to see if the Barnum & Bailey circus went marching into the apartment building.

He would have to take a chance and turn on the car. He was going to get frostbite, and the necessity of the defroster and windshield wipers outweighed the downside of someone hearing him.

Grimaldi pushed up on the sleeve of his down jacket with difficulty and peered at his watch. Twelve thirty. Okay, so a car starts at twelve thirty in the morning. Big deal. Still, he held his breath as he turned the key in the ignition as if it would help soften the sound.

No lights popped on in the apartment building, no sirens wailed, no heads burst out of windows. *Silent night, holy night,* he thought.

From his position near the back recesses of the parking lot, Grimaldi had a straight-on view of the apartment building. Even better, he had a clear shot, at least when snow wasn't in the way, of Quinn's corner apartment on the top floor of the building. It looked like there may be some kind of roof access. He would have to check that out with the building management the following day. He really should have done it already, but he did have to make an occasional appearance at his regular job, which he had been trying to do between naps in the last few days. His sleep had been spotty at best.

The lights in Quinn's apartment were off. The corner had been dark for many hours, unlike the previous nights when there seemed to be at least one light on throughout the night. This day, the shortest day of the year, Grimaldi hadn't seen a single lamp switch on. It was unlikely, given how terrorized she was, that Quinn would have left the premises. He knew she was there. Probably huddled under her blankets or hiding in the back of the closet.

Fortunately for Grimaldi, considering the darkness of the night, the building management had decided on a festive, holiday look for the building and had placed a gigantic wreath on the front facade and turned flood lamps onto it, bathing the building in a crisp white light. The floodlights were a godsend. They threw the entire building into sharp relief. No one was getting in or out—at least through the front entrance—without Grimaldi seeing them.

As the heater finally kicked in, the windshield cleared but Grimaldi was still cold. He took off his gloves and blew on his hands, then held them close to the vent. No wonder he was freezing. The air rushing out was barely lukewarm. Damned piece of junk. He waited a few minutes and turned off the car.

Grimaldi put his gloves back on, sticking his hands under his armpits. If Joe and Quinn were correct, this should have been straightforward. According to them, Dennis Price had some kind of special powers and knowledge of everything in Quinn Carlisle's life. Therefore, Price would have been aware that the boyfriend had left town, and, they reasoned, would seize this opportunity to attack Quinn.

There was only one problem with their reasoning, Grimaldi thought. Here it was, the third night, and no Dennis Price. A third night of zero sleep and freezing his ass off and not a whiff of Price.

The cold was penetrating his bones. He was going to have to turn the heater on again, such as it was. Grimaldi's hand was on the ignition key, ready to turn the engine over, when he spotted a figure on the upper corner of the building.

Damn, Grimaldi thought. He must have come up from the rear of the building. One second it was simply the same sharp angled corner that he had been staring at for hours. The next, Spiderman was making his way along the roof.

The figure, which had been sort of crouched, now stood straight, clearly visible in the floodlights. Grimaldi grabbed his binoculars. The figure was dressed all in black with what appeared to be a black ski mask covering his face.

Maybe there was something to hear as well as see. Grimaldi rolled down the car window just in time to hear the soft tinkle of glass. The black clad figure disappeared over Quinn's dark apartment.

Grimaldi checked for his weapons as he fumbled for the door. "He's in. And we're on," he said quietly into the frosty air and took off in pursuit.

The bed was on fire. It took a moment to process this fact. At least I was no longer considering it from my previous position, which was in the bed that was on fire. I had bolted out as soon as I realized that there were flames.

A small metal wastebasket I ordinarily kept in the corner by the dresser was now on its side atop the bed. The fire appeared to be emanating from it. I gaped at the flames licking the bedclothes and heading toward the footboard a few seconds before it all sunk in: someone had entered my room, lit a fire in the wastebasket, then set the bin on top of my bed. I wondered if this was an out-of-body experience and if I was already dead.

I raced for the bedroom closet where, out of our growing paranoia, Joe and I had positioned one of the many fire extinguishers scattered about the apartment. I was shaking and praying, praying and shaking. Please, God, let that extinguisher be there, please let it work. Please don't let Dennis Price be hiding in the closet.

My prayers were answered. I was able to find the fire extinguisher in the dark, pull the ring, and spray foam over the bed. Soon there was only a smoking mess. Blood must have been roaring in my ears, because when the extinguisher emptied, my head also grew silent.

Still holding the extinguisher, I stood stock still and listened for movement, either in the room or on the other side of the door. My eyes had adjusted to the dim light, although the smoke made it difficult to see that well. Choking back the urge to cough, I saw that the bedroom door was closed. That accounted for the absence of an alarm—the smoke detectors were in the hallway outside the bedroom.

I counted to thirty. Still no sound. But that didn't mean that Price had gone. He was in the apartment somewhere, and I couldn't lock the bedroom door until I was sure he wasn't in the room.

I took a deep breath. This was the moment we prepared for. Holding the empty metal extinguisher like a bat, I crept closer to the bed. Price wasn't likely to hide under a burning bed, but I couldn't take any chances. I was hoping he wasn't under the bed because that's where I had left the gun, in a spot hidden by the bed skirt but where I figured I could reach down and grab it.

Seconds ticked by. Finally I was by the bed, ready to jump back if a hand reached out from below. I snatched a can of pepper spray from under the pillows, at the same time dropping the extinguisher softly on the bed. With the pepper spray canister readied, I knelt and stuck my other hand under the bed, gingerly feeling for the gun. I was too afraid to look.

My hand moved tentatively at first, then more desperately, swiping back and forth across the carpet. The gun was gone.

I sat back on my heels, in a near panic. He must be there, under the bed with my gun and ready to shoot me in the face.

I drew a shaky breath and forced myself to think rationally. First of all, if he were still in the room, he wouldn't have been stupid enough to stand by while I extinguished the fire and gathered weapons. The gun must be there and I was just missing it in the dark. No doubt he set the fire and was waiting for me to burn to death or die from smoke inhalation. But Dennis Price wasn't the type to leave things to chance. It was likely that he was still in the apartment. Sooner or later he would realize the bedroom wasn't on fire and he would come back.

With this thought, my eyes swung to the bedroom door. It was still shut and unmoving. In one swift movement I was at the door, turning the lock on the knob. I ran back and pulled open the nightstand drawer, dragged out a flashlight, and shone it under the bed. There was the gun, right where I had left it, a little above where I had been searching.

The gun gave me new courage and helped calm my rapid breathing. But my thoughts came in a jumble: *Joe was right to get this gun. Thank God he insisted I learn how to use it. I hope to God I don't have to. Please, God, let me get out of this without pulling the trigger.*

With slow deliberate movements, I gently placed the flashlight on the bed, the light facing away from the crack under the door. I took the safety off the gun and positioned the pistol in my right hand and the pepper spray in my left.

I inched toward the bedroom door, which in my mind had taken on a persona of its own. It was an almost evil thing, incorporating the awfulness of Dennis Price, who was somewhere on the other side of it. I didn't want to touch the door, but I had to. Holding my breath, I pressed my ear to the door for as long as I could stand it. I heard nothing.

Still pointing my weapons, using the stance I had learned in my training, I stepped back and set to watching the door.

I bit my lip. *Think, think. That's what will get you through this.* It seemed to work—my heart rate slowed a notch. I realized I still had a few choices. I could open the door and jump out, gun and pepper spray blazing. Logistically, that would be difficult. I would have to move one weapon to the other hand in order to unlock and open the door, then quickly readjust.

And I had no idea where Price was in the apartment. *He could be anywhere. Advantage, Price.*

Another option would be to do nothing. I could wait it out behind the locked door. But he had set a fire in my bedroom. What if he started another fire somewhere else in the apartment? I had no escape route from my windowless bedroom.

There was a third option. Draw him out and see how brave he is when he has to face the barrel of a gun.

There really was no choice. I had to go with option number three. Just the thought of it made me sweat. Before I could change my mind, I used the hand holding the pepper spray to unlock the door. Nothing happened.

Okay, I thought, *after a few seconds. If this is going to work, I need to get his attention.*

I considered kicking the door. But my feet, especially the right foot, must have gotten burned in the bed fire. In spite of the adrenaline coursing through my system, I could feel them beginning to throb with pain, and it hurt just to stand. Kicking was out. Maybe I could body slam the door. I thought if I hit it from the left side and hopped down on my left foot, I could recover enough to be prepared for his entrance.

Like a diver, I filled my lungs with air and rushed the door, letting out a banshee yell. My scream seemed loud enough to wake the dead or at least the neighbors as I rammed the door with my shoulder. It hurt, but it gave a satisfying bang. I hopped back in pain, expecting the door to swing open immediately.

Perspiration dripped from my chin. I pointed my weapons at the door and bent my head a little each way to swipe my face against my upper arms. I squinted at the door. Still nothing.

Now what? I couldn't repeat the bone-crushing attack of the door. I was sure he heard it, certain that he was out there waiting, probably waiting for me to exit.

So I waited. The sweat was gone and I had turned cold with dread. Yet I stood at attention, arms outstretched, holding the pistol and the pepper spray, for what seemed an eternity. My arms grew so tired that they started to shake. I wondered how long a person could remain this way, on high alert. With that thought, I became flooded with doubt. All the training, all the preparation, the self-defense moves—it was running out of me like water from a faucet. *I can't do this*, I thought. Slowly I lowered my hands and shut my eyes.

Dear God, what am I supposed to do? Be the next victim? Tears burned the insides of my eyelids. *Tell me what to do*, I begged, *because I'm lost here.*

A thought popped into my head as clear as if someone said it: open your eyes.

My lids fluttered open just in time to see the doorknob slowly, almost imperceptibly, turn.

Michael Grimaldi wasn't running. He refused to run. But he was striding purposefully and rather quickly toward the apartment building. He had parked the farthest distance away in order to remain inconspicuous, and he had a lot of distance to cover. He also didn't want to arrive too soon.

He was halfway to the building when a car pulled into the lot and sped down the same aisle Grimaldi was walking. The driver was going fast, too fast. Grimaldi was forced to jump out of the way.

What the hell, Grimaldi thought as he rubbed the knee he had banged on the fender of a parked car. *Where's this guy going at one a.m.?*

The car stopped, moved almost as rapidly in reverse, then screeched to a halt. The driver hopped out, calling to Grimaldi.

"Are you okay? I'm sorry, but I wasn't expecting anyone—"

Joe stopped and stared as Grimaldi became visible in the street lamps. "Wow," Joe said finally. "I didn't think you would really . . ." His voice trailed off.

"Well, I didn't think I was going to keep watch over your girlfriend either. My superiors would have my ass if they knew. I'm sort of doing this on my own."

Joe continued to gape. "I don't know what to say."

"You can start by telling me what the hell you're doing flying in here like a bat out of hell in the middle of the night. I thought you weren't due back for another day or two. Did you get a distress signal or something?"

"No, I didn't get a call. Other than talking with Quinn today, as usual. My meetings ended earlier than scheduled, and I've been worried about her. So I decided to drive back tonight." He looked at Grimaldi sheepishly. "I thought I'd surprise her."

"Timing is everything. The one you surprised was our friend Price." Even in the weak light, he could see Joe blanch.

"What?" Joe began to look about wildly. "Am I too late? I knew I should have come sooner."

"Do you think I'd be out here if it was too late? No, Price just showed up. At least I'm assuming it's him. Can't think of anyone else who would be on the roof of the building in the middle of the night."

Joe followed Grimaldi's pointing finger to the outline of the top of the building.

"I just can't figure out how he could get into the apartment from the roof," Grimaldi said, bemused. "Maybe he's wandering around up there still."

"The skylight," Joe said, partly to himself. "There's a big skylight in her studio."

Before Grimaldi could form a response, Joe had dashed toward the building, and was bounding up the steps two at a time.

But Grimaldi was fast—faster than someone who had picked up smoking again had the right to be. He caught up to Joe and grabbed his arm as Joe was about to pull open the door.

"Hold up." Grimaldi had calmly managed to insert himself between Joe and the door, somehow wedging his foot against the entrance.

"Hey!" Joe yelled.

Grimaldi's grip was like a vise. "Listen for a moment, okay? I just want to tell you something before we go storming in there. It will only take thirty seconds, I promise."

Joe stopped struggling but was still breathing hard.

"First," Grimaldi started, "I wouldn't even be here if I didn't have your girlfriend's interests at heart. I think that by working together we have a shot at catching Price. That's what this whole thing is about, after all. And Quinn has an opportunity to play an important role in that."

He looked closely at Joe. "Ideally, I would like to catch Price in the commission of a crime."

"I know! You brought that up before and I don't know why I thought that was a good idea but—"

Grimaldi tightened his grip even more and Joe stopped. "Here's the thing," Grimaldi continued as if Joe hadn't spoken. "No one has been able to stop this guy for a very long time. I think we could find him literally standing over a body with a smoking gun, and he still would manage to get off."

Joe made a strangled noise that Grimaldi ignored.

"My preference would be to capture him alive, but . . . you know how these things go. You said you and Quinn were training, going to a shooting range? So let's assume she can take him. He wouldn't be expecting that. Maybe she wounds him, maybe she offs him. But she gets her justice, I get my DNA, I can close my case, and all is right with the world."

Finally Joe spoke. "Terrible idea," he choked out.

"What? What's terrible?"

"She's no match for him. She couldn't take him down. I was just trying . . . defend herself . . ."

Grimaldi slowly pulled his hand from Joe, who, unmoving, continued to stare at him.

Good. He's not running, Grimaldi thought. He started to pull out another cigarette because he could think better when he was smoking.

"How long has it been since he 'disappeared' off the roof?" Joe's voice was suddenly calm.

Grimaldi made a great show of squinting at his wristwatch in the bluish light. "I guess counting the time we've been talking, maybe fifteen, twenty minutes."

Joe's eyes bulged. "Are you crazy? That's plenty long enough to kill her." This time Grimaldi underestimated Joe's quick reaction. In one swift move, Joe kicked Grimaldi's foot out of the way and darted into the building.

Cursing, Grimaldi tossed aside his empty pack of cigarettes and headed in after him.

Maybe five minutes had passed since I had seen the doorknob slowly turn. Maybe five seconds. I was still staring at it, resisting the urge to glance over at the alarm clock, trying not to blink.

The more I focused, the larger the door loomed before me. In my mind, it took on fantastic proportions. What little courage I had mustered was gone.

Still, nothing was happening. The doorknob had stopped twisting. I shifted. My foot hurt and my muscles ached from the tension. I wondered if I should rush the door. No. That was what he was waiting for, the hunter waiting for his prey.

I pictured him, waiting just as I was, on the other side of the door. He was undoubtedly armed, too; only he would have no compunction about using his weapon.

I nearly slapped my forehead with the hand holding the gun. What a dumb ass I was. This was an emergency if there ever was one. Why hadn't I called 911?

I literally leapt to the door. Clutching the doorknob, I turned the lock back to the on position, then fled to the night-stand and grabbed the phone.

"9-1-1. What's your emergency?" I had the receiver pressed tightly to my head, but the voice sounded very distant. The voice was repeating something, but it was drawing farther and farther away, because then I was only hearing the sound of blood rushing in my ears and then a loud bang! I watched the door bulge inward as if it were taking a breath.

He was trying to kick in the door.

The 911 operator was patiently saying something from the other end of the tunnel. Another bang. The door was going to splinter at any moment.

That was when I found my voice. It came out in hoarse screams. I gave my address, begged them to hurry. Then I added only, "He's here."

I didn't hang up, I just dropped the phone on what was left of the mattress. Once again I prepared myself and turned to face the door.

It took several long, agonizing minutes for Price to kick in the door, much longer than I expected. I could hear squawking from the 911 operator coming from the open phone line on the bed, but I couldn't spend time thinking about that. Nervously I checked and rechecked my weapons amid the crashing and the banging. Pepper spray pointed out. Safety off. Legs spread for balance, as I had been taught. Don't stand too close but not too far away either. Keep calm. Stick with the plan.

Inevitably, the thin panel near the doorknob began to splinter from the repeated pounding. I could no longer hear the 911 operator, but she may have been drowned out by the noise, which was thunderous. Finally, a boot emerged, kicking through the rest of the panel. Then a hand was reaching, searching, and finding the doorknob.

From there it was a matter of seconds. The lock turned, the hand withdrew, the door swung open.

He appeared as a shadow at first because of the dim light and because he was wearing all black, including some sort of watch cap. It made him look less like a ninja, and more like a lowlife burglar.

He stopped short, apparently startled, which in turn startled me. Then I remembered that I was pointing a gun at him.

If there had been anyone there to observe, it might have struck them as odd, this frozen tableau of attacker and would-be victim, each trying to stare the other down. There was no mistaking him, even though I hadn't seen him in a decade. It was Dennis Price all right.

Despite his dark getup, he was visible in the moonlight that streamed through the open doorway from the living room windows and the skylight beyond. While he took in the weapons I held, I felt, rather than saw, the knife in his hand. I took a risk and broke my gaze to glance down.

Bastard, I thought. He had done it again. He had gotten his weapon from me. He was holding one of my serrated knives from the kitchen. Then I saw something behind him like knives glinting, a million of them.

I recognized it. Glass. There were shards of glass scattered about the apartment and tracked into the carpet, glass reflecting the brilliant moonbeam streaming through the hole that used to be the skylight. That's how he had gotten into the apartment. He had broken through the skylight when I finally succumbed to sleep, then he had come into the bedroom and started the fire.

We stared at each other in what seemed an infinite showdown. It was Price who broke the spell.

"You think you have the guts to shoot me?"

The taunting was so typical for him, and all too reminiscent of the first attack, when he had dared me to use my knife. Yet something was missing . . . then it struck me. There was no arrogant grin.

He's bluffing, I thought. *Maybe he's thinking that I may very well pull the trigger. Maybe he's actually scared.* The realization gave me courage.

"Try me." My finger rewrapped more snugly around the trigger.

I could have sworn I saw him swallow hard.

Instantly, a headiness spread through me, like whiskey in the veins. *I'm in control!* In the same instant I saw another brilliant flash and, confused, thought I was seeing glitter from the glass again. But it wasn't glass—it was the flash of his knife. I had just enough time to register that he was not in the least intimidated by the gun I was pointing at him, and that he was only trying to fake me out by pretending to be frightened. He was using his own weapon, one that I had known he would have no qualms about using.

These thoughts clicked rapidly through my brain, but not fast enough. There was not enough time to dodge, not completely anyway, as the blade came down and caught the side of my forehead and cheek.

Without thinking, without even looking as I reflexively shut my eyes against the knife slash, I squeezed the trigger in the hand that held the pepper spray.

Somehow I managed to score a direct hit, right in Price's face. He fell to his knees, clutching his head and screaming that he was blind. Something warm trickled down my face—blood, I supposed—and I watched Price writhe in pain as if I were watching a movie. Slowly, I leveled the gun and pointed it at Price.

I should shoot. I could end the madness, right here.

Price rolled on the floor, raspy breaths rattling from him. I wondered if this was another act.

The steel of the gun in my hand was cold—surprising me because I was gripping it so hard I would have thought the metal would be warm. My arm felt incredibly heavy, and my fingers were numb. I couldn't shoot even if I wanted to.

Price had stopped his rolling around and was lying still. Instinctively I knew that this was not good. His stillness was not a sign of defeat, only a sign that my window of opportunity— my time of being the one in control—was now most likely shut. I couldn't continue to just stand there, agonizing over what to do. I had to act.

I jumped over Price's prostrate form and ran down the short hallway to the front door. My bare burned feet slapped the hardwood floor, pain in every step. Hands shaking, I fumbled with the complex system of locks, all of which were still in place. My hands were slippery with sweat.

Finally, the last lock. This was the one that opened with the small key I carried on the chain around my neck. I grabbed for the key, missing once, at the same time feeling for the slot on the lock. It was very dark by the door. Something (sweat? blood?) dripped into my eye. No time to wipe it away. I blinked, concentrating on the lock. The key scraped it, missing its mark. I tried to aim the key, using my fingers to feel the lock. "Please, God, please, God," I whispered in desperation.

The key slid in on the third try. I could feel the bolt slide back. I was almost there. Just as I turned the key back to slide it back out of the lock, it popped out of its own accord. The key flew up the chain, and the chain was pressed against my neck. Now the chain and the key were no longer my escape hatch but a weapon, choking me. Harsh words sounded in my ear. He was calling me a bitch, he was pulling hard on the chain, he had hold of my hair, he was so close that he might suffocate me even if the chain didn't. Dennis Price was choking me to death just a step away from the door that was now unlocked.

I choked and gagged, arms flailing wildly. I tried to focus on inserting a finger, even a fingernail, under the chain. But it was too tightly wound. I shuffled my feet to try to get some leverage. Maybe I could get lucky and hook his leg. Amazingly, my feet lifted completely off the ground. I wasn't levitating; he was lifting me by the chain around my neck. I had a moment of panic, thinking that I might be decapitated before he finished strangling me.

What about the gun? I had a gun. At least I had been in possession of the gun when I ran out of the room. I began to see sparkles of light again from the lack of oxygen getting to my brain. I tried to grope at my clothes and pockets, praying that the gun or the pepper spray or something had remained magically affixed to my person. Nothing. And I was running out of time.

The idea that it might all be over and that I would drift into blackness let me draw on some deep well of resourcefulness. It's what gave me the strength—what seemed in that moment a superhuman strength—to lift a leg and kick behind me.

The kick must have barely made an impact. There was no lessening of the pressure around my neck. I was thinking I had blown my chance when it occurred to me that he had moved. It was only the slightest shift but I could feel his foot planted against mine.

This gave me the sense of place I needed. I drew up my knee again and brought my foot down hard on what I hoped was his instep.

I must have managed to nail a sensitive area, maybe the delicate mesh of bones where the toes are connected to the foot. I heard cracking before I heard him scream. He reflexively loosened his grip on the chain. In a single motion, I was able to pull the chain away from my throat, drag it over the top of my head, and toss it away. Once again I lunged for the door. I could see the brass of the locks in the dim light. The door was that close, freedom just a step further.

I stretched to touch it and it fell away. No, no, I tried to cry out, the words wouldn't come. Price was dragging me back by the hair. I finally was able to give voice to my desperation and was screaming, "No!" when he slit my throat.

I felt him jerking my head back, could actually feel the knife passing along my neck. I knew I was going to die. I was aware of it all; aware that I had lost, aware that the door was so close. I could see it, the symbol of my failure.

It was in this moment of abject failure, when I wasn't quite sure if I was dead yet, that the door flew open. A dark form burst in, hurtling over me and tackling Price.

I let myself fall away. I was only vaguely aware of the desperate fight behind me. *Thank God someone is here to take up the struggle.*

I managed to half-crawl, half-drag myself out of the way, curling up in a ball in a dark corner of the hallway. I was mostly hidden behind the door, which was why I never saw the second person enter. But I heard the gunshot. It reverberated through the apartment. There was no time to process whether I had been hit by the bullet before I passed out.

EPILOGUE

It turned out I was still alive. I hadn't escaped without injury, of course. But—as the medical professionals repeatedly told me—I had been extremely lucky. The near strangulation and slitting of my throat had caused only temporary damage, as he had missed my artery. I would have some scarring from the knife wounds. *Just add that to the pile of other scars*, I thought. I had also suffered a third-degree burn on my left foot and more minor burns on the other.

"Could have been worse," one attending physician said each time he made rounds in the hospital. "Much, much worse." I was sure he meant his comments to be comforting, but instead I felt annoyed and guilty. I thought perhaps he was implying: you had no business surviving when others hadn't.

During the first confusing hours after I regained consciousness, I was uncertain about what exactly had happened at the end of the long nightmare. At one point, I had woken briefly to find myself in an ambulance en route to the hospital. I saw Joe looking tense and anxious. I tried to ask questions, but my throat hurt too badly. I even struggled to sit up. The paramedic gently pushed me back into place on the stretcher. As the ambulance rocked along the streets, I settled down again, comforted by the knowledge that I did have: I had survived, Joe miraculously was there, and Price wasn't. I fell into the blackness again.

I woke again to the chaos of the emergency room. I kept checking for Joe. He always was there.

When I opened my eyes again, it was the next morning. Joe was standing with his back to me, looking out the window. Even from the bed, I could tell there wasn't much of a view. Yet he seemed engrossed in it. He must have felt my gaze, because he soon turned.

"Hi." It came out as a croak. My throat was still very sore. I tried to smile brightly, but I must have looked ghastly because Joe appeared even more concerned.

"How are you feeling? No, wait, don't talk." He moved to the bed and retrieved a notebook and a pen from the side table. "The doctors said you might have suffered some damage to your larynx, maybe even fractured it, so you need to rest your voice for a few days. You can use this to communicate. Pretty high-tech, huh?"

Awkwardly, I arranged the pad on my knees and positioned the pen. I hesitated. I wasn't sure what I wanted to know.

"Who came? 911?" I scrawled finally.

Joe twisted to see what I had written. "You mean who came bursting in shooting? It wasn't 911. The crazy guy who tackled Price was me. The one who did the sharpshooting? That was Grimaldi."

Joe described how his anxiety over what might happen had gotten the best of him while he was away. As soon as his business meetings wrapped up, he had rented a car and raced home. He described how he had run into Grimaldi in the parking lot, and discovered that the investigator had been staked out there each night that week.

I was astonished that Grimaldi has shown up at all. Joe said he hadn't told me about his little visit with the detective because he was pretty sure that he knew exactly what Grimaldi would do: absolutely nothing.

As I listened to what had happened in the hallway of my apartment, it occurred to me that Grimaldi had done far more than nothing. Joe was explaining that while he and Price were grappling on the floor, Grimaldi had managed not only to avoid shooting Joe, but also to only wound Price. The injuries weren't minor—Price had been shot in the leg with the first bullet and the gut with the second—but he was expected to survive. Joe said this with a trace of wistfulness.

A day later, Grimaldi showed up at the foot of my hospital bed. It was morning, before official visiting hours began. He probably timed his visit to occur when Joe was absent, but he needn't have bothered. Joe had gone back to work.

I had been dozing, and when my lids fluttered open, I saw an impassive Grimaldi, standing at attention. In that moment I both wondered how long had he been standing there, and realized that it must have been Grimaldi who I felt watching me when I looked out at my apartment window.

Grimaldi had never seemed one for small talk, but as he stood there awkwardly, he didn't seem inclined to speak at all. My throat was improving, but I was still having difficulty speaking. I picked up the pad from the table next to the bed and began writing.

"Were you going to intervene if Joe didn't show up?" I wrote and handed the paper to Grimaldi.

Grimaldi read the message and looked annoyed. "I guess Joe's been talking," he said.

I took the tablet back and scribbled. "He glossed over everything."

"Well, it worked out, didn't it? Anyway, you would have been able to handle it if we weren't there."

The rage rose so unexpectedly and violently that I spoke without thinking. "You think I was handling him?" It came out somewhere between a screech and a squeak. I was probably reinjuring myself but the anger bubbled from deep inside, from some buried container that was in danger of exploding. Breathing hard, I wrote rapidly on the pad. "I never stood a chance."

I handed him the pad with a shaking hand. Grimaldi glanced at it, then at me.

"You don't care, do you?" I croaked.

Oddly, with this statement, the defensiveness seemed to seep out of him. His jaw grew less tense, his stiffly squared shoulders slumped just a bit. Even stranger, his normal stern expression began to crumble. He quickly composed himself, but for that brief moment I could decipher his self-doubts. Then the curtain came down again.

"You know there's going to be a trial," he said.

A trial. It was my turn to be deflated. The anger ran out of me like steam until I was flat and exhausted. More courtroom proceedings simply hadn't crossed my mind. I thought it was over. But it refused to be over.

I picked up the pad again.

"Why?" As I wrote the word, tears came and I didn't even let him try to answer this unanswerable question before I lay back on the pillows and turned my head away. Grimaldi launched into an explanation, but I just let it wash over me. Through DNA evidence, he was saying, the state police were able to connect Price to the state park murder case. He would stand trial for that crime, and I would likely be called as a witness for my role in leading the authorities to him. In addition, there was a good possibility that the state would tack on charges for the break-in and attack on me.

Curled up on my side, I stared at the blank white wall of the hospital room and wished Grimaldi would stop talking and go away. I wished all of this would just go away. But a procession of the faces of his victims—of Judith, of the girl in the state park, other faces of other victims—seemed to crowd the wall. *What do you want from me,* I thought, and closed my eyes.

A long time, perhaps an hour, seemed to pass. Maybe I had drifted off again. I opened my eyes to a silent room. Even the hospital corridor outside the door, usually a constant buzz, was quiet. Grimaldi must have gone, departing as silently as he had entered.

"Now I know how Billy O'Brien felt," I whispered to the wall.

"Who's Billy O'Brien?"

I stiffened. Damn. He was still there. Instead of turning toward him, I shifted my face further into the pillow so that my voice was nearly muffled. "Could you leave now?"

"I will. But I just want to make sure you're clear about everything. I know you want it be done with, but the fact is, it isn't over yet. One way or another, you'll need to testify. And I don't get why you're not happy about it. You seemed to want there to be some justice, didn't you?" His voice switched from authoritative to slightly puzzled at the last part.

I let the air in my lungs escape in a long sigh. With difficulty I shifted in the bed to face him.

"Why didn't you shoot to kill?"

For the first time in my dealings with him, Michael Grimaldi looked uncertain. He seemed to struggle with an answer.

"Maybe that's just wishful thinking on your part," he said finally.

I shut my eyes again. "Look, I appreciate that you saved me. I really do. But right now I need you to leave. Please."

"Quinn—" he began.

"I said, get out!" My throat burned.

At last I heard the whisper of the hospital door closing behind Grimaldi.

My hospital stay lasted more than a week, after which my mother insisted that I come and stay with her while I recuperated.

I had some trepidation about how close quarters with my mother would work out. I thought she might spend a lot of time rehashing and second-guessing Joe's and my actions. There probably would be a lot of quizzing about why I hadn't told her anything of what we'd discovered about Dennis Price. In particular, I knew she would feel guilty about not taking me seriously when I called her after the state park murder. When I looked back on it, I could understand my mother's reaction. I had long since forgiven her.

Instead, my mother didn't broach the topic for days. She spent her time clucking over me, but I could see how much it bothered her that she hadn't supported me, and how close she had come to losing me again.

Finally, I brought it up.

"I was thinking about that night I called you in a panic, after I heard about the girl who was found dead in the state park. I would have thought I was paranoid, too, if I were in your shoes." I gave her a wry look. "It was a stretch, wasn't it?"

Rather than smiling or teasing, my mother burst into tears. But it opened the floodgates. After that, we spent much of our time together talking about it, dissecting what happened, and consoling each other.

Nearly a month passed. Although my mother was reluctant to let me go, I insisted I was well enough to return home. I missed Joe.

The morning I left, my mother hugged me good-bye, tears in her eyes, and told me she was sorry she hadn't supported me before.

"Don't feel guilty, Mom," I whispered in her ear. "I've been carrying enough of that around for both of us."

Bundled into the car with the vegetarian casseroles my mother had insisted I take with me, I started the ignition and immediately locked all the doors. *Just a sound habit. There could be danger anywhere, even if Dennis Price is out of the picture,* I thought a little defensively as I waved to my mother and drove off.

At the end of the street, I glanced in the rearview mirror. My mother was still standing on the sidewalk, waving. I had to stop myself from turning back and shouting to her to run in the house and lock her own doors.

My homecoming included a surprise from Joe. Order had been restored to the apartment. The skylight had been repaired and rebuilt with heavier plexiglass. Joe had even installed a lock. The carpeting had been shampooed, and all the rooms thoroughly cleaned. The biggest gift, though, was a bedroom makeover. Joe had furnished the room with a dark walnut bedroom set and recessed lighting with a small spotlight over one of my paintings, which he had framed and hung on one of the bedroom walls. I wandered from room to room in awe, before walking over to inspect the artwork.

"It was like you painted it just for this room," Joe said.

"Or it could be that somebody designed the room to match the painting." I turned to him and smiled. "How in the world did you convince the apartment management to do all this?"

"It's easy if you offer to pay for it."

I was horrified. "You paid for all of this?"

He looked embarrassed and shrugged. "Not all of it. The skylight and the smoke damage was covered by the insurance. Anyway, look at it this way; if you move, the furnishings will always be yours. Ours."

"Ours," I repeated, touching the smooth wood of the dresser. "I like the way that sounds."

In the months that followed, we rarely talked about Dennis Price and all that had consumed us for so long. I told Joe how helpful it was to talk it out with my mother. "It was better than going to a therapist," I told Joe. Every so often we would promise each other a long discussion, but we never seemed to get around to it. It seemed better to leave all that unpleasantness in the past.

We spent all our free time together, and grew so comfortable we forgot what it was like not to be a couple. While Joe was at work, I took up my art again with a vengeance.

After weeks of frenzied painting, I made an impulsive call to a friend who worked at a gallery in Baltimore. She put me in touch with the owner, who eventually agreed to meet with me. At the end of the meeting—a tense affair where he reviewed my portfolio with pursed lips while I held my breath—the owner looked at me. "I'm going to have to insist," he said, "that we start planning an exhibition of your work."

"Can you imagine? My art, actually in a show." That evening we sat together on the sofa, my legs tucked tightly under me. "He even implied that he thought some clients might be interested in buying my work. Wouldn't that be great?" Childish or not, I bounced a bit on the cushion.

Joe laughed and pulled me to him. He whispered in my hair, "It's so nice to see you this happy. I'm not sure if what I have to say . . ." His voice trailed off.

I pulled back and looked at him in alarm. "Why? What do you have to say?"

"It's not bad. At least, I hope you won't think it's bad." He rose suddenly, unceremoniously dumping me back onto the other side of the sofa, and disappeared into the bedroom. He returned with his briefcase and, setting it on the coffee table, pulled out a small jewelry box. He turned to face me.

"I've been carrying this around for weeks, trying to find the right time. I think you're supposed to do something romantic but, well . . ." He opened the box. The diamond ring inside reflected the lamplight like a miniature chandelier. "I'm hoping that today, which has been such a good day for you, might get even better. That is, if the idea of marrying me makes you happy."

I gaped at him, at the ring, and then at him again.

A blank look fell over Joe. "I shouldn't have assumed," he said tightly and closed the box.

I pressed my hands to my face in distress. "I love you. More than anything, if you want to know. That's why it wouldn't be fair to you to make this permanent."

Joe's laugh was mirthless. "Is that a line to get out of a marriage proposal?"

"No, I'm serious. Remember a long time ago I told you I was damaged goods? Everything that's happened has helped me to resolve things. Some big things. But there's still so much scar tissue, and I'm still, well . . . I'm screwed up. And that's not fair to you." I flushed at my own admission. "This is embarrassing," I muttered and reached blindly for the box of tissues, dripping tears on the coffee table.

Joe handed me the tissues. "But I thought things were resolved. You said they were."

"Not everything."

"I keep telling you, Quinn, you're too hard on yourself. You wouldn't be normal if you didn't struggle with what happened. The question is what you do about it."

Joe got up and retrieved his keys from the kitchen counter where he always left them, and then turned back.

"I'll give you some space for a while. If you think about it and the answer is no, I'll understand."

The door had no sooner shut quietly behind him before I was outright weeping.

It was ironic that I had immediately sought counsel from my friend Suzy. Although Suzy considered herself a matchmaker, she was never concerned with the nuances of relationships. So it was unexpected that Suzy was insightful and gave better advice, as earthy as it was, than probably anyone else would have.

"So you're saying that he showed you this mammoth diamond and you didn't immediately jump up and down and shout, 'Yes, yes, yes'?" Suzy asked wryly.

On my end of the phone, I was rolling my eyes. "Something like that."

"And you think that you're an emotional wreck and not wife material, huh?"

I didn't respond and Suzy sighed heavily. I waited.

"Okay," Suzy said. "Here's the thing. You don't think you're good enough for him because of quote-unquote these *issues*, but you also can't stand the thought of giving up this relationship and him walking away. So, clearly, what you gotta do is fix your issues." Suzy was triumphant.

"But how?"

"Go to a therapist, dimwit. You need to see someone to help you sort through this stuff. Actually I'm surprised you're not in therapy now. I would be."

"I did see someone for a few years after the attack in college. My mother's idea. It was a good idea, I guess, but I never got much out of it."

"Well, then get a better therapist," Suzy said. "Really, they're a lot like hairstylists. Sometimes you have to look around for the one who's right for you. So, it's very simple: work on your problems and, for God's sake, marry the guy. And I better be the first one you call when you get engaged."

It didn't happen quite as smoothly as Suzy said it would, but it happened. With my mother's help, I found a no-nonsense therapist who specialized in treating victims of crime and abuse. And after much discussion, Joe and I got engaged and began planning a small September wedding.

I felt more joy than I thought was possible, and definitely more than I thought I deserved. "It's because you're working things out," Suzy said, ever practical. Maybe she was right. I loved my therapist, and as spring grew into summer, I was making progress even if the sessions were far from easy. More than once I would return home and throw my bag across the room, announcing I was quitting.

But I persisted. One day I returned from a session and collapsed on the sofa, exhausted but glowing, and announced that I had achieved a breakthrough. "You know, in the end," I said to Joe, "it was so simple. I just had to give myself permission to be myself."

That might have been the end of it all, and I might have thought myself cured, had it not been for the prospect of having to testify in Dennis Price's trial. I had heard nothing about plans to prosecute him since Grimaldi had visited me in the hospital, but the idea of testifying hung like the sword of Damocles over my head. I knew I wouldn't be able to weather the emotional turmoil of another courtroom experience, especially one where I would have to face Price yet again. I feared it could reverse all that I had accomplished.

As the months passed and the specter of the trial loomed larger, I sometimes felt the old fear and anxiety starting to gnaw at me. The overwhelming dread threatened to drag me down into the abyss again. Part of me wanted to get the trial over with, and a bigger part hoped the delay would continue indefinitely.

One day the phone rang with the call I was dreading. It was Michael Grimaldi. *This is when he tells me that a trial date has been set*, I thought.

But Grimaldi didn't say anything like that. He made an awkward, uncharacteristic attempt at small talk, even asking about my health. After we had run out of inconsequential things to talk about, there was an uncomfortable silence. I was trying to think of something to break it when Grimaldi blurted, "He's dead."

"Dead?" For a moment I was mystified. Then the picture suddenly cleared. "Dennis Price is dead? How?"

"He hanged himself in his jail cell."

I didn't respond.

"You're the first person I've called about this," he admitted. "I thought you should know."

"I'm honored." I didn't have to pretend to say it with conviction because I meant it. I hung up, giddy with relief.

That night, Joe and I celebrated at a nice restaurant. We toasted with champagne as I wondered aloud whether I deserved to be this happy.

"Quinn, look at me," Joe demanded. "Now, repeat after me: I deserve to be happy. I deserve to survive. It's time to celebrate some good luck for a change." He smiled. "And not just good luck. Awesome luck. You have me."

I couldn't answer because of the lump in my throat. I settled for a wavering smile and reaching for his hand.

The very next day, the final letter from Billy O'Brien arrived. After I read it I thought that what Joe had alluded to the previous night was true, that maybe even a long string of bad luck was bound to balance out in the end.

I was glad to hear from Billy. I felt such a kinship to him. Although Billy's case had nothing to do with mine, our shared experiences with the crooked judge and our similar attempts to find some measure of justice had bonded us. I knew this communication from him closed that chapter in our lives. Because as soon as I began reading his handwritten note in what seemed to be a cover letter for a thicker document, I knew it would be the last time I would ever hear from Billy O'Brien.

"Dear Quinn," I read.

I know what you're thinking. Why is this guy writing to me again? But it seems that while I can't talk to the people I'm closest with, like my wife, about this subject, I have no trouble spilling my guts to you.

Speaking of my wife Mary, we worked things out, thank God, after I decided to go back to court and testify again. It was what was needed to help us set things right.

So in a way, communicating with you helped me get back together with my wife and kids. They're my life. They make me whole. So—thank you.

But the real reason I'm writing is that I want you to know that it's done. I went and testified to the truth. They say the truth will set you free. I guess that's what happened to me because this time the S.O.B. was found guilty and this time the judge did not set *him* free. As soon as I heard the guilty verdict I felt totally released. Praise God.

I wanted to tell you this good news but also wanted to send you something else. I got the chance to make what they call a victim impact statement. I figured this was my chance to say what I needed to say. They wrote down everything I said and gave me a copy. I thought you would understand and even get something out of this.

So here it is. I made the biggest, most important lawyer make an extra copy of it. He probably made the poor slobs who work for him do it, but I get a laugh out of that anyway.

Love and peace, BILLY

I carefully unfolded the double-spaced typed legal document. It appeared to be a court transcript. The name of the defendant had been blacked out.

Victim Impact Statement of William O'Brien

Mr. O'Brien: First, Your Honor, I want to let you know that I really appreciate the chance to speak my mind about the sentence you are going to give to ████████, the man who murdered my brother. It's been a long time. By that I mean not only has this thing dragged on for years, but it just seems like it's taken forever, truly forever, for there to be justice. I have to tell you, I almost gave up on that happening. I almost gave in to the despair.

There were some desperate times for my family and myself. After I testified in the first trial, our lives were threatened. My kids were only 6 and 4 at the time. They were ready to kill toddlers. It got so bad we had to go into a witness protection program and had to uproot the kids and live like gypsies. I was so upset I started drinking a lot. That wasn't good. Eventually my marriage fell apart.

I take responsibility for my actions and how I failed. Believe me, I failed. But one fact remains and that's the fact that this was all set into motion with the murder of my brother. There didn't seem to be any hope because the killer was set free and my brother was still dead.

Because I've had a lot of time to think about it, I started thinking of the idea of justice as a beam of light. A very long light saber that can bend and move. And maybe if there's enough time, it can bend right around and go back to the beginning. I see justice like a perfect circle of light because what goes around, comes around.

That's what happened in this case and it's still hard for me to believe that the Supreme Court actually ruled that it was okay to try him again. And then, finally, he was found guilty. The chance to find justice has helped me pull myself together again. I'm not tortured anymore by what went wrong or how unfair it all was. My wife and I patched things up. I'm cleaned up. Life, once again, is good.

But what about my brother? What about his justice, his life?

I've thought a lot about this too. And I've been thinking, yeah, as bad as things got for me and my family, as unfair as it all was, it still isn't as bad as being dead. Shot with a shotgun until you're nothing but a bloody mess of tissue and bones on a cold garage floor. Even if my brother got mixed up in something he shouldn't have, and I don't know that he did, but even if he did, well, he certainly didn't deserve to die. Not like that. No way can I lose sight of the fact that my brother was murdered.

But you know what else I think? I think my brother is pleased as punch that the other judge came clean and the courts saw fit to try this man again. He's probably high-fiving someone up in heaven that we got a conviction. It's dawned on me that my brother wants justice, but not revenge.

So, Your Honor, if you're looking to me, and through me to my brother sort of, to figure out what sentence to give this killer, I can't help you. Our part in this—my brother, my family, me—we're done. We're happy the system worked, but it's obvious that we never controlled it. It had to run its course.

I'm very grateful for how things turned out and that the justice system worked in the end. It was a strange series of events, but I probably wouldn't have seen things for what they are if these events hadn't happened. So for that I'm grateful too.

Guess you never had a victim be this thankful, huh? But that's what I am. Sad my brother is gone, but thankful that I still have a chance to live whatever life God has in store for me.

My eyes burned as I gently refolded the papers and inserted them with Billy's note into their envelope. I pressed it to my cheek briefly, then rose, went to the file cabinet, and placed the envelope in a special file marked "Billy O'Brien." I shut the drawer and, head bowed, said a little prayer. It seemed only right.

I went to my studio to work and pulled out the painting that for a long time now I had kept setting aside in favor of other projects. It was an intricate scene of monarch butterflies lifting in vast, majestic waves over mountains and valleys toward a single tree in Mexico.

It's probably like when someone is seriously hurt in a car crash, I thought as I prepared my oils and adjusted the canvas on the easel. If the victim pulls through, they're far more grateful to be alive than someone who just had a minor injury. The greater the hurt, the more you get from the healing.

I tilted my head, considering the path of the butterflies, and smiled. Finally, I knew where I was going. The painting was almost complete.

ACKNOWLEDGMENTS

This book has been a long time in the making, and I would like to express my deepest gratitude to family, friends, and coworkers who encouraged me, read manuscripts, offered ideas, listened, and supported. There are many but I especially want to acknowledge Karl Green, Dan Callahan, Jim Callahan, Joanne Bowes, Mark Green, Sandy Kazinetz, Rachel Caldwell, Jim Nelson, and Wayne Moser—and, in particular, my husband Jack McKeon for his unwavering support. Special acknowledgment and thanks go to everyone at NY Book Editors.

ABOUT THE AUTHOR

Marie Green McKeon has been a journalist, an advertising and marketing copywriter, and an editor, as well as an author of fiction. She lives near Valley Forge, Pennsylvania.

CPSIA information can be obtained at www.ICGtesting.com
Printed in the USA
BVOW03s1744140914

366580BV00004B/18/P